"I'm adopting her."

"What about the baby's family? Shouldn't they have a say?"

Mack blinked at the unexpected question. "Sarah's mother gave her up."

Thea leveled pleading blue eyes at him. "Maybe she thought she didn't have a choice."

Mack straightened and crossed his arms over his chest. "Why have you been nosing around Ms. Aurora's the last two days?"

"It has to do with my sister—when she came back to Marietta last spring."

Eileen Miller was in Marietta last spring? Not possible. "The night of the accident was the first time I'd seen her in years."

"Eileen probably kept out of sight due to her condition."

Mack turned sharply to stare at her. "She was pregnant? Where's the baby?"

"That's just it, Mack. Momma says the baby has been stolen."

"That's why you've been spying on Aurora's place." The pieces began to fall into place. "You think Sarah is Eileen's baby?"

"Sarah's the spitting image of Eileen." Sorrow along with another emotion—determination?—stared back at him. "That child you want to adopt is my niece, Mack. And I want to take her home."

Patty Smith Hall has been making up stories since she was knee-high to a grasshopper. Now she's thrilled to share her love of history and her storytelling skills with everyone, including her hero of thirty-one years, Danny, two beautiful daughters and a wonderful future son-in-law. She resides in northeast Georgia. Patty loves to hear from her readers! You can contact her at pattysmithhall.com.

Books by Patty Smith Hall

Love Inspired Historical

Hearts in Flight
Hearts in Hiding
Hearts Rekindled
The Baby Barter

Visit the Author Profile page at Harlequin.com.

PATTY SMITH HALL

The Baby Barter

HARLEQUIN® LOVE INSPIRED® HISTORICAL

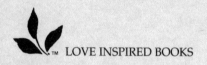 LOVE INSPIRED BOOKS

Recycling programs
for this product may
not exist in your area.

ISBN-13: 978-0-373-28345-3

The Baby Barter

Copyright © 2016 by Patty Smith Hall

www.Harlequin.com

Printed in U.S.A.

And we know that God causes all things to work together for good to those who love God, to those who are called according to His purpose.
—*Romans* 8:28

To Rose Smith. Your humble spirit and servant heart make you a rare beauty in today's world, sweet sister. You are a rare jewel indeed!

Chapter One

Marietta, Georgia
Fall, 1945

Sheriff Mack Worthington made it his business to notice people.

And the woman standing in the shadows of the massive oak tree at the edge of Merrilee Davenport's backyard had sent his senses on high alert. Not that he could see her all that well. The brim of her felt hat covered most of her face, leaving him at a distinct disadvantage.

But it was the little things that made him question her reasons for being there. In the tan skirt and white blouse she wore, she looked more prepared for a trip to the market than attendance at a wedding. And why did her fingers unconsciously dig into the sides of her purse as if she were holding on to it for dear life? Tension held her ramrod straight, reminding him of a soldier ready for battle.

What fight did this woman expect to face here?

"What's got you twisting around in your chair like a kite in a tornado?"

Mack glanced at the older lady to his right and felt the knots in his stomach relax. Ms. Aurora's tone had just the right combination of chastisement and concern that came from years of caring for other people's children. He straightened in his seat. "Nothing, Ms. Aurora."

She studied him a long moment until he felt himself start to squirm again. "It don't look like nothing to me."

Billy Warner, the oldest of Aurora's current batch of foster children at twelve years old, pushed himself out of his chair, his cane anchored against his side as he stretched up to get a better look down the rows of chairs that lined the makeshift aisle. "Is Claire up to something? I knew she'd get bored with all this wishy-washy romantic stuff."

Mack's lips twitched as he put his free hand on the boy's shoulder and gently pushed him back into his seat. "Claire is on her best behavior today. That girl's been looking forward to seeing her parents get remarried since her daddy showed up back in town." John and Merrilee had a troubled past—filled with misunderstandings and manipulations by her family meant to keep them apart. But they'd triumphed over it all, as this wedding proved. And their twelve-year-old daughter couldn't be happier.

"Maybe." Billy blew out a snort. "But the ceremony's been over for a good five minutes, and we're still sitting here when we could be eating some of that spread Miss Merrilee has been cooking for the last week. I'm starving."

Mack shook his head. The boy had a lot to learn about the female of the species over the next few years, particularly when it came to things like romance and marriage. Not that Mack was any kind of expert. His few attempts at romance had been shot down in flames. Maybe women and the workings of their hearts were the only mystery he wouldn't ever solve.

A faint whimper drew his gaze, and Mack found himself staring into a pair of pale blue eyes wide with just a slight hint of irritation, plump baby fingers reaching for him, her tiny body squirming in Ms. Aurora's arms. Technically, little Sarah was in Ms. Aurora's care until the adoption was approved, but both Mack and the baby knew the truth—he was the one who had been there for her, loving her since she was dropped into his arms on the day she was born. He was her father in every way that mattered. If only he could push Judge Wakefield to make it legal.

Ms. Aurora shifted the child in her arms and held her out to Mack. "Looks like someone wants to see her daddy."

"Come here, doodlebug." Mack scooped up the baby, her warm little body instantly nestling against his chest. She reached up and Mack caught the tips of her fingers between his lips, nibbling gently, enjoying this new game Sarah had discovered in the past day or two. Her lips turned up in a gaping smile, the jagged pink line just under her nose the only evidence of her most recent surgery to fix the cleft palate she'd been born with. A wave of love like nothing he'd ever known speared through him.

"Really, Sheriff," Ms. Aurora whispered as she caught the baby's hands and wiped her tiny fingers dry with a billowy cotton cloth. "You need to teach her to keep her hands to herself."

"It's just a game we play." Mack held out a finger to the baby, who eyed it for a moment before grasping it between her palms and drawing it to her gaping mouth. "Besides, I think she's teething. At least, that's what it sounds like from all the books I've read."

The elderly woman shook her head as she extracted his finger from the little girl's grip. "You're spoiling her silly, Mack."

"I can't help it." He lifted her up, brushed a quick kiss against Sarah's silky hair, then smiled. "And what girl doesn't deserve a little bit of spoiling?"

"Not every moment of every day," the older woman scolded.

Mack silently disagreed. They'd almost lost Sarah during her last surgery to correct the disfigurement to her mouth and nose, and there was still one more surgery to come. It would be a hard trial for anyone to face, particularly a baby who had already faced too much pain and rejection in her short life.

She'd been abandoned by her young mother just hours after she'd been born. Mack had gotten the call to pick up the baby that day—Victory in Europe Day—and deliver her to the only place that would take a child with such severe anomalies. In the short half-hour drive to Ms. Aurora's, Mack had found his attention riveted to the tiny infant lying swaddled in a ragged blanket in a cardboard box fashioned into a makeshift crib. By the time they'd turned into the dirt driveway leading to the older woman's home, he'd known he wanted to adopt this child and raise her as his own daughter.

As if she had a window into his worries, Ms. Aurora laid a comforting hand on his arm. "You heard anything from Judge Wakefield about when you can finally take Sarah home?"

Mack shook his head. "Not yet."

"That's Ethan for you. Taking his ever-loving sweet time about things." The older woman gave a little huff. "I swear that man is as slow as molasses in the dead of winter."

Mack couldn't argue with her there. Judge Wakefield was known in town for his persnickety approach to his duties, but Mack had an inkling this situation was related more to the man's personal dislike of him.

"Well, what's Red doing to get the adoption finalized? I figured with all the money you're paying that boy, he would have closed this case by now."

Mack's lips twitched. Red had never grown up from being "that boy" to Ms. Aurora, not since he'd filled up the town fountain with laundry soap when he was just ten years old. She didn't seem to realize that he had become one of the leading attorneys in the state.

But Aurora did have a point. Red should have gotten everything resolved by now. Since taking this case, one thing after another had gotten in the way of finalizing the adoption. "He's supposed to be here today. I thought I'd corner him with a piece of Merrilee's juicy chocolate cake and see what the holdup is."

"The way things are going, Sarah will be a woman fully grown before you take her home." Ms. Aurora gently patted the baby's back.

Billy turned to them, his finger pressed against his lips. "Claire's giving us the eye."

Mack glanced up to where the wedding party had gathered. Claire stood beside her mother, her lips drawn into a stern line. Boy, John and Merrilee would have their hands full with that one, especially when the boys began to come courting.

Mack leaned back in his chair, a smile threatening along the corners of his mouth. What would Sarah be like at that age? Full of sass and determination? A tomboy more interested in Atlanta Crackers baseball games than school dances? Or would she love frills and lace and girly stuff Mack didn't know a thing about?

Mack's gaze fell to the bundle of ribbons and bows perched on his lap. Was he being selfish, wanting to raise Sarah without the benefit of a mother, no feminine hand to lead her through those challenging years of becoming a woman? He shifted in his seat. It wasn't that he hadn't tried to find a wife. A number of nice women had moved into town since the bomber plant had opened. He'd even dated one or two, but things never seemed to work out.

He touched the scar just under the hairline next to his left ear. Probably for the best. If God wanted him to have a wife, He would have sent someone who could look beyond his limitations, one who would love him just as he was, deaf ear and all. Until then, he and Sarah would do just fine on their own.

A slight pressure against his right side jarred him away from his thought, and he turned to see Ms. Aurora's worried expression. Her pale eyes darkened into stormy gray as she stole a glance over her shoulder, her body rigid.

Mack lifted Sarah and nestled her against his shoulder. "What is it, Ms. Aurora?"

"I'm probably just imagining things."

Mack doubted it. Aurora Adair was one of the most sensible and down-to-earth people he knew. If she felt something was amiss, nine times out of ten she was right. "Let me be the judge of that."

She pressed her lips together as if deciding whether to tell him or not. "Remember a couple of days ago when I told you I felt like someone was watching the house?"

His heart rate kicked up a notch. "Yes."

"I didn't worry much about it. I like to think some of the families of the children who were left with me might try to get a glimpse of them, just to make sure they're all right. But this one..." The viselike grip she had on his arm put all Mack's instincts on alert. "She's been watching the house for the last two days, and now, she's here."

"Point her out to me."

Ms. Aurora gave him an annoyed look. "I can't do that. That's just plain rude."

"Then how am I—"

"She's toward the back, underneath that big old oak tree one of the children got stuck in last July. Remember?"

Yes, he remembered. Took him two hours to get that little firecracker Ellie off that high-hanging branch. "There's a crowd over there, Ms. Aurora. Which lady are you talking about?"

"The girl in the plain tan skirt with a white blouse and a brown felt hat. Doesn't look like she knew there was going to be a wedding today."

Knots began to form in the pit of Mack's stomach. He'd known the woman was trouble but just *who* was she? Mack shifted sideways to get a good long look at her. The brim of her hat still flopped over most of her face, but now he caught a glimpse of golden-brown curls clinging to the nape of her neck. She tilted her head back, casting a nervous glance at the crowd before her gaze fell on him. A dull ache settled in Mack's left jaw, and he reached for the jagged scar once again.

Thea Miller had come home.

Thea's palms grew moist inside her bleached cotton gloves, her gaze fixed on the impossibly handsome man glaring back at her. She immediately recognized Mack Worthington, football team captain, all-around good guy. And the only boy in high school she would have given a second glance. Or a third. Her heart hammered against her ribs just thinking about the crush she'd nursed for him her junior and senior years.

She didn't have time to reminisce about the good old days, not with the trouble she'd found when she'd returned home from England three days ago. Thea drew in a slow breath, then released it, her heart settling back into a normal rhythm. That silly girl with a shameful family and a hopeless crush had made something of herself, serving her country as a nurse on the front lines in Europe. If she could face those dangers, then facing down a boy she used to like should be the least of her worries.

But maybe he could help her. Someone in town had mentioned Mack had taken Sheriff Clay's place after the older man had enlisted. The news had shocked Thea at first. Knowing how protective Mack could be, she'd thought he'd enlist the day after Pearl Harbor was bombed. What had kept him in Marietta rather than serving his country overseas?

Thea shook her head. What did it matter? Mack was the town's sheriff. Maybe it was time to get the police involved if Momma's allegations were true.

Aurora Adair stole your sister's baby.

Momma's words twisted the knots in her stomach as tight as a tourniquet. The scenario sounded eerily familiar—her kid sister, Eileen, pregnant and unmarried, the child missing soon after birth, the frantic search that turned up nothing, a promise from Thea to find the baby and return it home. Her chest tightened. A promise she'd never been able to keep. Of course, she'd been little more than a child herself, barely seventeen. Eight unbearable years she'd waited to come home, thwarting the promise she'd made to her sister and had been unable to keep.

Not this time.

Besides, this was a completely different situation. Eight years ago, it had been their mother who had made the decision to give away Eileen's baby, her pride unable to handle the prospect of the town discovering that her unwed, teenage daughter had become a mother. But this time, her mother said that she'd wanted the baby—that she'd helped Eileen prepare. And Thea herself had seen the evidence: tiny sweaters and booties recently knitted, a cupboard full of washed and sterilized baby bottles and all the makings for homemade formula.

This time, they could have made things work, truly pulled together as a family in a way they hadn't done in years. But Eileen had died not long after, in a car accident. The baby had been taken from them. And Thea had returned home to find nothing left of her family but her mother—and even she was sadly changed.

All Thea could hope for now was to find her sister's baby, take her home and raise the child herself. Have a real family again.

Which might be more difficult than she'd first thought. Aurora Adair hadn't left her house once in the two days since Thea had started monitoring her movements, hoping for a chance to meet her on the street. She refused to knock on the woman's front door to deliver her accusation. It had been an answer to prayer when she'd learned Ms. Adair would be at the Daniels's place today. A public venue might give Thea her only opportunity to get this mess straightened out. She wanted badly to believe that this had all been some kind of misunderstanding, and that Ms. Aurora would be happy to return the baby to her loving family. Hopefully a quick conversation would be all it would take.

But crashing a wedding had never been part of the plan.

Thea stole back into the cool shadows of the tree and waited until the wedding guests made their way toward the house. The festive atmosphere didn't really agree with her. Not when she was still caught up in mourning for Eileen. It had been weeks since the fatal car accident, but Thea had only learned about it a few days before.

A fresh wave of sadness caught her by surprise, punching her in the midsection like a fist. It still didn't seem real, her baby sister gone. Guilt warred with grief inside Thea's heart. Maybe if she'd returned home, instead of staying away out of guilt over her broken promise, she could have kept an eye on Eileen. Maybe then she wouldn't have jumped into that car with Eddie Huffman, wouldn't have been killed when Eddie lost control.

An ache settled in the pit of Thea's stomach. She might have let Eileen down but she'd make up for it, raise her sister's baby as her own. Which meant getting the baby back.

Thea pushed away from the tree and scanned the Daniels's front yard as people lingered along the makeshift aisle, following the path the newly remarried couple had taken just moments ago. She wobbled forward and instantly yearned for the sturdy comfort of her army boots, the new heels she'd bought this morning shifting on the unlevel ground. Omaha Beach hadn't given her as much trouble as these silly shoes.

"Thea Miller?"

Thea felt her shoulders stiffen. Any hope of getting through the day unnoticed vanished. It had been a foolish hope, anyway. Nothing ever stayed hidden in Marietta. Her mother and sister had taught her that. Thea turned, her skirts whispering softly around her legs, making her long for the confidence she'd always felt in her army greens or nursing whites. An auburn-haired woman waddled toward her, the loose pleats of her dress floating over her swollen belly as she slowly moved down the row.

Thea's mouth turned up in an unexpected smile. "Maggie Daniels?"

"I thought that was you! How are you?" Maggie smiled as if she was truly happy to see her. "It's Maggie Hicks now." She caressed a loving hand against the swell of her stomach. "This here's Peanut."

"Family name?"

Maggie's smile widened. "On my husband's side."

The soft chuckles that rasped against her throat startled Thea. How long had it been since she'd truly laughed? Not since before the war, maybe even longer. "Congratulations, Maggie."

"Thank you, but what about you? Last time I talked to your mother, you were in nursing school in Memphis."

Thea nodded. So her mother hadn't told anyone in town she'd joined the Army Nurse Corps. At least she'd read Thea's letters and knew where her daughter had gone. She'd never written back, so Thea had wondered if the letters had been thrown away, her mother still holding a grudge about the way Thea had left home. Though, what had her mother expected after what she'd done, giving Eileen's first baby to a total stranger? "I joined the Army Nurse Corps a year after graduation."

"Where were you stationed?"

"Stateside at first, then I was sent to Sheffield, England."

"Really?" Her friend's green eyes warmed. "My husband's grandfather owned an airfield outside York for many years but he's been in the States for a while now."

"It must have been lovely then." Before the army barracks and field hospitals had filled the lush green fields surrounding the quaint buildings that formed the town's center. Thea closed her eyes. So much damage to that lovely land and the people who lived there. So many families torn apart, extinguished, never to be together again in this life. The need to see her own family had driven her these last few weeks, across the Atlantic then down the East Coast.

But where was home now, and who could she count as family since her baby sister was gone and her mother seemed to be a shell of herself? But then look at what Momma had lost in the past few months, her daughter and grandchild. Who could blame her for being quiet and withdrawn?

"I was so sorry to hear about Eileen."

Thea swallowed against the lump in her throat. Condolences weren't easy to hear. "Me, too."

"I didn't even know she was in town until I heard about the accident."

That little piece of news surprised Thea. "Where else would she be?"

Maggie frowned in confusion. "Didn't you know? She left for Atlanta right about the time you took off for school. This past summer was the first time she'd been back since then."

What had Eileen been doing in Atlanta? Why had she come back here to have her baby? "She must have been visiting Momma."

"Your momma must treasure that time now."

Thea drew in a deep sigh. "She doesn't talk about it much."

"I couldn't imagine, losing my child like that. It must be hard to talk about it with the pain still fresh." Maggie rubbed her hand over her swollen middle as if holding her unborn child close.

"Maybe." Or maybe not. Momma had never shown much emotion or warmth toward either her or her sister, especially after their father had died in a farming accident when she'd been only four and Eileen no more than three. Thea had taken over mothering Eileen then, rocking her back to sleep when she woke up from a bad dream, making sure Eileen was fed before she'd head off to school in the morning. As she grew older, Eileen and their mother had started to fight. When Eileen's wild ways blossomed in her early teens and proved to be embarrassing, the arguments had grown worse. Thea could only imagine how bad things had gotten after Momma had given Eileen's baby away. Maybe it wasn't that surprising that Eileen had decided to leave town. Why had she come home to deliver her second baby? Maybe she and Momma had made things right between them.

"They're ready to cut the cake!"

Both women turned to where a boy of about twelve stood on the porch at the top of the stairs, a wooden cane bearing the weight of his lean frame. Scowling, he fidgeted with his tie, leaving it slightly off center. His dark coat sat precariously on his shoulders, as if the boy hadn't decided whether to fling it off or not.

"He looks happy to be here," Thea commented.

Maggie's warm laughter coaxed another rare smile

from her. "Billy's not quite sure about this wedding stuff, but give him a plate of Aunt Merrilee's cooking and he's happier than a puppy with two tails."

Thea relaxed a bit. She'd always liked Maggie, liked her plain talk and friendly way of treating everyone the same, no matter their social status. "Please tell your aunt congratulations from me."

"You can tell her yourself." Before Thea had a chance to respond, Maggie tucked her hand into Thea's arm and pulled her out of the shadows.

Thea glanced around, praying no one else would notice her. "I'm not exactly dressed for a wedding."

"You look fine, and I refuse to let a woman who served our boys overseas get away without a piece of Merrilee's wedding cake. It's the first time she's baked anything since they stopped rationing sugar and eggs."

The thought of such a sweet delight after four long years was almost too much for Thea to bear. But staying for the reception felt too awkward. She'd approach Ms. Aurora another time, maybe get up the nerve to go to her door and ask about Eileen's baby. She may not know the woman personally, but she'd heard enough about her kindness and generosity to the children she'd taken in to her home, disabled children who'd been abandoned, to hope that this had all been a simple misunderstanding. One they could resolve easily... after which, she'd be able to bring Eileen's baby home.

A screen door slapped shut in front of her, and she found herself staring into the dark wool of a man's suit coat. She lifted her gaze and admired the taut muscles of the man's broad shoulders, his tanned neck, the thick mop of dark hair that reminded Thea of walnuts ready to be shaken from the tree. He turned slightly, and a soft gasp rose in her throat, just as it had when she'd caught sight of Mack early today. The young boy she'd admired as a teenager had grown into an amazingly handsome man.

Who was more than likely married, Thea reminded herself. A faint sense of disappointment settled over her. Best if she kept her distance. No sense giving folks around here any more reason to talk about the Miller girls if she could help it.

A soft sound, something between a coo and a whimper, drew her attention to a tiny bundle of pale pink ribbons and ivory lace squirming in his arms. A baby? Well, of course, he'd have a child if he were married. Even in high school he'd talked of settling down and having a large family. But wait, she'd seen this child before—recognized the ribbons and lace of her outfit. Yet it hadn't been Mack holding the little girl when Thea had seen her before. She was certain of that. So who had it been?

There was something distinctly familiar about this child, about the sunny blond curls that hugged her head like a Sunday bonnet. Mack lifted the baby to his shoulder and the little girl staring out at the small crowd, her piercing blue eyes watchful, absorbing everything around her. Recognition caused Thea's lungs to constrict in her chest, a joy so overwhelming, it threatened to shoot out of her fingertips and her toes.

She recognized the outfit from seeing that precious baby with Aurora Adair. The baby in Mack's arms was the mirror imagine of her sister, Eileen.

Chapter Two

"Look who I found wondering around the yard."

Mack turned at Maggie's exclamation, his heart picking up tempo as he raked a glance over Thea, startled to find blue eyes the color of a summer storm staring back at him, causing the muscles in his shoulders to bunch and tighten. An uneasiness gathered in the pit of his stomach. Why was Thea here?

And why had she been nosing around Ms. Aurora's place?

"Can you believe it, Mack? Thea's finally come home!" Maggie pulled Thea closer. Had the two of them been good friends in school? He couldn't remember. Thea had pretty much kept to herself between classes. He'd only gotten to know her during her junior year when they'd both worked at the movie house in town.

Maggie was right. No one, especially not him, had ever expected Thea to come back to Marietta. What had brought her back home now? Settling his hand against the baby's back, he took a step back to put some breathing room between them. "Theodora."

Thea stiffened, her delicate chin lifting at a stubborn angle. "Sheriff Worthington."

He didn't know why but the sound of his professional title on her lips felt like more of a dig than a proper show of respect. Maybe she'd done it because he'd used her proper name rather than the nickname she preferred. He'd have to tread lightly, then. No sense starting a war with the woman, not until he had some idea as to why she'd been snooping around Aurora's. Mack forced what he hoped was a relaxed smile against his lips. "Welcome home."

She gave him a curt nod that reminded him of the pretty teacher he'd had a crush on back in fourth grade. "Thank you. I just wish I was here under better circumstances."

"That's an odd statement seeing how we're at a wedding."

Her fingers clamped down on her purse like a vise. "I mean…"

Thea still had that same little habit of nibbling at her lower lip when she was uncertain about how to act or what to say. Whatever had brought her here made her uncomfortable.

"Always suspicious, aren't you, Mack?" Maggie tilted her head slightly toward Thea as if to share a well-kept secret. "I guess that's a good trait for a sheriff to have. Probably why the town council hired him in the first place."

That, and the fact he'd been about the only man left after Pearl Harbor was bombed and men shipped out to serve in the war. Mack turned to Thea. "Sorry about that. Occupational hazard."

She nodded, then turned her attention to Sarah, the tension he'd noted in her earlier softening as the little girl reached out for the slender finger Thea held up for her. "How old is she?"

Mack studied her for a long second. Most people chose to ignore Sarah, or worse, asked questions about the bright pink scar that had connected her nose to her mouth. Why hadn't Thea fallen into that pattern? "Five months. She was born on Victory in Europe Day."

A gentle smile bloomed across Thea's face as the baby grasped her finger and gave a playful squeal. "She's so beautiful."

"Thank you." Mack narrowed his gaze. Sarah had been called many things in her short life, but never anything close to beautiful—at least, not by anyone but him.

"We were just talking about what happened to Eileen," Maggie said, patting the baby's back. "Maybe you could answer some of her questions about that night."

"You were there?"

"Yes." Mack's gut tightened at the note of sadness in Thea's voice. As the top law enforcement agent in the county, he'd seen his share of car accidents, most fender benders, others deadly. But the scene he came upon the night Eileen died had haunted him for weeks after the accident. Two people just a couple of years younger than he lost in the blink of an eye, so close to the happiness they both spent most of their lives in search of, only to lose it in one unthinkable instant.

Of all the losses the town had suffered during the

war, watching Eileen Miller die was the one that had driven him to his knees.

"Why don't I take Sarah while you two talk?" Maggie slipped her hands beneath the baby's arms and lifted her away from Mack's shoulder. "I need the practice, anyway."

They stood in awkward silence as Maggie shifted the child. Oddly enough, Thea seemed to drink in even the slightest movement Sarah made until the child was nestled against Maggie's shoulder.

"Goodbye, sweet pea. See you again soon," Thea whispered as Maggie carried Sarah down the stairs and out into the yard. Soft strands of blond curls fell against Thea's shoulders as she tilted her head back to meet his gaze. "So you're a...daddy?"

The words brought a smile to Mack's face despite himself. "Not yet, but I will be soon."

A tiny line of confusion creased the smooth area between Thea's brows. "How...?"

"I'm adopting her."

Thea's pleasant chuckle felt good to his ears. "You make it sound like your wife doesn't have anything to say about it."

Was she fishing to find out if he was married? The thought sparked a warmth in his chest that he immediately tamped down. It had been years since he was a smitten teenager who cared what Thea Miller thought of him—he wouldn't make that mistake again. "Considering I don't have one, she doesn't."

Thea stared wide-eyed at him as if she were searching for answers and coming up short. How could he have forgotten the soft silver sparks that rimmed the deepest blue around her irises, turning the color from indigo to violet? He found himself noticing the tiny dimple in her right cheek, the different facets of pink that colored her bottom lip, the pale scar high on her forehead.

"What about the baby's family? Shouldn't they have a say in the matter?"

Mack blinked at the unexpected questions. Most people had wondered why he wanted to take on the responsibility of raising a child, especially a baby with special needs, not worried about the family who'd abandoned her before she'd barely taken her first breath. "Sarah's mother gave her up when she was just a few minutes old."

The mouth he'd been fascinated with just seconds before went taut. "Poor woman. Probably didn't know what to think after what she'd gone through."

Mack's throat tightened. Was Thea implying the woman had been coerced into letting the baby go? "Sarah's mother could have kept her."

Thea leveled pleading blue eyes at him. "Maybe she thought she didn't have a choice."

Oh, people had choices. Mack saw it in his work all the time. And when they got caught making the wrong one, they had to face the consequences. Thea had never understood that, especially where her wayward sister was concerned. Mack straightened and crossed his arms over his chest, his suit coat pulled uncomfortably tight. "Why have you been nosing around Ms. Aurora's the last two days?"

Her brows drew together slightly. "How did you know about that?"

At least she had the good sense not to deny it. "It's my business to know what's going on in this county."

"Ms. Adair reported me."

If he hadn't been so annoyed, he would have laughed. Thea had always been quick to call things as they were, except in the case of her sister. "You still haven't answered the question."

She closed her eyes, her fingers tightening around the straps of her purse. Her words were a soft whisper, as if in prayer. "Lord, I don't know where to begin."

Unease knotted in Mack's stomach. Thea had never been one to cry uncle, not even when the burdens her family placed on her fragile shoulders seemed to be too much to carry. What could have happened that would shake her this badly? *Lord, give me the wisdom to handle this situation with Thea. Help me treat her fairly no matter what happened in the past.* Mack rested a hand against the small of her back and gently pushed her toward a row of empty chairs. "Why don't we go over here and sit down?"

Faint color gathered in her cheeks as he held out a chair for her then took the place beside her. "The bad guys don't stand a chance with you, do they, Sheriff?"

A stall tactic, but he remained quiet, ready to listen. Thea would open up about whatever was bothering her when she was ready.

She cleared her throat. "It has to do with what was going on with my sister the last few months of her life."

"You mean the accident?"

Golden curls shimmered against the pale skin of her neck as she shook her head. "No, I mean…before the accident. When she came back to Marietta last spring."

Eileen Miller was in Marietta last spring? Not possible. Mack would have noticed. The woman had always been the type to stand out, draw attention—so different from her sister. "The night of the accident was the first time I'd seen her in years."

She drew in a deep breath as if to snap at him, then must have thought better of it. "But she was here in town last spring. In particular, around May eighth."

Sarah's birthday. The best day Mack had had in years, falling head over heels with the abandoned baby who had been placed in his arms—and deciding to adopt her. While everyone else celebrated the end of the conflict in Europe, Mack celebrated the beginning of his new role, that of Sarah's father. "Eileen had a way of making her presence felt. If she was here, Thea, I would have noticed it."

"I know she was here, Mack. She wrote in a journal she kept that she was out at the farm with Momma on VE Day."

Mack blinked. That wasn't possible. How had Eileen snuck back into town without him being aware of it? Granted, last spring had felt like a roller-coaster ride with President Roosevelt's unexpected death, then the war ending in Europe, not to mention the Bell Bomber Plant laying off some of the women workers. What else had happened right under his nose that he'd been unaware of?

"Don't beat yourself up over it, Mack. Eileen probably kept out of sight due to her condition."

Mack turned sharply to stare at her. "She was pregnant?"

The news wasn't truly a surprise. Eileen had been

trouble since the moment she started powdering her nose and wearing high heels. Mrs. Miller had always been very stiff, very proper. She wasn't a warm person, not even with her daughters, but she'd been tolerably friendly, participating in community events and active in the church until the gossip surrounding her younger daughter's antics had begun. After that, she'd rarely come to town. Whenever Eileen got into trouble, it was always her big sister who came to bail her out.

But it seemed odd he hadn't heard about Eileen coming back in the spring or having a baby. Odder still that the few times he'd been called out to tend to Mrs. Miller, who had grown increasingly rattled and confused as age set in, never once had the woman mentioned a child. Mack scrubbed his jaw. "Where's the baby then?"

"That's just it, Mack. Momma says the baby has been stolen, and I need to go and bring her home."

Another mess for Thea to clean up. Hadn't that always been the way with Mrs. Miller and Eileen? Well, this was one problem he could help her clear up. Mack shoved his hand into his coat pocket and pulled out the small notebook and stubby pencil he kept on him for moments like this. "Do you know the name of the baby's father? I could check with him, see if he or his family have the child."

"No, but…" She hesitated, what color she had in her cheeks fading, though her chin still arched at a determined angle. Whatever she was about to say, Mack knew he wouldn't like it. "Momma knows who has the baby."

"Who?"

"Ms. Adair."

"Aurora?"

Thea gave him a certain nod. "Momma said she knew it the first time she saw Ms. Adair in town after the baby was born."

"That's why you've been spying on Aurora's place." The pieces began to fall into place for Mack. "You think Sarah is Eileen's baby?"

"It makes sense. Sarah looks to be about the right age, and she's the spitting image of Eileen when she was a baby. Momma said it would be like Ms. Adair to take her." Sorrow along with another emotion— determination?—stared back at him. "That child you want to adopt is my niece, Mack. And I want to take her home."

For a moment Mack's eyes went wide with shock, and he didn't seem to be breathing. Then he huffed a laugh and shook his head.

Surprise shot through Thea. He thought her claim was so ridiculous that he was laughing at her? Not very gallant for the boy who'd protected her from the ugly whispers her sister's behavior had generated around their high school campus, who'd listened as she'd poured out her heart over her mother's indifference, who'd been more than her friend.

He was the only one who ever seemed to understand her—and he knew how much her family meant to her. Eileen was gone, but her sweet baby was here, and all Thea wanted was to give that darling girl a home with her family. Why was that so difficult to understand? Shouldn't Mack be happy that someone from Sarah's birth family wanted to claim her now? Instead, he seemed to find the very idea laughable. "Maggie would have your hide if she heard you laughing at me like that."

"Maybe," Mack replied, giving her an unrepentant smile that made her heart trip over itself. "But she'd have to catch me first."

A smile tugged at the corner of Thea's mouth, but she caught herself before she made a complete idiot out of herself and smiled back. What on earth was she doing, almost flirting with the man! She had to make him understand the situation. Otherwise, Eileen's baby would be adopted by him, and the opportunity to raise her sister's child would be forever lost to her. "I don't think what I said was that funny."

"It wasn't." A weak grin tugged at his lips. "It's just that Ms. Aurora has a hard enough time providing the necessaries for the children left in her care without going out and stealing more of them to spread her resources even thinner."

"Maybe there was a misunderstanding," Thea argued. "Maybe Eileen was upset, or overwhelmed, and considered giving up her baby. But Momma says she changed her mind. She just didn't get a chance to take her back before the car accident. This isn't an abandoned baby anymore—this is a little girl whose family wants her. Momma and I are entitled to have her."

Thea glanced into blue eyes studying her intensely as if he were staring straight into the very heart of her soul. She swallowed. No wonder the people of Marietta trusted Mack to watch over their town. He could probably drum a confession out of the most hardened criminal, let alone a young girl still haunted by the cries of her sister, years ago, longing for the first child she'd borne—a child she had held only once before the baby was whisked away in the night, never to be returned. Thea had left town to find that baby…and she had failed. This was her chance to make things right, and she wasn't going to let it go. How could she make Mack at least listen to what she had to say? "Have you ever known me to lie, Mack?"

He glanced down at her, the lines in his face taut. This was killing him. Thea knew it, but wasn't it better to learn the truth now than after the adoption had gone through? "What kind of proof do you have to back up your allegations that Sarah is Eileen's child?" Mack asked. "A birth certificate? An entry in the family Bible?"

"I haven't checked with the courthouse about a birth certificate yet." She'd never seen a family Bible around the house but that didn't mean her mother didn't have one stashed somewhere. "But I do have Eileen's journal. She wrote about delivering a little girl, just as everyone was celebrating the end of the war."

"Which will only prove she had a baby around VE Day." Mack leaned close enough so that only she could hear him. "Until you have some kind of proof that Sarah is that baby, I'd suggest you keep your claims to yourself."

"Then will you promise to hold off on the adoption until we've figured out this situation?" she countered.

A muscle in Mack's jaw jerked slightly, then he relaxed. "I'm not sure there is anything to figure out,

Miss Miller. According to the courts, Sarah has been abandoned and can legally be adopted."

"Miss Miller," was she? So, he'd dug in his heels. Well, she could be just as stubborn. Thea crushed her fingers into the leather sides of her purse. She'd need a new one after the punishment this one had taken today. "You can't think I'm just going to let you adopt my niece without putting up a fight."

"We still haven't established Sarah is Eileen's child."

"It's like I told you. Sarah's the right age, and she has the same sandy-blond hair and blue eyes that Eileen did when she was a baby."

"That's all circumstantial evidence, Thea. You're going to have to do better than that."

She knew that, but the more she thought about the situation, the more convinced she was that the little girl Mack aimed to adopt was her niece, especially considering what her mother had told her of the baby's abnormalities. "According to Momma, she was born on May eighth. I'm sure the birth certificate will back that up, once I locate it."

"She probably wasn't the only kid born that day," Mack replied, though his cheeks had gone slightly pale beneath his tanned complexion, as if the news had hit a sore spot. Clearly, that was Sarah's birthdate, as well. "And finding the official record might not be as easy as you think. It can take months for a birth certificate to be filed, and I happened to know Mrs. Williams left to stay with her sick sister up in Tennessee not two days after Sarah was born."

"The preacher's wife delivered Sarah?"

Mack nodded. "Placed that precious girl in my arms no more than an hour after she was born."

It felt as if the air had been sucked out of her lungs. "You were there?"

"Mrs. Williams called me at the station. Said the girl and her family didn't want anything to do with the baby so could I come by her house and take the baby to the hospital until Dr. Adams could get someone from the state to take over her care."

Thea's world tilted slightly, a dark mist settling over her eyes. "Why didn't you do something? Did you try to talk Eileen out of giving her baby up? Or at least convince her to wait a day or two before she made such a huge decision?"

Thea didn't realize she was shaking until Mack rested his hands on her shoulders. "First—" he spoke to her in that calm way of his that had always made her feel so safe "—why would I have any reason to believe Eileen was the one giving up Sarah? I didn't even know she was back in town. I certainly didn't go back into the delivery room to see the mother—that wouldn't have been appropriate. And secondly, Mrs. Williams takes her position as midwife very seriously. She wouldn't turn a child over to the authorities without being absolutely certain the mother understood exactly what she was doing."

Mack had a very real point. The protocol Mrs. Williams had followed was the same they used in the hospital. Still, she couldn't help her suspicions, especially after what she'd seen years ago, in her dealings with Miss Tann. Maybe Mack could answer a few questions she still had about the night Sarah was born. "How did the baby end up with Ms. Adair instead of at the hospital with Dr. Adams?"

Mack's lips flatlined. "I took her there."

"Why?"

"Because once he heard about her condition, Dr. Adams wanted to send her away." Mack glanced around. Some of the guests had begun drifting out of the house and back into the yard. Thea wondered what tales about her and the sheriff would be making the rounds about town tomorrow.

Well, if they wanted something to talk about, she'd sure enough give it to them. "He wanted to put her in an institution because she had a cleft palate."

His stony gaze sent a chill up her spine. Being on the wrong side of the law would be a hazardous business with this man in charge. "What did you say?" he asked, his voice low and dangerous.

"Whoever did her first surgery did a good job, but from the sounds she was making, I suspect she'll need more. Momma's been so worried about how the baby would survive with…a defect so severe. There are new procedures that could give Sarah a normal life."

"I know. There will be time for those later."

Thea blinked. Why was he waiting? Hadn't the surgeon explained to him that the risk of complications rose as the baby grew and the bones of the head and face fused? Did he not have the authority to arrange for the surgery since the adoption had not yet gone through?

"I think you need to go," Mack said.

She had hit a tender nerve. "I'm not just going to go away. We need to discuss this."

"Maybe, but not with all these people around." Mack thought for a moment. "I'll look at my calendar back at the office and figure out a good time to sit down together."

Sounded like a stall tactic to her. Thea would have to stand her ground. "I'm open any day this week. But I'm not giving up. I fully intend to gain custody of my niece and raise her as my own."

His steely blue-gray gaze bored into her, and Thea's heart tumbled into the pit of her stomach. "Not if I have anything to say about it."

Chapter Three

The walk home took longer than Thea remembered, though whether it was the unusual warmth of the late-October day or the heavy weight on her heart that slowed her steps, she wasn't sure. A ride might have been nice, but there wasn't money for even bus fare right now, at least, not until she secured a job. Even then she'd have to be careful. Raising a child cost money, and her mother's income barely covered her own expenses.

Just another mess Eileen had left for her to clean up.

Thea shook the thought away. She shouldn't feel that way, but she did. It was one of the reasons she'd stayed away for eight long years. There had been a degree of peace in knowing she could go back to her quarters without some kind of family catastrophe waiting for her when she got home. But then, there had been no one to come home to, no one to call family, no one to reminisce with over the old days.

Mack's image flashed through her mind. Her childhood friend had grown up to be every bit the man she'd expected him to be while they were in high school. Eyes and ears peeled for any trouble, he'd always carried the responsibility of protecting those around him. She was a little surprised that he'd ended up as sheriff—going to law school had always been his dream, and he'd been full of grand plans as to how he could help people with his law degree. But it was clear to see how well his current job suited him. It was as if he had been born to the job of being sheriff, an ease about him generated confidence from the community he served, the same trust he'd earned from his classmates in high school. It was one of the qualities that had attracted Thea to him in the first place.

If only he wasn't so closed-minded where Sarah was concerned. Thea sighed. At least he'd been willing to talk to her. Most folks wouldn't have given her the time of day, not when the topic was her wayward sister. If only folks could have known Eileen as she had, confused and scared, questioning why the father she'd adored had been taken away, why her mother was never warm or affectionate the way other people's mothers were. Seeking that affection from others, especially from boys, had led to a worsening reputation and more heartache—the misery, the anger her sister had felt toward herself each time she'd fallen for another man's lies when all she'd ever wanted was to be loved.

Had she found love, at last, with Sarah's father? Thea couldn't know for sure. All she could do now was love and care for her sister's baby—the only piece she had left of Eileen.

Thea drew in a deep breath and sighed. This was not what she'd expected when she'd decided to come back to Marietta. Though what she *had* expected, she couldn't say. Her sister to be alive, for certain. Momma, the same as she'd always been, maybe more mellowed with age. Not butting heads with Mack Worthington. He'd had always been reasonable, even if it meant being proved wrong. But he was a man now, with a man's pride and the law on his side. Would he accept the truth if it meant giving up a child he obviously loved?

Thea's heart tumbled over in her chest. No matter what happened, someone was going to get hurt. *Lord, haven't I lost enough without giving up what little family I have left?*

Just ahead in the bend in the path, the familiar gables of Momma's house came into view. Thea left the dirt road and climbed the steep embankment. Dandelions whispered softly against her ankles, their cottony seeds sticking to the hem of her skirt. If only she had a wish for each one she'd sent floating across the yard over the years. Then Eileen would be dancing alongside her as she use to do as a girl, her baby in her arms, cooing at the spectacle her mother and aunt were making. Momma would be happy and loving, and Thea would have the family she'd always wanted.

A screen door slammed shut in the distance, and her stomach sank as the reality of the situation set in again. Eileen's death, Momma's sorrow and the way the years seemed to weigh on her these days. This was what her life consisted of now, her family. And that included Sarah. She'd prove that the baby Ms. Adair was caring for was her niece. It was the least she owed Eileen after failing her so miserably all those years ago.

The wooden planks squawked beneath her feet as

she climbed the three steps to the porch and pulled open the screen door. "Momma?"

The sound of hurried footsteps from the back of the house clipped through the paper-thin walls until finally Mildred Miller burst out of the kitchen into the hallway, wiping her hands on her blue-and-white checkered apron. "Where have you been? You were supposed to be home hours ago."

Thea tugged at the worn fingertips of her gloves and folded them over the top of her purse. No hello or how have you been. Then, Momma had never been one for social pleasantries at home. No, those were reserved for Sunday-morning church service or a meeting of one of her ladies' clubs in town. But wouldn't it be nice if Momma greeted her with a welcoming hello, as if she were truly glad to see her? "I went to see Ms. Adair about Eileen's baby. Remember?"

"Eileen's baby?" Dull gray eyes met Thea's in the oval hall mirror, faded blond eyebrows bunched together in confusion, a common expression on her mother's face these days. Long moments passed before Momma's face finally relaxed a bit. "Oh, yes. Your sister. She had a baby."

Thea swallowed down the slight unease she felt at her mother's behavior. True, Momma hadn't been at her best since Thea had returned to town, but that was hardly surprising. How could she expect her mother to go on unaffected after all the losses she'd suffered, first Daddy then Eileen? Did losing her daughter bring on this forgetfulness that seemed to have settled like a thick fog over her memories? Or maybe forgetting the past had made it easier for Momma to live in the present. "I'm meeting with Sheriff Worthington sometime this week to discuss it more."

"Mack Worthington?"

Her mother's response surprised her. Momma had never had much time for Thea or Eileen's friends. "You remember Mack?"

"Of course, I do, silly child. The two of you have gone to school together since you were just a little bit of a girl." Momma studied her over the rim of her glasses, a slight smile lifting the corners of her mouth. "He's that nice boy you have a little crush on."

What in the world had caused her mother to remember that particular piece of the past? And why did she talk as if Thea was still in saddle shoes and knee socks? A cold chill skated up Thea's spine. "That was a long time ago, Momma. Back before I left home to go off to nursing school, remember?"

"Oh, yes, that's right." She buried her hands in her apron pockets, her eyes fixed on a point just over Thea's shoulder, as if she'd found something more interesting to look at than her daughter. "So what did you find out about the baby?"

"Ms. Adair does have a baby girl who is the same age Eileen's baby would be."

"Then you'll be bringing her home soon?"

If only it were that easy. "There are some complications, Momma."

"What kind of complications?" Her mother pressed her lips together in that annoyed way Thea remembered well.

She'd never please her mother, would she? The muscles in Thea's shoulders bunched together, a heavy

weight pressing her down into the scarred oak floors. "Well, Mack would like to see the baby's birth certificate to prove that Sarah is Eileen's child before he drags Ms. Adair into the matter."

"But that baby is ours!" Momma stepped closer to Thea. "You told him that, didn't you?"

"Yes, Momma, but a birth certificate would go a long way to proving that the baby belongs with us." Thea rested her hands on her mother's shoulders and stared into her eyes. "Do you know if Eileen filed the baby's birth certificate with the county?"

"Your sister was too busy to spend a day down at the courthouse." Momma fidgeted with the long strings of her apron. "She was always too busy for anything useful or important."

Thea ignored the implication. "What about Mrs. Williams? She delivered the baby, right? Would she have filed the paperwork?"

"I doubt it, but then again, I didn't ask her to. I figured we'd eventually get around to taking care of it ourselves."

Which meant the baby's birth certificate likely hadn't been filed. Thea turned and leaned back against the table, gripping the edges in her hands. How could she prove that Sarah was her niece if the only witness of her birth had left town for who knew how long? Where else would Eileen record the birth of her child? "Did Eileen have a Bible? Something she might have made a note in about the baby's birth?"

Momma shook her head. "Not that I know of, but you know how sneaky your sister was. Always hiding things away in her room. Secrets, she said." Her mother's thin lips flattened. "All she's ever brought home is trouble. Maybe if your father had lived…"

Thea nodded. If only Daddy had lived, Eileen wouldn't have turned wild. Thea wouldn't have been put in the middle of the violent arguments between her mother and sister. Maybe if Daddy had lived, Eileen wouldn't have had that child all those years ago, and there would have been no reason for Thea to leave home at age seventeen. Maybe she would have married some local boy, had a baby or two of her own. Thea shut her eyes on those thoughts. Daddy was gone, and wondering what might have been was just a waste of time.

This was her life. Mother, herself. Sarah. She'd best get busy living it. "I have an appointment at the hospital first thing in the morning to check on my job application but if you'd like to go, I thought maybe we could stop by the courthouse and look through some of their records just on the off chance Eileen filed a birth certificate."

"No!" Momma shook her head so hard, Thea worried she'd get whiplash. "I mean, that's all right. I've got so much to do around here, getting Eileen's old room ready for the baby and all." She gave Thea an uncertain smile. "You've always been so good at taking care of things, I'd rather leave the birth certificate up to you."

At least that hadn't changed. Momma and Eileen always left their messes for her to clean up. But her mother had never turned down a trip into town, not when the shops were open and ready for business.

"Are you sure? You haven't been out of this house

since I got home. Wouldn't you like to at least go into town with me? I heard Mr. Hice has some new material just perfect for the baby clothes you've talked about making."

Momma wrinkled her nose as if the thought of a trip into town disgusted her. "The square is just so crowded with all those people from over at the bomber plant wandering around." She shook her head again. "No, I think I'd rather stay here. That's all right with you, isn't it?"

Thea blinked. Momma never asked her permission for anything, had always been too busy passing out orders or barking out commands. "That's fine, but I might be gone for most of the day. I'm going to try to catch up with Mack at his office after I spend some time looking through the county records."

"You should have been here to take care of your sister." Momma turned away from Thea and started down the hall. She'd almost reached the kitchen when she turned around and gave Thea a forced smile. "If you had been here, you would have talked Eileen out of going with that boy. But you weren't, and now your sister's dead."

Thea closed her eyes, her muscles weighed down with the fatigue of the past few days as well as an equally heavy dose of guilt. The events of the afternoon had finally caught up with her, stripped her of all her energy. The practical part of Thea knew she shouldn't take anything her mother said personally. Momma always lashed out when she was upset. She mourned the child she'd lost, the grandchild she'd never held. Her mother was grieving, that was all. Her fingers tightened around the edges of the scarred hall table until she thought they would break. *Lord, please let it be nothing more than that. Don't take Momma away from me just yet.*

Maybe losing Eileen had been too much for her mother to handle, maybe the presence of a little one in the house was what Momma needed to find some joy in living again. Recovering her sister's baby was the answer. Then Momma would have a reason to fight, and it would give Thea a chance to right a terrible wrong. To bring her sister's baby back home.

This time.

Mack usually used his morning walks before the town came to life to meditate on the Scriptures or pray for the men and women who would soon be filling the streets of Marietta for another day on the job. He'd pray that no harm would come to them and that they would make wise choices. For the folks who visited their city, he prayed that they would have peaceful spirits and that he would handle those bent on making trouble with respect and honesty.

But this morning the peaceful spirit he needed in order to meditate or pray was out of his reach. His thoughts were scattered like the crimson-and-gold leaves gathered up by the harsh wind that had blown in late last night, yet his mind never strayed far from his conversation with Thea Miller yesterday. The bookish girl he'd known in high school had certainly changed. The way she'd stood her ground against him, her refusal to back down from her claim that Sarah was her niece and her plans to raise the child didn't make him

she was killed in that wreck out on Drag Strip Road."
Beau thought for a moment. "Wasn't that just a couple
of weeks after Sarah was born?"

"I'll have to go back and look at the accident report
but I thought it was maybe a week or ten days later."
Which meant Eileen *could* have been home when
Sarah was born. The thought made his heart tremble.
"I didn't even put the two together."

"Well, you still don't know if they're related yet. It
could just be a coincidence."

Mack wasn't buying that, not when the Miller girls,
particularly Thea, had caused him so much trouble.
"I'd already be Sarah's father if Judge Wakefield hadn't
dragged out the whole adoption process. I wouldn't
have to worry about any of Thea Miller's claims then."

"You'd still worry, because you're a decent man.
If you thought for a moment there might be a chance
what Thea is saying is true, you'd do everything you
could to set the record straight."

He might be decent, but that didn't stop him from
wanting go to Ms. Aurora's and steal his daughter
away. Hopefully Mrs. Williams would respond to his
letter quickly and lay this matter to rest.

Beau glanced up at the pale blue sky. "I'd better get
moving. Edie will be up soon."

"Tell her I hope she gets to feeling better."

"I will." Beau clapped Mack on his back as he
walked by. "You want to meet for lunch later? Maybe
over at Smith's Diner around one?"

"That works for me." Mack watched his friend walk
to the corner, then with one last wave, head toward the
parking lot. Beau had turned out to be a good man, de-

spite his father. Though Mack had heard James Daniels had changed his ways while in prison and turned to the Lord, much to his family's delight. Beau had even visited his dad a time or two, and Mack got a sense that the hard feelings between the two had softened. Beau had a bright future in the career he loved, a beautiful wife and a baby on the way—everything Mack had wanted for himself before Thea and the accident had robbed him of his dreams.

He may not have a wife or the law degree he'd always hoped for, but he could make a home, have a family with Sarah as his daughter.

Mack walked down Cherokee Street, past the courthouse, until he came to a row of quaint little homes just outside the main town square. Brilliant violet-and-gold pansies glistened with early-morning dew as they stretched to sun themselves, and the grass was still an emerald green, even in mid-October. A bird twittered his wake-up song overhead, drawing a reluctant smile from Mack.

He'd longed for a home in this neighborhood for as far back as he could remember. The idea of adopting Sarah had finally pushed him into putting a down payment on the small three-bedroom cottage at the end of the street. Nothing fancy, just a yard big enough for a swing set and a room where she could play with her stuffed animals and dolls in the years to come. A home where they could put down roots, where Mack could give Sarah the kind of childhood his parents had given him.

But not if Thea took her away.

He wouldn't let her, not without a fight. Sarah was

his daughter, had been since the moment Mrs. Williams had placed the squirming little newborn in his arms all those months ago. One look into Sarah's inquisitive sapphire-blue eyes and he'd lost his heart.

Blue eyes, now that he thought about it, that looked very much like Thea's.

Lots of babies had blue eyes, he reminded himself. Mack shook off the thought as he turned up a side street toward his attorney's office. Maybe Red would have some good news about the adoption for him.

His footsteps echoed against the brick-paved walkway that led up to Redmond McIntyre's ranch-style home. Mack raised his fist, then hesitated. The sun had barely risen. Would Red be up yet? Well, if Mack came across as rude, so be it. The situation warranted it. His knuckles rapped against the wooden door.

A heavy bolt slid seconds before the door flew open. Red stood framed in the doorway, a coffee cup in one hand, his tie hanging loose around his unbuttoned collar. "Mack, how are you doing this morning? You don't have one of my clients waiting down at the jail, do you?"

"I'm not here on official business." Mack whipped his hat off and held it between clenched fingers. "I was hoping I could talk to you about Sarah for a moment."

"Sure, come on in," Red replied, pulling the door open wider as he stepped back. "Would you like a cup of coffee?"

Mack shook his head. Truth be told, he couldn't stomach anything right now, especially not some of Red's strong brew. He followed the man into a small sitting room just off the hallway and settled onto one side of the sofa while Red retrieved his file from his office.

"Are you sure I can't get you something? A glass of sweet tea, maybe?" Red strolled back into the room, a thick three-ringed folder neatly tucked under his arm.

"Nothing, thanks." Mack settled his elbows on the chair's arms and leaned forward. "I was hoping to talk to you yesterday at Merrliee's wedding but I never saw you."

"I had to go to Atlanta for a client at the last minute and didn't make it back in time. Did I miss anything exciting?"

Nothing Mack was ready to talk about, at least not until he did some research into Thea's claims. He shook his head. "I just want to see where we are with Judge Wakefield."

"Pretty much the same spot we've been for the last month." Red sat across from Mack, dropped the file on the coffee table and flipped it open. "As far as I've searched, there's no precedent in the State of Georgia for allowing a single person to adopt a minor child."

Red wasn't telling him anything he hadn't already heard, but Mack refused give up, not where Sarah was concerned. "But those cases didn't involve a child with the kind of health issues Sarah has."

"No, but that's because those children are usually committed to an institution."

"Or on the streets," Mack bit out. His stomach roiled at the thought of his daughter, or for that matter, any of Ms. Aurora's kids, left on the curb to fend for themselves. Who would do that to any child, flesh and blood or not? It made Mack wonder how many more children were out there on their own right now, hungry, cold and afraid. "Those kids deserve a family and a place to call home just like any other kid, Red."

Red lifted his hands up in mock surrender. "You don't have to convince me. And it appears from my discussions with Judge Wakefield that he sides with you on that point."

Mack nodded. The judge had never hidden his feelings about the need for adoptive parents for all children, even those with physical and mental disabilities, but he held fast to the notion that a child needed both a mother and a father. Mack could see his point, but no family would adopt a child with the type of medical issues Sarah had. Wasn't one loving parent better than no one at all?

"You've got a more pressing problem at the moment."

Mack settled back into the cushions. Had Red heard about Thea's claim, that Sarah was Eileen's child? "What might that be?"

Red shifted forward, resting his forearms on his thighs. "Ben Holbrook cornered me at the courthouse after I got back from Atlanta yesterday afternoon. It appears the city council is bent on restructuring the police department."

"Why haven't I heard about this?"

Red shrugged. "They just voted on it. With all these folks from the bomber factory making Marietta their home, the council wants to add more men to the force, maybe even devote entire departments to specific crimes. And there was some mention of adding more experienced men to the sheriff's department."

"What you mean is now that the boys are coming home, they want law enforcement jobs to give them." Not a bad idea. Able-bodied men with battlefield experience on the force were just what a growing town needed. "We *have* had an increase in petty crimes recently, mostly kids bored and getting into trouble. It would be good to have some additional help."

Red sat back, his lips mashed into a straight line. "From what I understand, they might be evaluating your work as sheriff."

Mack's world shifted beneath him. "Why? Are they thinking about firing me?"

"I don't think it's that dire—yet."

Mack rubbed his fingers against the raised scar high on his left cheek. "Did anybody mention where I might fit into all this restructured force?"

Red shook his head. "Not yet. I'm sure they'll take your exceptional service to the community into consideration when the decision is made."

Mack stretched out his legs and studied his old high school friend. "That sounds like lawyer talk for you've already put that information out there for them, but they didn't bother giving you an answer."

"Always looking out for my friends."

For that, Mack was grateful. "How does this affect the adoption?"

Red's smile dimmed. "With this hanging over your head, Judge Wakefield isn't likely to budge on the adoption anytime soon."

"What's the man waiting on? Does he want me to jump through hoops or something?" Mack snapped, raking his fingers through his hair.

"I don't know about him, but I'd pay good money to see you do that trick."

Mack snorted out a chuckle. "I'm sorry. I didn't mean to bite your head off like that."

"It's understandable. You love that little girl, and you're afraid you're going to lose her."

Another obvious statement but the gut-wrenching truth. Mack wouldn't give up. He couldn't. "So what do we do now?"

Red slid back in his chair. "Well, we're still going to need Sarah's birth certificate. Have you heard anything from Mrs. Williams? I figured she would have gotten back with you before now."

Mack shook his head. "From what I understand, her family lives deep in the mountains north of Knoxville. I don't think mail service is all that reliable out there. It could take some time to hear back from her." He patted his shirt pocket. "I'm sending her another letter just in case the first one was lost."

"If it were any other judge, I'd ask for the adoption to be pushed through without a record of the birth, but Judge Wakefield is a stickler about those things."

Mack nodded. How was he going to get his next question by the lawyer without raising his suspicions? "Will Sarah's parents be listed on the birth certificate?"

"Yes, but that information will be sealed by the court once the adoption is finalized. Then a new birth certificate with your name listed as Sarah's father will be registered with the state." Red studied him for a long moment. "Why do you ask?"

No sense alerting the lawyer to another possible

roadblock, at least not until he had more information. "Just thought I'd ask."

"Well, if you're planning on asking Flossie Williams who Sarah's parents are, good luck with that," Red chuckled. "That woman can be as tightlipped as a Mason jar during canning season."

Mack waited for the relief Red's answer should have given him, but felt vaguely disappointed instead. "I wonder if Mrs. Williams would respond quicker if I sent her a telegram."

"Does Western Union even deliver to the backwoods of Eastern Tennessee?"

Were lawyers paid to be killjoys, or was that just part of their nature? Maybe it was a good thing he never went to college and became an attorney as he'd planned. "It's worth looking into."

"Even if they don't, this lull gives you time to get your job situation worked out." Red hesitated, tipping the three-ringed folder shut. "Can I ask you a question?"

"Sure."

Red took a long sip of his coffee, as if to steel himself. "How far are you willing to go to adopt this child?"

An odd question, especially from a lawyer. "What do you mean?"

The distant song of birds waking up the neighborhood filled the seconds before Red answered. "There is another way to ensure the adoption goes through as planned."

Mack knew what the man was going to say. "I've told you marriage is not a possibility at the moment."

"Hear me out before you dismiss the idea, okay?"

Mack glared at the man but kept his seat. What other option did he have short of walking out on his friend and possibly the only lawyer in Marietta willing to take his case? "Go on."

"If you're so bound and determined to raise this baby, you need to consider finding a wife. It would solve the immediate problem with the judge."

"And who would I marry, Red?"

"You've got to know a woman who'd love the chance to help you raise Sarah. Someone who would love that baby as much as you do."

The image of Thea, her deep blue eyes staring up at him, drifted through his thoughts. No doubt Thea was in love with the idea of raising the baby right now, but what would happen when she learned Sarah wasn't Eileen's daughter? Would she up and leave town without a backward glance the way she'd done before? Mack couldn't risk his daughter losing her heart to the woman. Or maybe it was his own heart he was worried about getting stomped on again.

"It's just not possible, Red."

"Well, think about it," Red answered before he grabbed the folder and stood. "Because getting married might be your only hope of getting Judge Wakefield to budge on Sarah's adoption."

Chapter Four

Thea closed her eyes and relaxed into a cushioned chair in the hospital waiting room, her mind drifting aimlessly as fatigue settled into her bones. Sleep had been elusive these past few nights. She'd been on edge, too worried by thoughts of Eileen, of losing her last link with her sister, to find any rest. It didn't help that Momma had taken to pacing the halls at night. Each morning Thea got up with the same questions. Would this be the day she'd finally bring Eileen's baby home? Or would she and her mother be coping with another loss soon?

She drew a deep breath in through her nose, her body relaxing even further. Once she brought Eileen's baby home, everything would get better. Her mother would become alert and engaged again. Guilt would ease its weight off of Thea's shoulders. They'd all be happy. At least, that's what she hoped. How in the world would she take care of Sarah and work an eight-hour-a-day shift if her mother didn't snap out of this fog of sadness and confusion?

Thea forced her eyes open and glanced around the

hospital's waiting area. Maybe she could work part-time for a little while, at least until they figured out a routine at home. Maybe they'd be able to hire in a teenage girl to help when Thea couldn't be at home. There might not be any extra money for a lawyer if she needed one, but she'd figure that out when it came down to it.

She would manage. She didn't have much choice. Thea's eyes slid closed again. Just a few more minutes, a cat nap, and she could face her interview with the head nurse alert and fresh.

"Thea?"

She snuggled deeper into the chair, the rumbled whisper settling over her like a comfortable blanket. What was it about this deeply masculine voice that set her mind at ease? Familiar, with warm undertones, deep, almost dreamlike. She'd clung to the thought of that dark, manly voice throughout the long nights of the war, let it lull her as bombs burst in the distance. She hadn't been able to place it at first, but then she remembered the boy who'd once been her friend. Thea drew in a deep breath, felt a smile form on her lips.

Mack.

"Do you usually take naps in the hospital waiting room?"

There was a gentle sternness to his voice that caused her eyelids to flutter open to find the man standing in front of her. Tall and broad-shouldered, this Mack was the quintessential lawman, though she'd confess she'd never met an officer quite so handsome. "What happened?"

The cockeyed grin he gave her as he pushed back his hat had her sitting up in her chair. "You fell asleep."

Thea drew in a deep breath and blew it out, her fuzzy world coming into focus. "Old habits, I guess." At his confused look, she explained. "When you work the mobile surgical unit, you either learn to grab a nap anywhere you can or never sleep. Standing up in the corner. Sitting in mess hall." She smiled. "One of the girls in my unit got caught napping in the latrine."

"That must have been…interesting." Mack's voice deepened with mirth, his lips curved up into a slight smile. Then, as if he remembered who she was, he straightened, any evidence of a smile gone. "What are you doing here?"

Needing something to do with her hands, Thea opened her purse and pulled out her compact. "Interviewing for a position."

"A job?"

For some odd reason, the way he said it irritated her. She opened the lid and studied her reflection in the tiny mirror. Anything to keep from looking at him. "I have to put food on our table and keep a roof over our heads. Momma's income is really only enough for one person."

The space between them suddenly grew smaller as he pulled off his hat and sat down next to her. "And what about Sarah?"

"What about her?"

The clean tang of his aftershave swirled around her, making her head spin in a pleasant sort of way as he leaned closer. "How do you plan on taking care of Sarah if you're working?"

She leaned back and drew in a cleansing breath. It wasn't any of his business how she handled Sarah's care. "If I'm given custody of Eileen's baby, I'll work something out."

"Sarah is going to need special care, at least until she's old enough to have her second corrective surgery." He crossed his arms over his broad chest, glaring at Thea, looking every inch the protective father, the kind of daddy any girl would have been blessed to have.

Just not Sarah's daddy. Didn't he understand the little girl was the only link she had to the sister she'd lost? Mack could make gaining custody of the child difficult, there was no doubt about it. Well, she'd lived through one war. If Mack wanted to battle it out, she was ready. "What about you?"

He blinked. "Me?"

Ah, she'd caught him by surprise. Well, good! "*You* have a job. How do you plan to care for Sarah while you're off catching the bad guys?"

His blue eyes pierced her all the way to the depths of her soul. "Ms. Aurora has volunteered to take care of her during the day, but I'll have her at night. Plus, I'm turning one of the rooms in my house into an office so I can do most of my paperwork at home."

"So it's okay for you to have someone care for Sarah while you're at work, but not me." She slammed her compact shut and cocked her head to the side. "Why is that?"

Mack glared at her for a long moment, then much to her surprise, he gave a regretful chuckle. "Stuck my foot in it, didn't I?"

Thea's heart did a sudden flip at his crooked smile. Mack had always been a charmer. It would be best if she remembered that. "I'd say so."

"Sorry." He leaned back, leaving Thea suddenly bereft of his warmth. "Just had a rotten morning."

"Please say it's not the baby. She's not sick or something, is she?"

He shook his head, twirled his hat between nervous fingers. "Doodlebug is doing fine."

Now it was her turn to gawk. "You call her doodlebug?"

He cocked an eyebrow at her. "Is something wrong with that?"

No, quite the opposite. It was endearing, the sort of sweet name a man would give his baby girl. Thea shook her head. "It suits her."

He seemed glad she agreed with him, at least on his pet name for Sarah. "The first couple of days after I took her to Ms. Aurora, the kids fought over what to call her."

"I thought she'd always been Sarah."

He shook his head, the ghost of a memory playing along his smile. "That was Merrilee's idea. Ms. Aurora generally lets the kids decide what to call any new additions to their family."

The older woman let the children name the baby? "Isn't that like the prisoners running the jailhouse?"

Her heart fluttered when he turned the full effect of his smile on her. "Ms. Aurora wants them to feel like they have a say in their family. She gave them a few suggestions, and they voted for the baby to be named Sarah, though Ellie wasn't too happy about the choice."

Was Ellie one of Ms. Aurora's children? Or had Mack adopted other children? "Ellie?"

"A little six-year-old spitfire who has lived with Ms. Aurora since she was barely two weeks old." He sat down beside Thea then leaned toward her as if to whisper a secret. "They'd just gone to see a matinee of *The Wizard of Oz* and Ellie wanted the baby to be named after one of the characters."

"But Dorothy is a nice—"

He shook his head again. "Scarecrow."

Thea choked back a giggle. "You're serious."

"I had to bribe her with a day at the park to get her to agree to the name Sarah."

Oh, dear. If Mack succeeded in his adoption plans, little Sarah would have him wrapped around her pinky finger. *Lucky kid.* "The sheriff bribing small children. Isn't there a law against that?"

"Not yet. Besides, I like pushing the kids on the swing set in the park. Takes my mind off of work."

Thea studied him as he stared out over the empty room. This was the Mack she remembered, the guy who loved being outdoors, who found joy in simple pleasures like helping his neighbor or pushing a little girl on a swing. She was glad that growing up hadn't taken that away from him. But what about all his plans for adulthood? Why hadn't he followed through on his dream of playing football in college, becoming a lawyer like his father? Why had he never left Marietta?

She swallowed the questions burning on the tip of her tongue. It would only complicate the situation more if she learned who Mack had become, what had driven him to stay here, to abandon his dreams. For some unknown reason, she felt disappointed at the loss. "I never intended to hurt you, you know."

He stiffened, the pleasure of the last few minutes fading. "What do you mean by that?"

"It's just…" She hesitated, not sure how much to reveal. Maybe if she could make him understand, make him realize how important it was to her to raise Eileen's baby, it would be easier for him to let Sarah go. "I know you love Sarah, but I love her, too."

"You don't even know her."

"She's a part of Eileen. She's my family, Mack."

"You don't know that for certain," Mack said, her words obviously falling on deaf ears. "You're going to have to produce some proof to get a judge to listen to your claim."

Thea figured as much. She'd searched through Eileen's room, through her personal mail, even the journal she kept, but had found nothing except a brief entry a few days after her baby was born. Nothing to prove Thea's claim to Sarah. "I'd planned on visiting the courthouse after I finished my interview today."

"No sense wasting your time."

She glanced up at him. "Why would you say that?"

"Because if Mrs. Williams delivered Eileen's baby like you say, it wouldn't have been filed with the county and state yet." A look of frustration clouded his expression. "As I told you before, Mrs. Williams went up to Tennessee to take care of her sister shortly after Sarah was born. Sarah's birth certificate still hasn't been filed. If you're able to find a certificate on record for Eileen's baby, then that would be proof that she's *not* Sarah."

That wasn't the news Thea had expected to hear. She'd need a birth certificate to petition the court to stop the adoption. But if she needed one to prove Sarah's parentage, wouldn't Mack need one to get final approval for her adoption? "You can't adopt Sarah without a certificate, can you?"

His jaw tightened, and for a brief moment, Thea thought she'd have to pull an answer out of him. Then just as quickly, he relaxed—though only a bit. "No," he agreed, "I can't."

So he knew her frustration. "Have you been in touch with Mrs. Williams?"

He shrugged. "I've tried. I sent a letter when I learned she hadn't filed Sarah's birth certificate but she's a ways outside of the city limits so I figured it would take a while before I heard from her. I checked on sending her a telegram this morning but they don't deliver that far up into those mountains."

"I take it her sister doesn't have a phone." Thea didn't wait for an answer. She was thinking again what it must have been like for Eileen, delivering her baby all those months ago. "Do you think Mrs. Williams tried to talk any of those girls who gave up their children into keeping them?"

She felt his gaze shift to her. Could he see the pain that had consumed her in the days since she'd returned home, the fear that her only chance at a real family had died with Eileen? Or was he too centered on what losing Sarah would mean for him? His answer was to cover her hand with his, warmth to her cool skin, and she relaxed. "This thing with Eileen has really thrown you for a loop."

"I just…" She leaned her head back against the wall, her fingers threading automatically through his as if hanging on to him for dear life. "I don't understand why my sister would do such a thing. We weren't in touch for these past few years, but I've read her journal. She talked about how much she wanted a yard full of kids, babies she could love on." And who would love Eileen back, Thea suspected. "I can't see her giving her baby away."

"Maybe she realized she wasn't ready for that kind of responsibility. Maybe she did it out of love." Mack gently squeezed her hand.

She'd like to think her sister was that unselfish, but Eileen had spent her short life desperate for the affection she never got from their mother. Thea's love had never been enough for her—she had wanted more. Giving up her baby, a child who would grow to love her unconditionally, wasn't something Thea could see her sister doing. "She could have left the baby with Momma. I could have asked for an emergency discharge and come home…"

"And cleaned up the mess your sister made just like you always did?" Mack pulled his hand away as if he'd touched his fingers to a hot furnace.

"You don't understand." How could he? Mack had always had parents who loved him, who thought the sun and the stars rose in his every movement. How could he begin to fathom what she and Eileen had endured, living with a mother who always found fault, who only made time for them when it was convenient for her? "I'm not saying Eileen didn't make mistakes. I know she did, but I did, too, and when I messed up,

Eileen tried to be there for me. Sisters help each other out."

"You were too easy on her. Eileen took advantage of your sweet nature. She always did."

Thea grimaced. Yes, she probably had. But she had let Eileen down, too, at the time when her sister needed her the most. "You don't understand."

"I understand more than you think, Thea." Mack leaned a hair closer to her, just enough to see his blue eyes darken to a stormy indigo, pinning her in place.

Thea shook her head then caught herself. How could she explain her sister's behavior without Mack learning the whole truth, that this baby was not Eileen's first? That her own mother had been in cahoots with the likes of Georgia Tann, a woman who had browbeaten and threatened countless scores of women into give up their babies so that she, under the front of a charitable institution, could go on to sell those babies to the highest bidder.

To admit what her mother had done, and the circumstances leading to it, would betray the little good that was left of her sister's memory while revealing Thea's own failures. She shouldn't have taken the extra shift at work that night eight years ago, but she'd wanted to see Mack, work with him one more time before she quit to leave for college. If she had stayed home, she could have stopped her mother from ever going to the train station, before the exchange had been made with Georgia Tann.

Instead, she'd made a promise to her sister that she'd bring the baby home. And then the only option Thea'd had was to jump on that train and follow Miss Tann to the ends of the earth if need be. But it had been for nothing, and Eileen had lost whatever hope she'd held on to with the disappearance of her son, a baby boy their mother had sold to keep scandal away from their doorstep. The baby boy Thea had failed to retrieve, breaking her promise to her sister for the first time in her life—leaving her too ashamed to come home for eight long years.

Thea pushed away the awful memory. No. No matter how much Mack thought he understood her family's situation, he couldn't.

Not in a million years.

Finding Thea here at the hospital hadn't been what Mack had expected when he'd agreed to meet Beau for lunch. But these few moments he'd spent with her had given him time to get a read on her, to try to figure out what had brought her home after an eight-year absence. Only her reaction to his questions had confused him more. The woman held secrets close to the chest but her blue eyes revealed a storm of emotions that unsettled him, made him want to protect her from the pain and regret he'd found hidden in their depths. Why he felt this way, after the mess she'd left behind when she'd hopped that train out of town, after the damage she'd caused him, the loss of everything he'd ever hoped for, he couldn't explain.

No, she wasn't directly responsible for the car accident that had had such devastating consequences in his life. But he wouldn't have been out in his car that night—driving too fast to get home after dropping her off at the train station, trying to beat the curfew the coach insisted on so he'd be able to play in that weekend's big game—if she hadn't come to him, desperate, needing a ride.

If it hadn't been for her, he'd have been safely at home rather than out on the road. He'd have played in the big game instead of spending that weekend in the hospital. He'd have gone on to college, instead of losing his scholarship after the doctors said the partial deafness in one ear was permanent. He'd have lived the life he'd always planned instead of giving up his dreams.

He'd lost everything, all because he'd chosen to do a favor for a girl he'd thought was his friend. But what kind of friend would have left him behind so completely? He hadn't heard from her the entire time she was gone, even though she must have known about his accident. Not one call, or card, or even apology in eight years. Those years of silence should have been more than long enough for him to harden his heart against her.

But he couldn't deny that he still had a soft spot for Thea, maybe because he knew how tough she'd always had it at home. Probably just being overprotective, the same way he felt when he'd sworn to protect the citizens of Marietta.

And maybe President Truman plans to dance a jig in Marietta Square!

Mack stood and paced to the opposite side of the waiting room, needing to put some distance between them. Hadn't Thea taken enough from him? He touched the puckered skin just under the hairline at his ear. Nobody wanted a man who could barely hear, not even the armed services during the war, and they'd been desperate.

And now Thea was back, and this time she might cost him his child. The woman owed him a straight answer as to why she'd come home, and this time she couldn't run away.

Before he could get the question out, Thea spoke. "I'm sorry I snapped at you like that." She gave him a watery smile. "It's just…with finding out about Eileen, and well, everything, it's been a lot to deal with this last week."

Mack felt himself weaken. Poor woman. No doubt this was not quite the homecoming she'd hoped for. This situation with Eileen's baby couldn't be easy for her, either. "It's understandable. This whole thing with Sarah has got me walking around on pins and needles. I'm as grouchy as an old black bear."

"Well, maybe not that bad." Her lips twitched into a slight grin. "But almost."

He snorted out a short chuckle. That's one thing he could say for the woman. She always knew how to stop him from taking himself so seriously. But this was a serious situation. All his hopes for the future, a future that included raising Sarah, were at stake. "I love that little girl, you know."

"I know. You feel like she's your daughter."

Mack drew in a deep breath and waited. Surely she'd remind him that Sarah might be her niece and Thea intended to raise her as her own. But Thea remained quiet, as if acknowledging his love for the baby had taken what little energy she had left. He shouldn't be surprised. Thea had always been sensitive to every-one's feelings, especially her family's.

And now to his feelings, it seemed. It was a pity she couldn't have been bothered to show more care eight years ago, when he really could have used a friend. He watched her as she fidgeted with the clasp on her purse. The dark blue suit dress she wore gave her an air of de-pendability and professionalism while the black velvet hat turned her skin a luminous pink that matched the tiny pearls at her ears. Her brownish-blond hair had been pulled back into a loose knot at her nape, tiny tendrils caressed the smooth skin of her neck making his fingertips tingle. Would the silky strands feel as soft they looked?

Mack shook off the feeling. This was Thea, his old friend, the girl who'd robbed him of his future, and who had run away without a single glance back to the people who might need her. The woman who planned to steal his daughter.

"Why did you come back?"

Clutching tight to her purse, Thea lifted her head. "Excuse me?"

Mack took a step toward her, then stopped. He'd get no answers out of her if he intimidated her. "You've been gone for eight years, Thea. In all that time, you never came home, not once. So why now? What brought you back here after all this time?"

She gave a quick glance at her wristwatch as she bit her lower lip, pushed a tiny strand of hair behind her ear. Signs he took to mean Thea was nervous. She stood. "I must have misunderstood the head nurse about my appointment time. Or maybe she wanted to meet me in her office. That would make more sense."

The woman was going to make a run for it. How typical. Mack blocked her path to the exit. "Why is it so difficult for you to answer my question?"

"Why is it so important that you know?"

Why *was* it so important to him? For the sake of the baby, of course, but he knew that wasn't the entire reason he'd pushed her for an answer. Maybe if he opened up a little, Thea would feel comfortable enough to answer in return. "You left without a word to anyone except for maybe Eileen, and if she knew where you'd gone she didn't stick around long enough to tell anyone. I was surprised not to hear from you. I guess I thought we were friends back then."

He'd said too much, but once he'd started, the words had seemed to flow out of him before he could call a stop to them. What would Thea do now? Turn and walk away, or was she brave enough to answer his honesty with her own?

"I missed my family."

"After eight years?" All right, so that had been kind of mean, throwing that fact out there, but if Thea had wanted to see her family, why had she waited all this time to come back home? "You could have come to Marietta anytime."

"No, I couldn't," she snapped, then she jerked back as if the words had stung her. "I didn't mean…"

The guilt in her expression tugged at him. What had he expected? Even puppies snarl when you back them into a corner. But her answer had intrigued him. What was this great sin she had committed that made her think she wouldn't be welcomed back home?

The door behind Mack opened. "Miss, have you seen…" The man paused. "There you are, Mack. I've been looking all over for you."

Beau. Sparring with Thea had made Mack forget all about his lunch plans. "You must not have been looking too hard."

The man had the decency to smile at the good-humored ribbing. Beau turned to Thea. "I'm sorry about that, Miss. Mack here is a great sheriff but he's no Bob Hope."

"I don't know." Thea lifted her chin a notch higher, their gazes tangling as her eyes met his. "He can certainly hold your attention when he wants to."

The breathlessness in her response made Mack's palms sweat. This Thea was wiser, more confident. Yet, there was still a vulnerability about her that made him want to protect her, be her shelter in the storms that raged around her.

"You seem to know our sheriff rather well." Beau gave him a sly grin. "You ashamed of your old friends or did you want to keep your beautiful lady all to yourself?"

Mack rolled his eyes. Of course Beau would jump to conclusions. The man knew Mack had been searching for a wife, had even considered courting Edie Michaels until Beau had made it plain he wanted Edie for himself. But this woman? Mack had to set the record straight. "Thea is just a friend."

"Thea Miller?" Beau turned to study the woman in question with a more in-depth look. "Oh, my, it *is* you."

If Thea felt insulted, she didn't look it. "I know I didn't make much of a splash in high school, but I can't believe you don't recognize the girl who hung out with your cousin, Beau Daniels."

Beau squinted slightly then smiled, his eyes alight with recognition. "Maggie mentioned something about you being back in town. Of course, she forgot to mention how lovely you are."

Thea's cheeks turned a delicate pink. "That's mighty nice of you to say."

"I always believe in telling the truth."

Mack bit back a frown, an uncomfortable knot tightening in his gut. Beau didn't have to be quite so charming. "How's Edie doing? Still having problems this morning?"

Beau nodded, his smile dimmed somewhat, concern shadowing his eyes. "As long as we keep her in saltine crackers, she seems to be okay. I've told her to stay at home and not worry about work for right now, but my wife can be as stubborn as a mule. I'll be glad when she's a little bit further along."

Thea stepped forward and laid a hand on Beau's shoulder in a comforting gesture Mack had seen a million times from other nurses calming patients. Then why did the thought of her touching his friend, no matter how innocently, bother him to no end?

"Maggie mentioned your wife was having a rough time," Thea replied. "What is she? About two or three months along?"

"The baby's due at the end of April." Beau gave her a hesitant smile. "I just hate that I can't do anything to make her feel better right now."

"And being in medical school, you think you should be more prepared than most men?" She waited until Beau gave her a reluctant nod. "What you're feeling is what every other man with an expectant wife has felt, and it's okay. You know what you can do for her right now? Be there for her. Hug her when she's not quite sure why her emotions are all over the place. Tell her how much you love her. And pray for her, and for the family the two of you are making together."

"Thank you, Thea." The worry that had been in Beau's expression since the day they'd announced Edie's pregnancy eased slightly. "It's easy to see that you're very good at being a nurse."

"Thank you. I appreciate that."

Mack could tell by the color deepening in her cheeks that Thea wasn't accustomed to much praise. Why was that? She'd always been one of the smartest people he'd known, her nose always in a book, her acceptance into the finest nursing school in the Southeast proof of all her hard work. Why did she seem surprised when someone complimented her?

"Would you like to join us for lunch, Thea?"

Mack blinked at the invitation. Great, he'd hoped to talk, get some information out of Beau, maybe question him about the town council's decision to beef up the police department and where the decision might leave Mack. Now, with Thea tagging along, the conversation would be limited.

"I appreciate the offer, but I'm supposed to meet with the head nurse in a few minutes, then I have a few errands to do before I go home. It was nice to see you again, Beau, and I hope your wife gets to feeling better soon." Thea's gaze shifted to Mack. "Sheriff."

Mack was grateful for Beau's silence as Thea walked across the room, the sharp clip of her heels against the tile floor receding as she proceeded down the hall. It was only after he drew in a deep breath that Mack realized Beau was watching him. "What?"

"I could ask you the same question, my friend. There was so much tension between the two of you when I came in, you could have cut it with a scalpel."

Irritation slithered up Mack's neck. "Leave it alone."

But his friend wasn't one for listening. "You've been looking for marriage material and from what I could tell, Thea seems like a really nice girl."

Mack could hear the blood pulsing in his ears. "You're out of line."

Beau droned on. "Pretty, smart and she has a career to fall back on."

"Would you shut your pie hole?"

"And I happen to know you kind of had a thing for her back in high school."

That stopped Mack dead in his tracks. He jerked around toward his oldest friend in the world. "I never told you that."

"You didn't have to. You made it plain every time another guy thought about asking her out. How many did you threaten to pound if they so much as got near her? Five? Six?" Beau's mouth cocked up into a sly smile. "And here I thought you'd stayed friends because…well, a guy like you didn't date a girl with Thea's kind of background."

Mack had had enough. "Thea was and still is the

complete opposite of what her sister was like. As you said, she's a nice girl—and I'll have words with anyone who says otherwise. I didn't date her because we were good friends, nothing more. Okay?"

"Okay. All I'm saying is she seems to be someone who would have the kind of caring nature that would be good for…say, the mother of a young girl."

Mack sighed. Almost the exact statement his lawyer had made a few days before. "You've talked to Red."

Beau nodded, his expression suddenly somber. "He did drop by. Said you might need someone to talk to about the adoption and the mess with the town council. But something else came up this morning, and I think we need to talk about it first. Back in my office."

Whatever it was had Beau worried. Mack couldn't take much more bad news, not now. "Why don't you just spit it out?"

Beau glanced around the empty room, then motioned to a group of chairs in the far corner. Once Mack sat down, Beau seemed to transform from friend to one of the white-coated med students he'd seen around the hospital. Beau gathered his thoughts for a moment, then began. "Dr. Adams got a call from Dr. Medcalf over at the children's hospital this morning."

Mack's stomach churned. Winston Medcalf? The doctor who'd performed surgery on Sarah? When she'd almost died? "What did he have to say?"

"Dr. Adams mailed copies of Sarah's medical records over to Dr. Medcalf to keep him updated on Sarah's progress."

"He's keeping tabs on her?"

Beau's mouth twitched. "It's not like one of your undercover sting operations. Doctors need to exchange information on patients under our care."

Mack guessed that made sense. "What did Dr. Medcalf have to say?"

Beau leaned forward, resting his elbows on his knees. "He feels Sarah has matured enough to give the surgery another try."

"No."

"Come on, Mack. Sarah was barely three months old the last time Medcalf had her in the operating room. She's put on some weight, her lungs have matured a little bit." He steepled his fingers together. "She needs this surgery. Putting it off will just complicate the situation later."

An ache radiated through Mack's left jaw, and he unclenched his teeth. "She had a bad reaction to the anesthesia last time, and we almost lost her. What makes Medcalf think things will be different now?"

"I don't know. And that's not to say Sarah couldn't have another problem. But we're racing against the clock now, Mack. If she doesn't have the corrective surgery before her first birthday, the bones in her face will begin to set and make for a more complicated procedure in her future."

This was not what Mack needed to hear today. "But she's still such a tiny little thing. Couldn't we put the surgery off for at least another month or two? Give her a little bit more time to grow."

Beau dropped his chin to his chest, his fingers tightening into a knot. Whatever it was he had to say was hard on him, as if he had no other choices. When he finally lifted his head, he met Mack's gaze with an honesty that came from years of friendship. "You don't have a say in the matter, Mack. You're not Sarah's guardian."

No say in matters pertaining to Sarah? "But I'm in the middle of adopting Sarah, and Ms. Aurora, she's her guardian. She won't agree to this."

Beau shook his head. "She's not officially Sarah's guardian, not in the eyes of the law, and you…" He hesitated, as if the words hurt him to say. "We don't know how long it will be before Judge Wakefield signs those adoption papers—or if he ever will."

Mack fell back against the chair, his body numb from the news. A thought occurred to him. "Someone has to give the okay for the surgery. They can't operate without it."

"True, which is why the hospital got permission from Judge Wakefield this morning."

"Wakefield." Why didn't the news that the judge had gotten involved surprise him? Maybe because this mess smelled like something the judge would cook up. "Then I'll go to court. Get an injunction to stop the surgery."

"You think the judge is going to sign an injunction to stop a court order he signed himself?"

It did sound ridiculous when Beau said it like that. All Mack would do is poke the bear. And he couldn't afford to make the judge angry with him, not with the adoption still up in the air. "What am I supposed to do then? What if something happens to Sarah? How would I live with myself if I sat back and did nothing?"

"Have faith."

Why was it, when people don't have the answers,

they'd tell you to fall back on your faith? *Lord, help me in my disbelief. Keep Sarah safe. Help her through this.* "What you're telling me is that there's nothing I can do to stop this."

Beau shook his head. "All you can do now is be there for your daughter. Love her through it, and pray."

Mack drew in a steadying breath. "When have they scheduled the surgery?"

"A week from tomorrow. Sarah will be in the hospital at least a month, longer if there are any complications."

Mack threw down his hat on the chair beside him and raked both hands through his hair. "You know I can't afford to pay for that long a hospital stay, and I'd rather be skinned alive than allow someone else to foot the bill for my daughter."

Beau shifted to the seat right beside him. "I've been thinking about that. You've already paid for the surgery, right?"

Mack gave him a quick nod.

"Then the only bill you've got to worry about is for Sarah's convalescence, and that can be pretty much done at home under the right circumstances."

Home. Back to Ms. Aurora's. Why hadn't he thought of that? It was the perfect solution. Ms. Aurora could handle taking care of the baby during the day while he settled in for the night shift. But what about the other children in Ms. Aurora's care? They needed her almost as much as Sarah did now. Casting the extra work of caring for a recovering infant on the older lady wasn't fair to any of them, and Mack couldn't take time off to care for Sarah himself, not with his job already on the line.

"You're going to need help," Beau stated.

"I can't ask Ms. Aurora. She's got enough on her plate as it is."

"You couldn't take Sarah back there, anyway." Beau crossed his arms over his chest and stretched his back. "No matter how clean the woman keeps her home, those kids are walking incubators, bringing in who knows what kind of sicknesses. Even something as simple as a cold would complicate Sarah's recovery. We need to keep her well until the stitches in her mouth are somewhat healed."

Then Ms. Aurora's was out of the question. "My house, then?"

"It would be the best choice. She'd be isolated from other children there, and you can monitor who comes inside. The only problem now is finding a trained professional who can come in and take care of her during the day, while you're working."

"A trained professional? You mean like a nurse?"

"Exactly!" Beau nodded. "Sarah needs someone who can recognize any problems that could come up. Infection, busted sutures, stuff like that. A trained medical professional who would make herself available day or night."

"Her?"

"You'll have more of a chance at hiring a nurse, preferably one who's had some experience dealing with pediatric patients."

For some strange reason, Mack felt as if he'd just walked into a trap. "You have someone in mind?"

"As a matter of fact," Beau said, reaching into an interior pocket of his jacket and pulling out a folded sheet of paper. "I ran across this résumé yesterday and thought she'd be perfect for the job."

Mack unfolded the paper, glanced at the name at the top, then crumpled it into a ball. "You think I ought to consider hiring Thea as Sarah's nurse."

"Look, I know it's an uncomfortable situation, but her credentials are excellent."

Uncomfortable? Unbearable would be more like it. He tossed the wadded up sheet of paper back at Beau. "Then you know there is no way I'm letting her take care of my daughter."

"Hear me out." Beau unfolded the tight ball and pressed the paper against his thigh, rubbing out the creases with his hand. "This is a tough surgery, and Sarah already had enough problems the first time around. It would seem to me you'd want her to have the most experienced pediatric nurse available to care for her."

"And that's Thea."

Beau waved the crumpled paper at him. "She graduated near the top of her class and worked almost exclusively in pediatrics before she joined the Army Nurse Corps four years ago."

"And her references?"

Beau shook his head slowly, as if in disbelief. "She's even got one in there from General Patton."

Patton? It figured. Thea had never done anything halfway. When she'd decided to go to nursing school during her sophomore year of high school, she'd worked two jobs to stockpile money for school. But

Thea living in his house? Taking care of the child they both wanted?

And it wasn't just Thea. For propriety's sake, he'd have to invite Mrs. Miller to move in, too. Though, come to think of it, it might be better to have the older woman living in town, where he and Thea could work together to keep an eye on her, and other people would be able to check on her. From what he'd heard and witnessed himself, the woman had been having trouble lately. She often seemed confused and somewhat dazed. It might just be loneliness and old age wearing at her, living alone as she had before Thea's return. Or…it could be the first signs of a more serious condition. As the sworn protector of this community, he owed it to Mrs. Miller to make sure she was taken care of.

"Look, I know it's none of my business." Beau folded up the paper. "But you're not still holding a grudge against her about the accident, are you?"

Mack's chest tightened. "What are you talking about?"

"Maggie told me about the accident. About how you were out that night taking Thea to the train station before it happened, and that's why you were out on the road so late."

"That cousin of yours sure does like to shoot off her mouth a lot."

"Now, wait a minute, don't go blaming Maggie. I pestered the truth out of her. I wondered why you didn't join up with the military like everyone else and she let it slip that you couldn't because of your ear." Beau sucked in a breath through his nostrils. "She only told me because we're friends and she thought I could help."

Phrased like that, it made Mack feel as petty and as immature as a seventeen-year-old kid. Mack glanced around the room, slightly ashamed of himself, though he wasn't sure why. He'd done a nice thing to help Thea out and ended up losing his chance at a future. Surely *he* wasn't to blame for any of that. "Help how? The doctors said there was nothing to be done to save my hearing in that ear."

"No, but I could listen. I know how much being a lawyer like your dad meant to you. It must have hurt when the college pulled your scholarship."

"Water under the bridge." At least, that's what Mack told himself. He'd made a good life since then, and though it wasn't the one he'd planned on, he didn't have a reason to complain. It didn't matter if he was arguing a case in front of a jury or making an arrest. Keeping the town a safe haven in a rapidly changing world had always been his primary goal.

"What I want to know is why are you blaming this on Thea in the first place?"

Mack's jaw tightened, dumbstruck by Beau's question. "I wouldn't have been speeding home, trying to beat curfew, if Thea hadn't asked me to take her to the train station."

"You could have told her no."

He shook his head. "Thea didn't have anybody she could depend on. That night, she was frantic. I couldn't let her go by herself, even if she could have gotten a ride from someone else."

"So you made a choice."

Mack bristled at the smug look on his friend's face. Yes, he'd made the choice to help Thea that night. It didn't mean she shouldn't take some responsibility for what happened, for the way she'd abandoned him afterward, leaving him to deal with the crumbling of his dreams without even a token of her friendship. "Just like I have a choice right now whether to hire her to take care of Sarah or not."

Disappointment flashed in Beau's eyes then, just as quickly, fled. "If it were me, I'd want the best available care for my daughter."

Mack had never felt more between a rock and a hard place in his life. Of course he wanted what was best for Sarah, but why did that have to include Thea? He took the résumé from his friend. "If Thea's so good, why isn't the hospital hiring her?"

"Every nursing position is filled at the moment." Beau hesitated. "If the town council would decide to build a new hospital that could accommodate our growth, we wouldn't have to send good nurses like Thea away."

But Thea wasn't going away. She'd as much as told Mack that during their sparring match just a few minutes ago in this very room. She had a family to care for. But how would she keep a roof over their heads and food on their table if she didn't find a job to support them?

"And there's another good reason."

"What's that?"

"You could keep an eye on her. You know the old saying, hold your friends close and your enemies closer. If she's serious about getting custody of Sarah, and you have her working for you, you'll at least know what she's up to."

Beau had a point. He'd know every move Thea made, where she went and what evidence she'd collected to solidify her claim. Guilt flushed through him and just as quickly abated. What did he have to feel guilty about? The woman threatened his family. He had to do this, for Sarah's sake.

And if he was going to muddle waist high in Thea's affairs, he might as well go completely under. "Can I keep this résumé?"

"Sure, but what for?"

"I don't hire anyone without checking out their references myself."

Beau broke into a wide smile. "So you're going to hire her?"

"Maybe." If not, at least he might finally be able to find out more about what she'd been up to in the years since she left Marietta. Mack skimmed down the page, his gaze focused on the city where Thea had landed after leaving town, a bit startled by the answer he found. *Why in the world would Thea go to Memphis when the nursing school she'd planned to attend was on the other side of the state?*

Chapter Five

What was she going to do?

Thea pushed what was left of her dessert around on her plate, her nerves too much of a jumbled mess to stomach even Miss Lucille's famous peach cobbler. It had always been her favorite item on the Smith's Diner menu but not today. She finally gave up, put her fork and napkin on the plate and set it all to the side, her thoughts firmly on the interview she'd had with Sally Eison.

It had gone so well. At least, that's what Thea had thought. The head nurse had seemed quite impressed with her battlefield experience as well as her time on the pediatric floor at Methodist Hospital. An offer of employment seemed like just a formality after the hour-long interview.

But then there'd been no offer at all.

Apparently all nursing positions were filled. Even now, the words robbed Thea of breath. There was only one hospital in Marietta for now, though Nurse Eison had shared that plans were in the works to build a larger facility in the next few years. A lot of good that would do her and her family. They'd be living on the side of the road by then.

What was she going do? The next nearest hospital was a good hour away in Atlanta. Even if she considered taking a job there, it would mean a long commute every day, time she'd rather dedicate herself to Sarah's care, once the child was in her custody. There weren't enough hours in the day.

"Miss Lucille's cobbler not up to your likin' today?"

Exactly what I need right now. She stared up at Mack, his powerful, muscular frame blocking the sunlight, his face in shadows so she couldn't get a clear read on his expression. "Well, are you here for round three or did you just stop by to gloat?"

"I heard there weren't any openings."

There was a note of sympathy in his voice, as if he were truly sorry a position hadn't been available for her. The kind of sweet reaction Mack had always had, compassionate and caring. A good combination for a lawman.

A man who, at this moment, was staring at her. "Is there a problem, Sheriff?"

"Mind if I join you for a cup of coffee?"

Her heart gave a funny kick under her rib cage, though why, she wasn't sure. Probably because he'd already goaded her into one argument this morning and she wasn't in the mood for another one, not right now. But that didn't stop her from nodding her head toward the seat across from her.

"Thanks." Mack pulled off his hat and gently tossed it to the other end of the table before dropping down into the seat across from her. The cozy little booth she'd asked for suddenly seemed too small, his broad shoulders taking up almost the entire length of the table. The kind of shoulders a girl could lean on, the perfect pillow to rest her head after a long day of nursing sick people or caring for a growing baby.

Thea blinked. Where had those thoughts come from? She had enough on her plate without adding inappropriate feelings for this man to the mix. Thea leaned back into the vinyl seat. "You never answered my question."

Mack gave her a quizzical look. "What was that?"

"Is there a problem?"

"Well, yes. I mean, there could be."

A problem, and Mack was coming to her? That alone was enough to keep Thea glued to her seat. "What kind of problem?"

"It's Sarah."

Her pulse quickened, her chest suddenly tight, the feeling reminiscent of those first few moments before the ambulances arrived with a fresh batch of wounded men. Now, as she always did then, she needed to assess the situation. "What's wrong?"

He must have noticed he'd unsettled her because he reached across the table and covered her hand with his. "She's okay."

"Really?"

"I promise. She's perfect."

Thank You, Lord! Thea closed her eyes and released the breath she'd been holding. If something happened to Sarah… Her eyes shot open. "Wait, if she's all right, then what's the problem?"

"Well, um…" He hesitated as if trying to find the

right words and for a brief moment Thea felt herself soften at the uncertainty in Mack's expression. "I'm not really sure where to begin."

Thea motioned to the waitress who filled Mack's empty cup, then refilled Thea's. Once the girl had left, Thea reached for the creamer. "Well, I've heard the beginning is as good a place as any."

Mack watched as she poured a sizable amount of milk into her coffee. "Like a bit of coffee with your milk?"

Good, he was back to his irritatingly charming self. "It's the only way I can drink the stuff. What about you?"

"Three sugars." As if to confirm it, he reached for the sugar bowl. The spoon clicked against the side of the cup as he stirred three heaping spoonfuls into the steaming brew. "Sorry about that. It's been an interesting morning." Mack sat quietly for a long moment, studying her, as if trying to decide if he should tell her. Then, almost as if he didn't have any other choice, he gave a slight nod. "The doctor from the children's hospital has scheduled Sarah's surgery for next week."

Thea heaved out a relieved sigh. She'd been wondering why it was taking so long for the baby to get the surgery she needed. So why did Mack look at the prospect as a bad thing? "This is good news."

"Not to me, it isn't." Stormy blue eyes glared back at her from across the table.

She was confused. "You don't want Sarah to have corrective surgery?"

"Not until she's older. Stronger."

Thea pressed her lips together. She should have expected Mack to be an overprotective parent. He'd always guarded those around him he cared for, defending them as much as he could from the hurts this world inflicted. But this was going too far. The surgery and the recovery that came afterward might be hard on Sarah for a little while, but what she got in return would be worth it. Maybe if Thea could get him to talk about it, she could assure him surgery was the right thing for Sarah. "You do know this procedure will help her when she starts talking, not to mention helping now with her food intake."

"I'm not against the surgery. I'd just like to put it off for a few more months."

"Why?"

The muscles in his throat worked, as if he found the words almost impossible to say. "She could die, Thea. It almost happened last time they attempted this surgery. She had some trouble with the medicine they gave her to put her under. Dr. Medcalf had to stop before he barely got started because her heart rate dropped dangerously low."

No wonder Mack felt the way he did. The thought of sending Sarah into surgery now worried Thea more than a little bit. "Did he give you any reason as to why she could have reacted that way?"

Mack nodded. "He feels it had something to do with her weight, that maybe she was too small to handle the stress of the surgery."

The stoic sheriff was gone, replaced by a man deeply concerned about his child. Dark blond hair fell across his forehead, his brows knitted together in worry, his arms folded around himself as if protecting himself from a fatal blow. Emotions thickened in Thea's throat. She'd seen things during the war no man or woman should witness, had hardened her heart against her instinctive reactions so that she could do the job she'd been trained to do. So why did this man's pain pierce her heart like nothing she'd ever felt before?

"She could die." His voice was unsteady, as if saying the words made them so.

"I know." Thea touched his forearm, then settled her hand there when he didn't flinch. A nurse's touch, she reminded herself, unsure why the warmth of his bunched muscles beneath her fingers offered her comfort in return. "Dr. Medcalf must think that Sarah will be able to handle it now."

"But what if he's wrong?" His lips pressed into a hard line. "What if it happens to her again?"

Mack loved the little girl, thought she was perfect as she was, almost as if Sarah was already his daughter. What would happen when Thea finally found the evidence she needed to prove Sarah was her niece? She'd have to find ways to include Mack in the baby's life. But for now, he needed comforting. "You could always put off the procedure for a few more months. Give Sarah time to grow up a little bit more."

He shook his head. "I don't have a say in the matter."

Thea hadn't thought about that. "Then Ms. Aurora…"

"She doesn't have a say in it, either."

Then who? Her shoulders slumped slightly as the realization hit her. "Dr. Medcalf has gone to the judge and asked him to sign the consent forms on Sarah's behalf."

Mack sent her a hard stare. "How did you know that?"

"I've seen it done before on the pediatric floor where I worked when I was in nursing school," Thea answered, trying to quiet the painful memories. Going to the judge and having him sign off on authorizing procedures for the little ones she'd targeted for her Children Society had been a classic trick of Georgia Tann. At first, it had seemed like a godsend to desperate parents unable to pay for needed surgeries. But in return, Miss Tann took their children and sold them to the highest bidder. Of course, that wasn't the case here—but the memories were still painful.

"Thea, are you okay?"

She shook away the memory of Miss Tann and what she done with Eileen's first baby. Her concern right now was Sarah, and part of taking care of the girl meant calming Mack's fears so the necessary surgery could move forward. "I'm sure Dr. Medcalf will monitor Sarah very carefully after the last time."

But he was still focused on her. "Are you sure you're okay?"

"Of course I'm okay. Why do you ask?"

He nodded to a growing pile of torn paper in front of her. "That napkin you're holding didn't stand a chance."

"Oh." A flush of heat hit Thea's cheeks, and she dropped what was left of the napkin then brushed the lint off her hands. "I guess I'm more nervous than I thought."

Her confession brought a tender light to Mack's

eyes. "Little ones have a way of changing how a person thinks about everything."

"I can't disagree with you about that." Since she'd learned about this second chance to make things right with her sister's memory, Thea had thought of nothing but getting Sarah back home. Well, she admitted to herself as she stole a glance at Mack, *almost* nothing else. Even in the mist of their disagreements over Sarah, she'd caught glimpses of the boy she'd once known, teasing her, making her smile when that was the last thing on her mind. He should have women lining up at his door, begging to start the family he so obviously wanted. So why was he still alone?

Not that it mattered to her.

Thea straightened. "Don't worry, Mack. I'm certain Dr. Medcalf isn't going to take any undue risk with Sarah."

"Good." He relaxed slightly, but Thea sensed there was something else on his mind. "But that's not the entire problem."

"It's not?"

He sunk down into the seat, his voice low enough so that she struggled to hear him. "You know how long the recovery period is for a surgery like this."

Thea bent closer, narrowing the gap between them. "At least a month, maybe longer if there are complications. Why?"

"Can she be taken care of at home?"

"Yes, but…" Realization hit her. Corrective surgery was expensive all on its own. Adding in the cost of spending the recovery in the hospital made the price tag more than what most families made in a year's time. And Mack's case was complicated by the fact he was single. He could save money by having Sarah recuperate at home, but with no wife to care for the baby, he'd be forced to hire outside help. But how could she help? She didn't know any nurses in Marietta who were qualified to provide post-op for this procedure, and after their recent run-ins over Sarah, the man would never consider her. "If you're looking for a recommendation, I don't know any of the nurses who live around here."

"I already have a recommendation."

"You do?" Thea's midsection tightened into a painful knot. She wished she'd known Mack was looking for someone. If he'd asked her help with the search process then it would have given her a chance to interview the woman, find out if she was good with children and if she had the proper training to care for someone with Sarah's special needs.

"Nurse Eison spoke very highly of you. Said you were the most qualified person for the position."

The knot in Thea's stomach loosened slightly. She'd have to send the nurse a thank-you card for such kind words. There could be nothing as wonderful as spending each day with her sister's daughter, nursing her back to a normal life. But being recommended didn't necessarily mean Mack was on board with the decision, and he hadn't really offered her anything yet. "Are you saying you want me to take care of Sarah?"

He scrubbed an aggravated hand through his hair. "I'm not quite sure yet."

"But you're considering it."

"Yes, only because Nurse Eison says you're the best

pediatric nurse in town." He leaned slightly forward, his gaze catching and holding hers, concern darkening his blue eyes. "But I don't want Sarah caught in the middle of one of our 'discussions.' She may be a baby, but it can't be good for her to hear the folks caring for her arguing."

Thea understood that. "I agree."

"For this to work, we're going to have to set aside our differences."

"A truce?"

"Yes."

Mack watched her as if he expected her to argue the point. In fact, she felt grateful. To spend time with her niece, to be a part of her daily life, to nurse her back to health. It was an answer to prayer. "I think we can work something out."

"I was hoping you'd say that." He visibly relaxed, the lopsided grin he gave her kicking her heart into high gear. "What? You look surprised."

The man could absolutely read her like an open book! "I didn't expect you to agree so easily."

His smile slid into a more serious line, and she felt a pang of disappointment at its absence. "I'd move mountains for that little girl."

Thea didn't doubt it. If fact, she felt a tad envious. How would her life have been different if she'd had someone like Mack as a constant presence to protect and watch over her? To love her unconditionally without ever expecting anything in return? She wanted to give that to Sarah. It was what Eileen would have wanted.

"Then we agree. Truce?" Mack held his hand out to her.

"Truce." She slid her hand into his, sparks racing up her arm. Once the surgery was in the past and the situation with Sarah was settled, someone would nurse a broken heart.

Please, Lord, don't let it be mine.

"We'll need to explain the situation to Ms. Aurora. Will you come with me for that?"

Oh, dear. It was a reasonable request. Thea was the one with the medical background who could answer Ms. Adair's questions. And anyway, it would make sense that she'd have to face the woman eventually. How would she feel about Mack's plan for Thea to be involved in Sarah's recovery? "Yes, of course. When's a good time for you?"

"I'm going out there this afternoon."

She blinked. So soon? Would she have time to run home and check on her mother? But she couldn't fritter away this opportunity, either. "Right now?"

"Might as well get this over with." He nodded. "Just don't expect Ms. Aurora to feel comfortable with the surgery unless Dr. Medcalf can promise Sarah will be okay."

No doctor would ever make that kind of guarantee. Maybe she could explain the procedure in a way that would give Mack and Ms. Adair peace of mind. Convince them that this was the right thing to do for the little girl they only wanted the best for.

For now, they'd be working together to take care of Sarah. And as for what would happen later…they'd deal with that then.

Chapter Six

An hour later, Mack's doubts continued to dog him as the familiar landscape along the route to Ms. Aurora's flew by. What had he been thinking, asking Thea to nurse his daughter back to health after her operation? What would stop her from taking Sarah and stealing off to parts unknown? He'd have to keep her close to keep her in line.

Which could be a problem.

Mack glanced over at Thea. He hadn't known shaking a woman's hand—or maybe it was just *this* woman's hand—could set off a firestorm of emotions inside him. Attraction, yes, but something deeper, a feeling that threatened to endanger the well-thought-out plans he'd made for his life. He couldn't trust Thea for the long term, not when she'd let him down in the past. And Thea wouldn't want someone like him, anyway. No woman had after they'd learned of his disability.

"You've got that look on your face."

Had Thea figured out what he'd been thinking? Mack coaxed his features into a neutral expression, only his knuckles, gleaming white from their tight grip on the steering wheel, betrayed the turmoil he felt. "What look?"

Her skirts rustled softly as she turned toward him. "The look that says you're wondering if you've made a huge mistake, asking me to take care of Sarah."

She'd gotten all that from his expression? He couldn't imagine what hidden truths she'd have mined out of him if he'd given her a yes or no. "It would be unwise not to wonder if you've made the right decision at times."

"But you've always been so sure of yourself, so certain of the choices you made."

"We all have to grow up sometime." Mack stared out at the road in front of him. Yes, he'd been sure of himself, almost cocky back in those days, so certain of who he was and what the life ahead of him looked like. A football scholarship, then law school and a family of his own, almost the same path his father had taken, a journey Mack had been on since birth.

Had he done the right thing in hiring Thea?

"Is Ms. Aurora expecting us?"

He glanced at her, sitting so properly, her hands folded in a neat knot in her lap. She'd freshened her lipstick, a dusty rose that reminded him of the blooms he'd planted last spring just outside his bedroom window, lovely and dewy soft.

It seemed that handling this attraction he felt toward her was going to be more difficult that he'd thought. Mack flipped the blinker on. "Ms. Aurora knows I come out and see Sarah when I get off work."

"So *you're* expected. But what about me?"

"I didn't have time to call and let her know you'd

be coming, if that's what you mean." Which was the truth. Once he'd gotten back to his office after hammering out all the details with Thea, he'd had to track down paperwork for a bond hearing, then got called out for the weekly disturbance at Old Man Fletcher's house. The one time he had tried to call Ms. Aurora, she hadn't picked up. "But knowing Ms. Aurora, she'll be fine with it."

"I don't know." Thea's voice held a touch of doubt. "I mean, I can't be her favorite person. She thought I was spying on her and the kids."

"You *were* spying on her and the kids. But she is the most understanding soul I've ever met. It takes a lot to ruffle her feathers," Mack reassured her.

"She must be a saint." Thea rested back against the vinyl seat, crossing her arms over her tiny waist. "I'd be like an old momma bear if someone put my cubs at risk."

A faint memory played along the fringes of Mack's thoughts. "You always did have a soft spot for little ones. Remember how you got roped into nursery duty at church?"

"I can't believe you remember that."

Mack stole a glance at her. "Why wouldn't I? It's not everyone who can hush a room full of crying infants by just talking sweet to them."

Her cheeks turned a shade of soft pink. "I wasn't the only one who knew how to handle kids. Seems I recall you leading the boys in a raid on the toy chest more than once."

"The girls hogged all the cookies for your tea party.

What other alternative did we have?" he teased, then fell quiet. "Did you always want to take care of kids?"

She nodded. "For the most part. Children are easier to handle than adults. You love them, do everything you've been taught to make them feel better and they'll trust you with their life. They're open, honest. Not like adults."

Mack didn't know how to answer, only knew that Thea's words had tightened into a knot in the pit of his stomach. Somewhere along the way, someone had abused her trust, and it had scarred her like the puckered skin hidden in his hair next to his ear. But who? And what had they done to make Thea question everyone's motives?

"How did Ms. Aurora come to take in all these children?"

Mack turned the car down the dirt road to the Adair farm. "I don't know the whole story, just that she's owned this place and brought in kids no one else wanted for as long as I've known her. Before the kids, it must have seemed like a big house without anyone else living there."

"She never married?"

Mack shook his head. "I heard she was engaged to one of the coaches at the high school for a time but it didn't work out."

"So she committed herself to the kids, instead."

The way she said it, with an air of disbelief, grated Mack's nerves. "Ms. Aurora is like that, always doing for others before thinking of herself. It's just her way."

Thea gave a noncommittal "Hmm."

"You don't seem too impressed."

"Why should I be?" There was real surprise in her voice, as if she truly didn't understand why it mattered to him.

Why did it bother him what Thea thought of Ms. Aurora? Maybe because Ms. Aurora was the most loving person he'd ever met, someone who'd truly followed God's path despite the heartache and loneliness life held. She'd be a good example to Thea on how to find contentment in her life despite all of the challenges—contentment that Thea had never seemed to have for as long as Mack had known her.

"How many children has she adopted out?"

He shot a glance at her. Was she serious? These kids' own parents hadn't wanted them because of the physical and mental challenges they faced. Getting a stranger to agree to adopt them would be all but impossible. Was that why Thea wasn't impressed by Ms. Aurora? Because she had no idea the condition of the children the older woman cared for? "Sarah will be the first."

"Sarah will be the *first*?" she repeated.

Mack nodded. "Most of these kids were left on the streets to fend for themselves, or given to Aurora to avoid being admitted to an institution."

"I just thought…"

"What?"

Instead of giving him an answer, she went quiet, as if mulling over this new information. Was she measuring it against everything she'd seen in her years as a pediatric nurse and finding it hard to swallow? "People are cruel, aren't they," she said at last. "Abandoning their own kids like that."

The need to comfort her, to wrap her in his arms and whisper soothing words, to ease the desolation in her voice, slammed through him. Thea had never had it easy, not with her sister always in trouble, or a mother who didn't have a kind thought toward either of her children. Words would have to do for now. "I use to think of it that way, but now I look at the situation as a blessing."

He felt her staring at him and could imagine she probably thought he'd lost his mind. "How's that?"

"Maybe these kids had a rough start, but now they've got a home with someone who loves them as her very own, not to mention a family of aunts and uncles from the community." Mack maneuvered the turn into Ms. Aurora's driveway. "What someone thought of as a curse, God turned into a blessing."

"I guess that's the only way to look at it, isn't it?"

Mack frowned. Thea didn't sound convinced. Of course, she didn't know Ms. Aurora, didn't know what a Godly woman she was. Once Thea got to know her, she'd see that these children couldn't have been left in more capable hands.

"Maybe if I'd known Ms. Aurora before I left here," Thea whispered just loud enough for Mack to hear as he pulled the car to a stop near the front porch. "She might have known how to help us."

Mack's stomach lunged. What did Thea mean? What trouble could Thea have gotten into that she thought the older woman would have known how to handle?

A knock at his window surprised him out of his thoughts. Mack rolled down the glass to find Billy

Warner staring at him. "Are you going to get out or were you planning to sit in the car all day?"

A smile tickled Mack's lips. The boy might have limitations but his character—and his penchant for mischief—was like that of any other kid his age. Billy glanced beyond Mack to where Thea sat. "Did you finally get a girl to go out with you, Sheriff Mack?"

Mack tried to temper the heat rising up the back of his neck. His problems with the female population of Marietta must have been the topic of one of Merrilee and Ms. Aurora's hen talks. What would Thea think? When she'd left Marietta, Mack had still been the big man on campus, still had a future ahead of him.

Mack found out soon enough. "Then I must be a lucky woman indeed that those other girls didn't take him up on a date."

"That's what Ms. Aurora said—when the right girl came along, she'd snatch Mack up in a heartbeat." Billy grinned back at them as if he'd discovered penicillin or something.

Thea snorted softly, and the heat in Mack's cheeks flamed higher. Someone needed to have a long talk with the boy about using some tact, especially around women. He stole a glance at Thea but found no sign of pity in her expression, just a teasing warmth that melted away some of the residual anger he'd felt toward her.

Might as well face his embarrassment head-on. "As you can tell, things have changed since high school."

She gave him an understanding smile. "Truer words have never been spoken."

Mack nodded. Yes, the accident that had made him

partially deaf had molded him into the man he'd become, but what of Thea? What experiences had shaped her since she had left Marietta?

And why was it suddenly so important that he know? Because he was trusting her with Sarah, that had to be it. Or, at least, that's what he told himself as he opened the car door and stepped outside.

Thea was already out of the car by the time he walked around to open her door. She studied the house, almost as if it was a specimen she was looking at under a microscope. Mack took a long look at the two-story frame. It might not be much, with the paint peeling and the torn screens, but it was the only home these kids had ever known. "It's not much to look at, but Aurora has made it into a home."

She glanced back at him. "Does a blind child live here?"

Her question surprised Mack. "How did you know that?"

Thea pointed to the clothesline that connected the front porch to the barn and various parts of the front yard. "Rather ingenious, really. Gives the child a feeling of independence when they can get from place to place in their own home. And the ramps." She motioned to the angled boards that covered every step coming off the porch. "She's made it easier for Billy and the others to move around. From what I can see, Ms. Adair has converted her house to accommodate children with special needs."

"So the peeling paint doesn't bother you?"

Her brows furrowed. "Why would it?"

He'd been prepared to defend Ms. Aurora and how

much she put into making this a refuge and haven for her children. It was a little jarring to realize he didn't need to. Why had he assumed that Thea wouldn't understand? Was Beau right? Did he still blame her for the accident that night? Was that why he defaulted to assuming the worst of her? He wanted to move past it, had thought he had to a degree but could he possibly still hold her responsible for everything he had lost—and for the friendship she had abandoned on top of it all? An "I'm sorry" would go a long way to healing this gap between them, yet Thea held back. Why couldn't she at least give him that?

"Is something wrong, Sheriff Mack?"

Mack glanced down at the young boy balancing on his crutch beside him. "Why would you say that?"

"It's just you look…" Billy's gray eyes narrowed, a swatch of brownish blond falling carelessly across his forehead. "Pensive."

Pensive? Mack felt a smile form on his lips. "That's a mighty big word there, Billy."

The boy rolled his eyes. "I told Claire I'd sound like a sissy if I went around saying stuff like that, but she says if I want to go to college someday, I'd better start learning big words."

Ah, Mack should have known a woman would be involved, even if she was barely twelve and still wore pigtails. He settled his arm across the boy's lanky shoulders. "It won't do you any harm to learn a new word or two."

"Well, I think Claire is a very wise young lady."

Both he and Billy turned to look at Thea. Planting

the tip of his crutch on the ground, Billy took a step toward her. "You do?"

Thea tilted her head to the side and nodded. "It's never too soon to start planning for your future. Why, I started reading biology books from the minute I realized I wanted to be a nurse, and it helped me when I entered college."

"You went to college?" The admiration in the boy's voice was undeniable.

Thea's cheeks warmed to a delightful shade of pink. "Well, nursing school."

"But that's almost the same thing," Billy argued. The boy turned slightly and glanced back at Mack. "Did you go to college, too, Sheriff Mack?"

The question still caused a band to tighten around his heart, even after all these years.

Mack stepped forward and ruffled the boy's hair. "No, Billy, college wasn't in the cards for me."

"But I thought…"

Mack glanced over at Thea. Confusion and questions clouded her blue eyes. A whole lifetime of questions. But he didn't have the time or patience to give her any answers at the moment. "We ought to get up to the house or Ms. Aurora is going to be wondering where Billy took off to."

"I wouldn't want that." Billy hobbled off at a fast pace. "Last time I took off without telling her, Ms. Aurora put me in charge of Ellie all day long. Don't want to do that again."

"Is this the Ellie who took your bribe, Sheriff?" Thea tucked her purse under her arm as Mack took her elbow.

The feel of her soft skin beneath his fingertips sent a trail of warmth up his arm. "The very same. You'll meet her soon enough."

They followed Billy across the yard, onto the front porch and into the foyer, the water-stained walls hidden behind sheet after sheet of the children's artwork. At the door, a box held wooden blocks, Tinkertoys and baby dolls with their hair matted, their clothes dirty to show how often they'd joined the children outside to play. He picked up one rat-haired doll that looked ready for the garbage can. What kind of toys were these for Sarah to play with?

"Sheriff Mack!" A small warm body crashed into his legs, throwing him slightly off balance. He reached down to steady himself, his hand landing in a bed of soft curls.

"Ellie!" Billy scolded. "You almost knocked him over!"

The girl loosened her grasp and tilted her head back to look at him, her eyes wide with concern. "I sorry."

"The infamous Ellie, I take it."

The playful grin Thea gave him made his heart tumble around in his chest. Mack crouched down in front of the child, and touched the tip of Ellie's flat nose. "It's okay, gumdrop. I'm happy to see you, too."

The girl nodded, her curls bouncing against her shoulders. "Swing?"

"Mack?"

He glanced up to see all good-natured teasing in Thea's expression replaced by a growing look of concern. "What is it?"

Thea tossed her purse on a nearby bench and bent

down beside him. "Do you mind if I look at your arms, sweet pea?"

As if to answer, the child lifted her hands into the air, displaying a cluster of angry red bumps gathered under her arms spreading down to her elbows. Mack took a good look at Ellie's face, surprised to find the same red spots along her hairline and across her nose. "Did you get in a batch of poison ivy?"

Blond curls bounced when Ellie shook her head.

He pressed a hand against her forehead, then glanced up at Thea. "She's burning up."

"I thought as much." She tugged at the fingers of her gloves and pulled them off, then tossed them alongside her purse. "We need to get her upstairs and in a cool bath to get her fever down."

But Ellie had other ideas. The girl crossed her chubby arms over her chest, her expression one of mulish determination. "I want to swing."

"But you're burning up, sweetheart, and a bath will make you feel better," Mack pleaded.

"No!"

Thea kneeled down in front of the stubborn little mite. If she thought she'd convince Ellie to change her mind, she was about to get schooled in the ways of a certain six-year-old. "So you don't want to go for a swim?"

Ellie's body relaxed slightly. "But you said you were going to give me a bath."

"That's just what us big people call it." Thea leaned in closer, as if sharing a great secret with the child. "The truth is we're not small enough to go swimming in the bathtub when it gets too cold outside. But you!

You can make do by swimming around in the bathtub, instead."

The small girl didn't seem convinced. "I like to jump in the water."

"I know. I do, too. And you can't jump into a bathtub in the same way. But you can float on your back and splash around just as if you're pretending it's a hot summer day." Thea nodded her head toward the toy box. "I bet one of your baby dolls would like to go swimming with you, too."

"Really?" Ellie's bright blue eyes widened with excitement. "Grandma Aurora won't mind?"

Thea gifted her with a bright smile that Mack wished was aimed his way. "I'll tell her what a big girl you're being and ask."

"I'll be right back." Ellie started for the stairs.

Mack started after the child, but Thea's delicate hand on his shoulder locked him in place. "Where are you going, gumdrop?"

"I go put on my bathing suit!" Ellie crested the top of the stairs then disappeared down the hall.

Mack would have laughed at Miss Ellie's antics, but he was too worried. Praise the Lord, Thea had a certain way with kids, though Ms. Aurora might not appreciate the soaked floors and wet towels Ellie's "swim" was sure to generate. Right now, he'd mop the floors himself. The child's fever had scorched his hand. Between that and the bumps, what could be wrong with her?

He glanced back at Thea to find her rummaging through her purse before pulling out a stubby pencil and a pad of paper. "What are you doing?"

She didn't bother to lift her head to look at him. "Making a list. We're going to need supplies."

Riddles made more sense to Mack right now than this woman. He needed to get a handle on the situation before alarming Ms. Aurora, and the best way to do that was figure out what the little girl had gotten into. "What's wrong with her?"

Thea stopped writing and looked at him then, her expression calm yet tender, her eyes the most incredible shade of pale blue. She stepped toward him then stopped, as if she'd wanted to give him comfort, maybe even hold him in her embrace, then thought better of it. Instead, she settled for a gentle smile. "Ellie's going to be okay. I promise."

"But…" He couldn't stand thinking that Ellie might be in pain or uncomfortable. And what about Sarah and the other children? Were they in danger of catching what Ellie had?

Thea's warm hand in his scattered his thoughts, her delicate fingers strong and dependable as she gently squeezed his. She'd done this once before, when he'd missed his receiver downfield and lost the state playoff game. That was the first time he'd wondered if Thea might be part of his future.

As if she'd read his thoughts, Thea released his hand and stepped back, leaving him with a faint sense of loss. "Don't worry, Mack. We may have a minor epidemic on our hands but it's only chicken pox."

Chicken pox?

"Mack, I thought that was you." Ms. Aurora hurried down the hallway toward them, Sarah fussing on her shoulder. The tiny pink spots that dotted the baby's chubby legs sent Mack's stomach tumbling into his shoes. "I'm gonna need some help. The children have come down with chicken pox."

He hoped that didn't mean what he thought it did. "What kind of help do you need?"

The older woman thought for a moment. "I think I have enough oatmeal, but I could use a bottle of aspirin."

Thea stepped forward with her pencil and paper. "I thought I'd get the pharmacist to make up a couple of bottles of calamine lotion to help soothe the itching."

Mack nodded to Thea. "You remember Thea Miller? From Merrilee and John's wedding?"

"The young lady who's been spying on us for the last week." Ms. Aurora glared at him as if he'd brought a war criminal into the house.

"And I'm sorry about that. It was never my intention to worry you." Thea's expression softened as her gaze drifted to the child in Aurora's arms. "I wanted to see Sarah so very much. She looks so much like my sister." She reached out to touch the child, then pulled her hand back. "How could Eileen give such a precious little girl up?"

Ms. Aurora glanced at Mack, confusion deepening the lines around her eyes and mouth. "Your sister? I don't understand."

"It's a long story," Mack answered. One that he'd eventually have to share with the older lady. But at the moment they had more pressing matters. "How many of the kids do you think are sick?"

"Five so far. But Billy's never had it so it's just a matter of time."

Not necessarily. Mack had been exposed to the chicken pox a number of times and never got it. Maybe Billy was immune, too. Still, five sick kids were a lot, even if Billy wasn't added to the list. Ms. Aurora couldn't handle such a load on her own. She needed help, but who? Usually, Merrilee and John would be here, but they still had a few days left on their honeymoon, and the other Daniels women who would normally pitch in were expecting and couldn't be put at risk.

He was stumped. "Got any ideas who might be able to come and give you a hand over the next few days?"

"I can."

Thea. She'd be the logical choice with her nursing background, and he'd seen for himself she had a way of dealing with children. But was it asking too much of her to care for five, maybe even six sick kids?

Seven, if Mack came down with the virus, too.

But he wouldn't.

Would he?

Chapter Seven

Mack closed his eyes and drew in a deep breath, rubbing his arms to generate some heat in his extremities, his stomach and back itching as if a nest of mosquitoes had camped out under his shirt. Though the day was warm for October, a cold chill ran up his spine as he stood in the shade of Thea's front porch.

What could be taking Mrs. Miller so long? Mack rubbed the back of his neck where a headache had settled in. Packing an overnight case for her daughter couldn't be that difficult. Toothbrush, comb, a change of clothes. But then ladies needed more than the bare basics, didn't they? Though what Thea would need, he couldn't say. She had a natural beauty about her, eyes that sparked with humor and compassion, lips the perfect shade of pink to tempt a man beyond reason.

Sucking in another breath, Mack lifted his hand to his forehead, his palm wet with moisture. Fever. No wonder his mind had wandered into this dangerous attraction he felt for Thea.

The screen door squealed open behind Mack and Mrs. Miller poked her head out, pulling Mack's thoughts back to the matter at hand. "I'm sorry it's taking so long, Sheriff, but I can't seem to find a suitcase."

Truly? He'd been standing out here for a good twenty minutes, and she hadn't even started packing? Mack pulled the door open wider and followed the woman inside. "I usually keep mine in the hall closet."

"That sounds like a place Thea would hide it."

Odd way to put it, Mack thought. Almost as if Mrs. Miller thought Thea was concealing something. He watched the older woman hurry across the foyer, pass a door Mack knew to be the closet and head back up the stairs. He frowned. Mrs. Miller had always been a little scatterbrained but since Eileen's passing, she'd seemed different, more forgetful than usual. He'd put it down to the sorrow of losing a child but what if it was something else? What if there was something seriously wrong with her?

The idea worried Mack. Thea had already lost her sister and might never be able to track down her niece. Was she now at risk of losing her mother, too? Family had always been so important to her, even with all the problems they caused. Losing her last link to her family would break Thea's heart. Maybe her staying with Ms. Aurora—leaving her mother in this house alone—wasn't such a good idea, but there was no one else to help tend to a houseful of sick kids.

Well, if he couldn't bring Thea back to the mountain, he'd have to take the mountain to Thea. Mack walked over to the bottom of the stairway. "Mrs. Miller, why don't you come with me to Ms. Aurora's? Thea is going to need all the help she can get and Ms. Aurora would love the extra company, I'm sure."

The woman turned toward him, a wrinkle worrying her forehead. "I don't know. Thea's always done just fine on her own."

That was true, but then Thea hadn't had much choice with a younger sister running wild and an indifferent mother. She hadn't just taken care of herself—she'd taken care of them, too. Which was why Mack couldn't leave Mrs. Miller here, no matter how much she wanted to stay. "That's a lot of work, keeping all those kids from scratching themselves silly."

"What about the baby?"

Mack's heart sank. He'd hoped to get back to Ms. Aurora's without any mention of Sarah or her supposed relationship to Eileen but he didn't see any way around it. "She's covered in chicken pox, too."

Mrs. Miller's eyes went hazy, as if she was drifting in her own thoughts or memories. "So sad when babies get sick," she murmured. "And there's nothing... nothing you can do. Even when you try—but it's not my fault." She shook her head. "Not my fault that Eileen's baby passed."

Mack blinked. Had he heard her right or was it just the fever? Did Mrs. Miller almost slip up and say Eileen's child had died?

Thea leaned back against the wall, wiping off the last bits of wet oatmeal from her hands, her cuffed shirtsleeves damp around the edges. The past few hours had proved hectic as Thea examined first one child, then another, making notes—writing down each child's temperature, the extent of the blisters, the times she'd administered oatmeal baths. A second round of baths would need to start soon, and Thea had used the last of the oatmeal.

Where was Mack?

She glanced at the clock sitting on a nearby hall table. It had been over an hour since he'd left to get supplies at Mr. Galloway's drug store. Had he ran into problems finding some of the items on her list or had he been called out on police business? Maybe at this very moment he was struggling to disarm a person with a gun. Her stomach clenched into a sick knot at the thought.

Why had he gone into such a dangerous profession when he could have gone to college and earned his law degree the way he'd planned? Being a lawyer had been his dream, at least, the one he'd shared with her the most when they studied together at the library or worked the same shift at the movie theater. What had happened? How had his dream for the future gotten sidetracked?

A noise in the front hall pulled Thea to the top of the staircase, relief cascading through her at the sight of Mack setting two large grocery bags on the front table. He'd barely put them down before he turned and walked out the door again.

Where was he going? Thea hurried down the stairs and across the hall to the door, stopping briefly to confirm what she already knew, that everything they'd need from the druggist was in the two bags. Then what, she wondered as she moved to the door, did Mack have out in the car? He walked to the passenger-side door, opened it, then leaned down.

"Momma?" Thea stepped out on the porch, the sickening knot suddenly back in the pit of her stomach as she watched Mack help her mother from the car. "What are you doing here?"

"This nice police officer thought I might like to take a ride." She tilted her head back and stared up at Mack with a look of total adoration. "Wasn't that kind of him?"

"Yes, Momma, that was very kind of him, but…" Thea stared past her mother to where Mack extracted two suitcases from the backseat of his car. He shook his head slightly, cutting off any further questions she might have. He was right—that particular talk would have to wait. The children needed them at the moment.

"Why don't we get your mother settled, then we can make a plan of attack?"

We? Thea had figured Mack would drop off the supplies then head on home. The town couldn't do without their sheriff while he helped her tend to a bunch of sick kids, no matter how much she craved his presence. Ms. Aurora, God bless her, could have handled the children if Claire and Billy pitched in, but both of them had been confined to their beds, their temperatures spiking in the time Mack had been gone. Now with her mother, it was one more person to care for.

Ms. Aurora, looking tired and worried, met the group at the door. She perked up when she spied Thea's mother. "Mildred Miller, why, it's been a coon's age since I've seen you."

"Aurora Adair." Momma grasped the woman's hands as if they were long-lost friends newly found. "It's been forever. How have you been?"

"Why don't we go into the kitchen and have a cup of

coffee?" Ms. Aurora wrapped her skinny arm around Momma's plump one. "It'll give us time to catch up."

"What a lovely idea! You wouldn't happen to have any of those delicious macaroons you use to make? I never could get you to give me the recipe."

"No macaroons, but I baked some peanut butter cookies this morning." Their voices drifted off as they made their way down the hall and into the kitchen.

Thea spun around to face Mack. "What is she doing here?"

Mack set down the suitcases then straightened. "I went by your house on the way back from town. I figured you might need some things if you intended to stay here for the next few days. But when I got there, your mom seemed more confused than usual."

"What did you mean, more confused than *usual*? How would you know that?" Her eyes widened and her mouth fell open slightly. "You been called out to the house before, haven't you?"

Mack seemed almost reluctant to answer, as if telling her the truth would open up a new wound. "Your mother's next-door neighbor called me out there about a month ago."

"The Donohues?" They were a kind couple, Thea remembered. Always offered her a homemade biscuit every morning on her way to the school bus stop.

"Mr. Donohue came home from work and found your mother on the front porch, barefoot and in her nightgown. She was confused, Thea. Didn't have a clue where she was or how she'd gotten there."

"Oh." Thea felt like sinking into the floor. Needing something to steady her, she reached for the table and found Mack's warm arm instead. He pulled her against his broad chest, his strong arms anchoring her, keeping her safe. She buried her face in the curve of his neck. "I thought she was just rattled over losing Eileen and worried about the baby. Grief will do that to a person."

"It still could be the reason she's acting the way she is."

She felt the corners of her mouth lift slightly. Mack was being kind now, trying to ease her into the reality of her mother's situation. But Thea had always been a good diagnostician—when she didn't allow her emotions to get in the way. She knew what these lapses in memory were, what her mother's outbursts of anger and frustration meant.

I'm losing her a little at a time.

A whimper tore through her before she had a chance to react. All she had ever wanted, if she made it back from the war, was to have her family, flawed as they may be, around her again. She'd prayed about it, asked God to give her another chance to make things up to Eileen, to make her peace with Momma. It was the one hope that had gotten her through the endless line of young men that she'd sutured up and sent back out into the battle.

Who did she have now?

"You're not alone, sweetheart," Mack whispered near her ear, his hand tracing comforting circles against her shoulder blades, lulling her, making her wish she could press farther into his embrace. He'd always known how to comfort her, almost as if he had the instruction manual. If she could only have a man like Mack, someone to build a life with, and a family.

She'd spend the rest of her life showing him how precious he was to her, how much she loved him.

Love? The errant thought caught her off guard.
It had to be an overreaction to this crazy day. First,
the job interview, then Mack's idea to have her nurse
Sarah, not to mention tending a houseful of kids
breaking out in various degrees of chicken pox and,
of course, her mother's issues.

What man could possibly want to involve himself
in that?

Thea placed her hand on his chest and gently pushed
away from him. Love? How could she love a man who
threatened to take the only family she had left? Besides, Mack didn't deserve to be chained to the mess
her family had always been. And her problems with
her mother's deteriorating health were just beginning.

"You okay?"

"I'm fine." She wasn't really, but he didn't need to
know that. Walking over to the hall table, she bus-
ied herself unpacking the grocery sacks. "Did you get
ahold of Dr. Medcalf's office and let him know about
Sarah?"

"He wasn't too thrilled about the delay but what's
he going to do? Operate on her while she's infected?
Maybe he hasn't had chicken pox, either."

What did Mack mean by *either*? It wasn't possible,
was it? How could a grown man Mack's age have made
it through his youth without contracting the virus? She
sought his reflection in the mirror hanging over the
table and almost gasped. His skin was flushed, as if
he ran a low-grade fever, and she couldn't be sure but
a pink spot appeared to be forming high on his right

cheek. Thea jerked around. "Mack, you've had the chicken pox, haven't you?"

He shook his head, then rubbed the back of his neck as if he was nursing a headache. "Never caught it. Mom wanted me to catch it." He gave her a faint smile. "Even sent me over to friends' houses when they'd come down with it, hoping they'd pass it along. The doctor said I must have a natural-born immunity to it."

Without asking, she pressed her hand against his forehead, startled by the heat radiating through her fingers. "I think whoever told you that was wrong. You're on fire."

"Probably nothing." Mack swatted her hand away. "I've been running around for the last couple of hours trying to get everything settled, that's all. Just got overheated."

Well, she could add irritability to his symptoms. Grabbing his shirtsleeve, she tugged him into the dining room then pushed him into the nearest chair. "Be still while I check for more spots."

His dark blond brows furrowed together. "What do you mean *more*?"

"Well," she started, cupping his face with one hand and tilting it up toward the light. "You're got a small bump here." She brushed her fingertip along the outer curve of his right cheek.

Mack reached up to rub the spot but she swatted his hand away. "You're making a mountain out of an anthill," he complained.

"Maybe." The word came out on a shaky breath, the gentle scratch of his day-old beard against her palm sending pinpricks of awareness up her arm. Thea chided herself. She needed to focus. The man was obviously sick. "Well, I'm not taking any chances. Chicken pox can be serious business in adults. Understood?"

He gave her a reluctant nod.

That settled, Thea scanned his face, taking in every nuance: the tiny laugh lines around his eyes and mouth, the faded scar on his forehead he'd gotten when he'd taken a tumble on the fireplace when he'd been a toddler. Her gaze shifted downward, only to find him watching her.

"You have flecks of silver in your eyes."

Her heart did a funny pitter-pat in her chest. "I do?"

"Yeah." His irises turned a warmer shade of blue. "Almost like tiny bursts of starlight."

Thea felt her cheeks go warm as she ducked her head to check his exposed neck. "I don't remember you being so poetic, Sheriff Worthington."

"It's been known to happen on occasion, especially around a pretty nurse."

Oh, my. The man must have a higher fever than she'd thought to spout such sweet words to her. But even that knowledge didn't stop her heart from beating out a wild rhythm under her rib cage. Thea dropped her hand and moved to his side, still close enough to get a good look at any spots that might have formed. "Let me check your scalp. Sometimes the lesions like to hide in the hairline."

"If you have to."

She took a deep breath, then sank her hands into his neatly trimmed strands of blond hair, her fingers gently moving. How many times had she dreamed of doing exactly this when they'd been in high school, dreamed of feeling the weight and texture of every strand against her palms as she tugged him close for a kiss? Her mouth went dry. Girlish dreams. Mack had only ever looked on her as a friend, and now, a nurse. A nurse with a houseful of sick patients.

Mack closed his eyes and slumped down farther in the chair. "Mmm, that feels good."

A soft smile turned up the corners of her mouth. "Helping your headache any?"

"How did you know?"

"I'm a nurse, remember? It's what I do." She felt along the hairline at one ear, then the other, pausing when her fingertips skimmed over a small jagged line that puckered just under his hair. "What's this?"

"What?"

Thea tilted his head slightly to one side and pushed the hair away to get a better look. She uncovered a pale, almost whitish zigzag line about an inch in length. "It looks like a surgical scar."

The muscles beneath her fingertips tightened. "It is."

"What happened?"

Mack glanced up at her, the warmth in his blue eyes suddenly chilled. "Your mother didn't tell you?"

Thea felt the air drain from her lungs. There was a note of anger in his voice, as if it was a foregone conclusion she would know what had happened to him. How could she explain that, until a week ago, she'd spoken less than ten words to her mother over the past eight years? "You know Momma. She's never been one to keep up with the news around town."

"So you don't know about the car accident I was in the night you left town?"

A hard lump formed in the pit of Thea's stomach. "How bad was it?"

He hesitated, and for a moment she thought he wouldn't answer. "I was rounding a corner on Cunningham Road and skidded. Ended up wrapped around a tree in the Deavers's front yard. I'm just thankful I didn't hit anyone else."

"What a blessing that it wasn't any worse than it was." Thea breathed a sigh of relief. "You could have been killed."

"Sometimes, it felt like I was. At least, a part of me, anyway."

Fear tightened like a fist around her heart. Whatever had happened, clearly it was much worse than Mack had told her so far. Was the accident the reason why he'd never gone to college? Had his injures kept him for going overseas to fight?

Questions whirled around in her head like a children's top. And why had it seemed so important to him that her mother inform her about the accident? She hadn't lived in Marietta for eight years and had not kept in touch with anyone from her past.

Now was not the time for questions, not when Mack looked ready to drop any minute. Even in the short time she'd spent examining him, more spots had bloomed across his face and on his neck. She'd have to wait to get her answers.

Thea moved back, giving him room to stand. "Come on. We need to get you in bed."

Feverish eyes stared back at her. "But I can't have the chicken pox. My job…"

"Will still be there once you've recovered." Bending her knees, she lifted his arm and placed it across her shoulders, pressing herself against him to give her leverage to pull him to his feet. He tightened his hold, bringing her even closer, an odd feeling of belonging settling over her as if right here, next to him, was where she was supposed to be. Thea gave herself a mental shake. Just overwrought emotions after a long day.

"I can stand, you know."

Thea leaned her head back to glance up at him, her mouth suddenly dry again. How could the man be so adorably handsome with tiny bumps popping up all over his face? "I know, but humor me. Nurses like to feel like they're doing something to make people feel better."

"Well, then," Mack answered with a teasing note in his voice, his cheek against the top of her head, cocooning her in his warmth. "That's mighty fine with me."

Thea couldn't help the smile that formed on her lips. She'd take this minor reprieve in hostilities, might even savor it. But she wasn't fooling herself. Questions remained between them, about the accident, concerning Sarah. And the answers, Thea feared, could breach any truce they might have reached and lead to all-out war.

With a man she was coming to care for altogether too much.

There was a reason chicken pox was a childhood disease, Mack thought as he scooted up in the bed, the cotton sheets sticking to him, setting off small fires around the lesions on his back and legs. He reached down to scratch a particularly bad patch along his thigh, first stealing a glance at his bedroom door. Thea had threatened to wrap his hands in a pair of socks fastened with duct tape if she caught him scratching again, and he knew with a sinking certainty that the woman would really do it!

Better not chance it. Mack sank deeper into his pillows. Three days now, and he still felt like the gum on the bottom of some kid's shoe, the day hours filled with oatmeal baths, watery broth and gallons of the calamine lotion Mr. Galloway had mixed up. With the way Thea dabbed the pink goo over his exposed arms and chest, he'd begun to resemble a bag of cotton candy at the North Georgia State Fair.

But no more. Mack pulled himself up again, resolutely ignoring the new wave of pain slicing through him. Thea may think he needed another day in bed, but he'd had enough. His muscles ached from inactivity; the only daily exercise he'd had was the short walk to the bathroom for the oatmeal baths Thea had drawn for him.

Thea. She really was something, always patient, never complaining, even when he'd been at his worst these past few days. It had surprised him to find out she'd had no idea about his accident. For years, he'd felt hurt over the way she'd failed to live up to their friendship, never contacting him to check on his recovery. Now that he knew she'd never even been aware of his situation, he'd have to let that grudge go. As for whether he still blamed her for the accident itself...

he'd need to let that go, too, after all she'd done these past few days to nurse him back to health.

Besides, it wasn't all her fault. He'd driven too fast in poor weather conditions and missed the curve. Instead of focusing on the road, his mind had been on Thea and whatever trouble her sister had cooked up.

Trouble that had caused Thea to run away and not return for eight long years. He knew she'd come back for her family…but her mother was doing poorly, and if Mrs. Miller was to be believed, Eileen's baby hadn't survived. Would Thea leave town again when she learned Sarah wasn't her niece? Maybe not at first, she'd have her mother to care for, but he could only imagine the sadness she'd carry, the guilt that she could have done more to save her family. A knot formed in Mack's throat just thinking about it.

There was a light rap on the door before it opened, and the subject of his thoughts walked in. "You're not in here scratching yourself again, are you? I don't want you to be scarred."

"With you threatening me every five minutes, I don't think so."

She chuckled, a musical sound that seemed to vibrate through to his soul. "Well, at least you're getting your sense of humor back. Sounds like you're on the mend."

Should he chance asking her if he could see Sarah? Thea had given him almost hourly updates on the infant since he'd fallen ill, but he'd feel better if he could see his daughter for himself. "Think I could get out of bed for a while? Maybe walk a bit?"

"You mean see Sarah?" She moved quietly through

the room, placed a stack of freshly laundered towels on the dresser, tucked in an errant blanket at the corner of the bed before finally reaching for the glass thermometer on his bedside table. Loose curls trembled against her shoulders as she shook it, then held it up to his mouth. "Remember to put it under your tongue."

Mack grasped the thermometer between his lips while Thea continue to bustle around the room. Watching her had become his favorite pastime these past few mornings. There was an efficiency in her movements, a discipline that almost seemed as natural as breathing to her. Was that what had drawn her into nursing in the first place, this need to have some small area of her life under control?

Grasping the glass tube, she slid it out of his mouth and studied it before giving him a relieved smile. "Almost perfect."

"Good." Mack threw back the covers and sat up. He grasped the edge of the bed as the room spun around him and a dull ache started at the base of his skull.

"You tried to get up too fast. Just sit there for a minute, okay?"

He couldn't argue with her even if he wanted to. Mack closed his eyes. "Okay."

He drew in a deep breath, hoping to clear his head, but instead breathed in the heady mixture of Thea's personal scent, a combination of fresh cotton and Ivory soap that he thought smelled better than anything Mr. Hice had bottled in the perfume section of his department store. She was nearby, hovering over him as she had for the past few days, as if she were truly worried for his welfare. The thought made him feel off balance again but for an entirely different reason.

"Are you okay?"

He opened his eyes, and his heart tumbled around in his chest at the concern in her expressive face. No wonder injured soldiers fell in love with their nurses, especially if they were as beautiful as Thea was. It would be the easiest thing in the world.

If he'd let himself—which he wouldn't. She was determined to take his daughter away from him. "I'm fine."

"Good." The fabric of her cotton jumper rustled softly as she knelt down in front of him and reached for a pair of soft-soled shoes at the foot of the bed. "Let's get these on you. Don't want you to get cold."

"Are you this way with all of your patients?"

Thea chuckled as he shoved his foot into the house shoe. "Most times."

"No wonder General Patton gave you a reference letter."

She stood up and stepped back, a smile dancing along the corners of her mouth. On closer inspection, she looked pale, and the tender flesh under her eyes appeared bruised a purplish blue. She had to be tired, taking care of six children, seven if he counted himself. Exhausted was more like it, but she'd never said a word of complaint. Well, the epidemic would be all over soon.

"How's the baby?" Mack asked.

The tender smile that played along Thea's lips made his heart do a little flip in his chest. "She's fine. Not even a smidgen of fever this morning. She's still a little fussy. She tried to scratch at her spots so often, I finally had to tie a pair of socks on to her hands to keep her for tearing at her skin."

"Was that necessary? I mean, she's so little."

She stiffened. "She could scratch herself and end up with infected sores. We don't want that." Her voice wobbled a little, and he could tell she was hurt.

Guilt assailed him over his hasty words. Mack stood up, but this time when the room spun, he wasn't sure why but the only thought in his head was getting to Thea.

He cupped her chin in his hand, lifted her face until her gaze met his. Blue eyes shone with unshed tears. "Hey, it's okay."

"I'm just tired, that's all."

"Of course you are. While we've all been lying around, you've been running around taking care of us without one word of complaint." He brushed his thumb against the soft curve of her cheek, watched a rosy pink infuse her skin where his fingertips touched. "That couldn't have been easy."

"No. You were worse than the kids. At least they didn't snap at me."

There was that spark he'd grown to admire. "Maybe because I'm not use to having someone take care of me."

She seemed to think about that a moment. "I know the feeling."

He knew she did. Growing up, he'd at least had his parents to care for him, but Thea had been stuck in the role of caregiver since she was a child. Was that another reason she'd gone into nursing, because taking care of others was the only thing she'd ever known? "I still shouldn't have said what I did about how you nursed Sarah. You did what was best for her, and that's all I could have asked for."

"Really?" Her lips curved up into a tentative smile.

"Are you kidding? Nurse Eison told me you were the greatest thing since coffee beans when it came to taking care of little ones, and boy, if you didn't prove it. I'm just being an old grouch."

"Well, you have a right to be. You've been very sick." She chuckled weakly. "And I usually don't dissolve into a puddle, but I've never taken care of someone I've cared about so much before. It just about killed me to bind Sarah's tiny little hands in those socks but I've seen what an infection can do. Just the thought of what could happen to her…" She hiccuped.

"But she's fine." Thea's confession tugged at his emotions in a way he hadn't expected. Before he knew what he was doing, he pulled her close and wrapped his arms around her. "We're worrying over nothing. That's what loving a child does to you. I know not seeing Sarah these last few days has about driven me nuts."

"She's missed you, too."

Mack leaned back to look at her. "She has?"

Thea nodded. "I've noticed she watches the door in the evenings, like she's waiting on you."

Mack thought his heart would explode beneath his ribs. His baby girl missed him. "Thank you for telling me that."

"I think it would do the both of you some good if you spent a little time together today. Maybe give her her afternoon bottle and rock her to sleep?"

"You're okay with that?"

A tiny line formed between her lovely blue eyes. "You thought I wouldn't be?"

Shame sent a flash of heat up his neck. "I just figured with the both of us wanting to raise her, you'd want to keep me as far away from her as possible."

"I might have thought that way a couple of days ago," she said, moving back slightly as if she needed to put some space between them. "But you love her, and I believe she loves you, too. You're her family, and if it's proven that she's my niece, I'd want you to still be a part of her life. If that's what you want."

It was the most unselfish gift he'd ever received, the chance to be a part of Sarah's life even if Judge Wakefield denied the adoption. Filled with gratitude and wonder, he cupped her face in his hands, her skin warm beneath his fingertips. Thea breathed a soft sigh, and Mack followed the path to her slightly parted lips. For the briefest of moments, his thoughts wandered. What would it feel like to press his mouth against hers, to taste the sweetness that she lived out every day?

Her eyes widened, almost as if she'd read his thoughts, and without knowing what he intended to do, Mack lowered his head toward hers.

"Knock, knock."

Mack jerked his head around to find Beau Daniels standing in the doorway, his gaze traveling back and forth between them until he finally smiled. "If you want me to come back later..."

"A good long visit is exactly what the sheriff needs." Thea slid by Beau, She collected the dirty linens then headed for the door. "Maybe you can convince him to take it easy for another day or two."

"I'll give it my best try." They passed each other, Beau stepping toward the foot of the bed as Thea clicked the door shut behind her. He turned back to face Mack, a knowing smile plastered on his face. "Looks like Nurse Miller is taking very good care of you."

Mack didn't like the implication. "Don't say it like that. Thea isn't anything like her sister."

"I never thought she was." Beau walked over and sat down in the rocking chair next to the bed. "But the two of you did look mighty cozy when I came in."

"All right, so I almost kissed her." Still wanted to, if the truth be told. But kissing Thea would complicate matters, especially concerning Sarah's adoption. Mack grabbed the robe at the edge of the bed and shoved his arms into the sleeves; his bumps flared back to life. He sank back to sit on the bed. "Thea's had a rough couple of days, and I didn't help things by barking at her about Sarah's care."

"So you were only trying to comfort her?"

Mack nodded. That was as good an excuse as any he could think of at the moment.

"Fine." Beau studied him for a long moment, then shook his head. "Anyway, that's not what brought me out here."

True, Beau hadn't been to Ms. Aurora's for at least four months. It must have been something important to have brought him this far out of town now. "One of the kids hasn't taken a turn for the worse, have they?"

"No, from what I can see, Thea's done an excellent job nursing everyone through the chicken pox."

Mack didn't doubt it. His own care had been superior. "Then why are you here?"

Beau's expression turned serious. "The town council met last night to discuss their plans for reorganizing the police force."

Perfect, and him laid up in his sick bed. As if he didn't have enough to worry about. "They couldn't wait a week so that I could give them my insights on what direction the county needs to take?"

"It's my understanding that's exactly the reason why they held the meeting last night, so they could feel comfortable discussing their options without your input."

Mack didn't like where this conversation was going. "Did they come to any conclusions?"

"Not really." Beau's mouth twisted to the side as if he'd bit into an unripe persimmon. "To be honest, they seemed more interested in dissecting your personal life."

His personal life! Mack jumped to his feet, the world suddenly swirling around him again. He sucked in a deep breath and grabbed hold of the iron bed railing until the room slowed to a standstill. "What personal life? All I ever do is work and spend my evenings here visiting Sarah. My big day out is going to Sunday services then having lunch with your family at Merrilee's."

"I know. Kind of sad, isn't it?"

Quite more than sad. Just like his world had become. "Do they have a problem with me adopting a child?"

"No. Everyone on the council thinks it's a fine idea, you wanting to raise Sarah." Beau hesitated, his mouth turning up at one corner in a way that had always meant trouble. "Their concerns are more about your… recent behavior."

That made Mack forget about the itching. "What exactly is it about my behavior that has everybody in an uproar?"

Beau leaned forward and rested his forearms on his thighs. "Is it true you and Thea were holding hands and making goo-goo eyes at each other in the diner the other day?"

How did folks take an act of friendly comfort and turn it into something that sounded sordid and trashy? Didn't people have better things to do with their time than spread silly rumors around town? "We were talking about Sarah's surgery and she took my hand to comfort me, that's all." Only it had felt like more, at least to him. Even now, he remembered the spark of awareness that her touch had ignited. He shook the memory away. "Whoever saw us is making a mountain out of an anthill."

"You don't have to convince me. If you say there's nothing going on between the two of you, then I believe you."

Mack drew in a steadying breath. While Beau the boy hadn't been so dependable, the man who had returned from war was as solid as the granite under Kennesaw Mountain. Mack felt honored to have such a friend. "Didn't mean to take your head off."

"I'll give you a break this time." Mack gave him a slight grin. "You've been sick."

"Anything else I should know?"

Beau shook his head. "Just like a dog with a bone, aren't you?"

He was stalling. What had those old coots on the town council cooked up now? "What is it?"

There was a slight hesitation, then Beau sighed. "Truth is, most of the council members are a little uncomfortable with the fact that you've been out here with Thea for the last few days."

Mack didn't know whether to laugh or get spitting mad. "You're kidding me, right?"

"They feel that it looks inappropriate for the two of you to be out here together, especially after the hand-holding incident in town."

"We weren't holding hands!" Mack raked his hand through his hair then instantly regretted it as the sores on his scalp caught fire. "You did tell them that there are ten people in the house, including one of the most respected ladies in town and Thea's mother, right? How many chaperons do they think I need?"

"From the looks of what I just saw, a few more might be in order, Romeo."

"Aw, be quiet," Mack grumbled when Beau chuckled. He went to scrub his jaw then changed his mind. "I don't remember Merilee and John causing this much talk when they helped out Ms. Aurora earlier this year."

"No," Beau agreed. "But neither of them is a public official like you are. People hold you to a higher moral standard. Judge Wakefield himself said this incident flies in the face of every law-abiding, church-going citizen of Marietta. A little melodramatic but it gave those busybodies in town something to chew on."

Mack's shoulders slumped. Strange as it seemed, he understood exactly what Beau meant. The citizens looked to him, as the law in this county, to be an example of moral living, a standard to which others should aspire. Even though nothing inappropriate ever happened between him and Thea in this situation, there was the appearance that broke with that standard. Without meaning to, he'd let the people of Marietta down. He glanced over at his friend. "What do I have to do to make this right?"

"Well, I thought I could take you home and follow your recuperation myself." His friend eyed the door as if half expecting someone to pop in. "But after what I witnessed today, I'm wondering if there's not another option."

Mack's brows furrowed until realization set in. "I'm not marrying her."

"Now hear me out." Beau pressed his lips together. "If I hadn't interrupted when I did, you would have kissed that woman, and if news of that ever got around town, you'd either be fired from your position or standing in front of the Justice of the Peace."

Mack pulled his fist back, then plunged it into the mattress. The people who knew him would know the rumors of misbehavior weren't true, that he'd been isolated at Ms. Aurora's only to keep from spreading the chicken pox around town. But what could he do about those who didn't know him as well, those who would believe the rumors? What kind of standard did that set for the town if the sheriff was accused of immoral behavior?

And what of Thea? He'd witnessed the pain she'd gone through when talk centered on her sister's wild behavior, had comforted her when she'd been snubbed, watched her hold her head high even as people whispered around her. Even now, some of the old folk would have her wear a scarlet letter because of Eileen's actions. What would people say about Thea now? Would they listen to reason or brand her with the same ugly names they'd given her sister? Mack wouldn't sit by and watch her get hurt like that, not when a marriage would silence people's tongues.

That was if Thea would take him, disability and all.

"You both want to raise that little girl downstairs so why not team up? Get married and adopt her together," Beau said. "Judge Wakefield wouldn't have any reasons left for holding up the adoption then."

"You make marriage sound like I'd be joining the football team." Of course it all seemed that simple to Beau. He had the kind of marriage Mack had always wanted for himself, the kind of marriage his parents had had, a lifelong promise, a covenant between him and his bride to love, honor and cherish each other until the Lord called them home. A life with a woman who chose to be with him, to love him, to grow together in the good and bad times.

Not a woman forced into marriage because of public opinion or to skirt around the adoption laws.

He needed to talk to Thea. It was her reputation at risk. To leave her out of the conversation about her future, about *their* possible future with Sarah, felt just plain wrong.

Besides, the other option besides proposing was letting Beau take him home—and Mack couldn't leave now. Not after he'd seen the way that exhaustion wore on Thea. Sarah and the rest of the kids needed him. One desertion in a person's life was one too many. He couldn't do that to Thea or the kids. "How long does it usually take to get over chicken pox?"

"A week, give or take a day or two," Beau said. "Why?"

"Then come back in a couple of days and we'll talk again."

Beau stared at him for a long moment. "It would be better if I monitored you at your own home."

"Better for who? The town council? If they're so worried about my reputation, have them send somebody out here to help Thea with the kids. Because that's what I intend to do the next few days."

Beau shook his head. "They're not going to like this at all."

"Maybe not, but I wouldn't like myself too much if I didn't stay and help Thea care for these kids now that I'm feeling better." Mack scoffed. "Just because a bunch of old hens got a bee in their bonnet about the situation between me and Thea doesn't mean I'm going to turn my back on doing what's right for my daughter."

Concern clouded his friend's expression. "I understand, you know I do, but you're talking about your livelihood here. If you lose your job, no court in this country would consider giving you that baby."

Beau was right. Why win the battle if it meant losing the war? Compromise seemed the only viable solution, though it left a sour taste in his mouth. "Can you get me until tomorrow? Just long enough to spend some time with Sarah and make sure she's okay?" And Thea, too. She needed sleep, and he wanted to make sure she got some rest after being run ragged these past few days.

"That shouldn't be too hard. I'll let them know that unless they want a full-blown epidemic of the chicken pox right before Thanksgiving, they'd better let you stay put."

"Thanks."

"This may give you a short reprieve," Beau started. "But don't think that the town council is just going to drop this. I talked to several of them last night about the possibility that you'd hire Thea to be Sarah's nurse after her surgery, and that didn't go over very well. I didn't know someone could raise their eyebrows so high."

If Mack hadn't been the topic of conversation, he might have liked to have seen that. Instead, it felt as if he'd jumped on the Ferris wheel at the county fair and it was spinning out of his control. Once again, Thea had entered and wreaked havoc on his life. Only this time he wasn't helpless—there was something he could do. *If* Thea was willing to agree…

Mack closed his eyes. *Father in Heaven, You're going to have to sort out this mess that's my life right now. Give me wisdom and strength to follow You in all my ways. In Christ's name, Amen.*

Chapter Eight

Thea dried the last soup bowl and set it alongside the others. Sarah's sporadic cries from across the room as Ms. Aurora walked her around the kitchen table tore Thea's heart to shreds. She wiped her palms on the skirt of the apron she'd borrowed, then turned and held out her hands. "Let me take her for a little while and give you a break."

Ms. Aurora shifted the baby's weight on her hip. "You could use a break, too. The kids have run you in circles since the rooster crowed this morning."

Sarah tilted sideways, waving her arms in the air, a signal Thea recognized. The baby wanted Thea to hold her. She scooped the baby up, the now-familiar scent of calamine lotion floating in the air between them. Sarah curled up into her, her warm body a sweet weight. "I've worked long hours before."

"On the front line over in Europe during the war," the woman said softly as she walked over to the cupboard and opened it. "Weren't you afraid you'd get killed?"

"Constantly." Thea rested her cheek against a patch

of the pale blond hair that swirled around Sarah's head and held her tight. But the prospect of death wasn't as horrible as the fear of being alone, of having no one to come home to. That fear had driven Thea back to Marietta, ready to see her mother and sister again, to try and put their grievances in the past.

But there'd been no family to come home to. Eileen was gone, and Momma… The thought made her heart contract into a painful knot.

Thea glanced down at the baby nuzzled against her shoulder, her deep, steady breathing a comfort after so many sleepless nights. Watching this child suffer had torn a hole through her. Thea would have gladly borne the itching and fevers Sarah had endured to give the child relief. How in the world would she bear the weeks of pain this baby would go through recovering from the surgery to correct her mouth and nose?

Mack would be there to lean on for support.

Her heart fluttered as she remembered how close he'd come to kissing her. She'd wanted his kiss, had almost stretched up on her toes to breach the distance between them and cover his lips with hers. What would Mack have thought? Would he have branded her as wild as her sister? He'd probably laugh if he knew the truth, that in all her twenty-six years Thea had still never experienced a real kiss. Wouldn't it have been lovely if Mack had been her first?

But not with the question of Sarah's parentage hanging over their heads. No, it was best for everyone that Beau had interrupted when he had.

"You're deep in thought over there," Ms. Aurora said as she walked over to the cupboard.

Thea rocked the baby in her arms. "Just letting my mind wander. I'm too tired to think too much."

"I could do with a cup of coffee." Ms. Aurora opened the cabinet door and took a cup and saucer down. "How about you?"

"I'd love one," Thea whispered on a shaky breath, Sarah finally asleep. "But the children…"

The older woman held up a delicate hand. "The little ones are napping while Claire and Billy keep Ellie occupied in her room."

"My mother…"

"Upstairs napping, as well." She extracted another cup and closed the cabinet. "Being around all these children has about worn the woman slap out."

"We could all use a good night's sleep." Thea yawned as the baby snuggled deeper into the crook of her neck.

Ms. Aurora chuckled as she carried the cups and laid them on the linen-covered table. "That doesn't happen much around here, even when all of the children are well."

Nights with no sleep for someone of Ms. Aurora's advancing years had to be wearing on her health. Yet Thea had seen that she loved these children with a joy and patience most parents didn't demonstrate. Shame knotted in the pit of Thea's stomach. She had severely misjudged the woman. Cradling Sarah tightly against her shoulder, Thea maneuvered herself onto a chair at the table. "I owe you an apology, Ms. Aurora."

The older woman looked at her with startled eyes. "Whatever for?"

Thea swallowed. This was harder than she'd thought

it would be. "I judged you based on someone else I knew, a woman who wasn't kind to the children she took in."

"Who in the world would do something like that?"

Georgia Tann. "Just someone I knew from my nursing school days."

"I hope you reported her to the authorities."

Repeatedly, for all the good it did her. "Anyway, I'm sorry for judging you."

Ms. Aurora gave her the same sweet smile Thea had seen her give the children time and again. "It's all right. If I'd seen someone mistreating a child like you have, I'd be suspicious, too."

No wonder everyone thought so highly of Ms. Aurora. Thea sat back in her chair, the weight on her heart a little less heavy now that she had the older woman's forgiveness. "I do have a couple of questions."

"I'll answer anything you like as long as it's my story to tell."

"Well," Thea began, "what made you decide to take in all these kids?"

"If you mean did I go out looking for these children, I didn't." She opened the silverware drawer and pulled out two spoons. "God just put them in my path."

"I don't understand."

Ms. Aurora returned to the table with a coffeepot and sat it on a crocheted pot holder in front of her before taking a seat. "When I was growing up, I didn't have the opportunities to marry. I was in the hospital during the time most girls are courted. By the time I was released, I was more interested in enjoying my freedom than being chained up again."

Why had Ms. Aurora been hospitalized for such a long time? Or had she been in an institution? Thea decided not to ask. "But if you wanted your freedom…"

"I know. Silly me!" Ms. Aurora chuckled. "But God knew the real desires of my heart. He knew that I wanted a family even if that didn't include a husband."

"That must have been very difficult for your parents to understand."

Sadness blew across the woman's expressive face then just as quickly, dissipated. "They were gone from my life by then. Anyway, here I was, unmarried and yearning for a family of my own. So I did what I'd always done. I asked for God to provide me with a child if it was His will."

"You asked God for a baby, and He gave you one?"

"Well, not a baby, but two little boys." Ms. Aurora reached for the coffeepot and poured Thea a cup before pouring her own. "I was at the grocery store one day and saw a little boy stealing a loaf of bread. John, that's Claire's daddy, was about ten years old then." She shook her head. "That boy, he had my heart even before he told me he'd only taken the bread to feed his little brother. Their daddy deserted them after their mother died. John was fine, but his little brother, Matthew, was severely crippled."

The thought of those boys left to the streets to fend for themselves caused an ache to well up in Thea's soul. "Did the police ever find their father? Was he brought up on charges for abandoning them?"

"No." The woman must have sensed Thea's outrage and continued. "Taking it to the courts would have put the boys in danger of being sent to one of the state institutions, and we couldn't chance that. So Mr. Worthington and I worked out a plan. The grocer wouldn't press charges and I'd take the boys home and give them a place to live."

"Mr. Worthington?"

"Mack's daddy, and a very good man. I don't even think Mack knows this but his father used to bring us groceries every week so we wouldn't have to do without." A soft smile lit her face. "Mack's done the same thing since he became sheriff four years ago. Sometimes I wondered how that boy managed to put food on his own table when he gave most of his ration stamps to us."

Yes, Mack would do that. Even as a boy, he'd always put others' needs first. That was how they had become friends in the first place—he'd shared his lunch when there had been nothing at home for Thea to eat. "How did Sarah come to live here?"

"That was a sad situation." Ms. Aurora spooned a heaping tablespoon of sugar into her steaming cup. "Mack showed up with that little baby, only a few hours old, and it was so plain to see he was just heart-broken at the thought of her mother not wanting her. He'd fallen in love right from the start. He'd been told that the daddy was killed overseas and that her momma was all set to keep the child, until she saw Sarah's condition. Once she realized the full extent of her problems, she asked to have the baby taken away."

Thea flinched at Ms. Aurora's words. Would her sister give up her own child simply because she wasn't physically perfect? Thea feared she knew the answer, but there had been no one to tell Eileen there were medical procedures to correct her baby's misshaped mouth and nose.

"I'm so sorry. I shouldn't have spoken so harshly about Sarah's mother, not knowing if…"

"It's all right, Ms. Aurora. I know my sister wasn't a saint." Thea hesitated, shame washing over her. "I'm just going on the belief she wasn't in her right frame of mind when she gave the baby up."

"That's a possibility, as rough a time as your mother said she had."

That startled Thea, considering she'd had to drag any information out of her mother. "Momma talked to you about my sister's delivery?"

The woman nodded. "She said that Eileen was in labor for almost three days before your mother finally drove her over to Mrs. Williams to see what was taking the baby so long. Said it was the most scared she'd ever been."

Three days! Why hadn't Momma called for help sooner, or better yet, called for an ambulance to take Eileen to the hospital? Was her mother already suffering confusion and poor decision-making then that had put her sister and niece in danger? Thea held the sleeping child closer. If she'd been there, she would have taken control of the situation, comforted her sister, maybe kept Eileen from making a terrible mistake. Sarah whimpered.

"You're holding her too tight. Ease up a bit," Ms. Aurora instructed in a gentle tone.

Thea released her hold on the baby slightly. "I'm sorry, darling girl."

Sarah's answer was to stick her sock-covered fingers into her mouth and curl back into Thea's neck.

"You mind if I ask you a question?"

Thea braced herself. If there was one thing she'd learned about Aurora Adair in the last three days, it was that she was as blunt as a dull scalpel. "What would that be?"

"I can't help but wonder what's the real reason you're all fired up to raise Sarah."

Thea brushed a lock of Sarah's silky soft hair away from her face. "I believe she's my niece, so of course I want to raise her."

"Not everyone would. I mean, it's a lot of responsibility to take on, raising a child. Especially a child with special needs. Alone, for the most part." The older woman brought her coffee cup to her mouth.

Thea stared at the sleeping child resting in her arms. Yes, she'd thought about all the hardships of raising this baby with no help from anyone but Momma—and a diminishing amount of help to be expected even from her. She'd have to deal with the constant worry about money, the stigma that went along with being a single mother. But it would be worth it to have the chance to raise this precious girl. She owed it to her sister.

She wanted it for herself.

Thea looked over at the older woman, a mournful smile on her lips. "What is it?" Thea asked.

"You love that little girl," Ms. Aurora answered quietly.

"Yes, I do." Though if someone had told Thea a month ago she'd be here, back in Marietta, nursing a houseful of people with the chicken pox, falling in love with her niece, she would have thought they'd lost their marbles. But why did Ms. Aurora seem so sad at the prospect? "Don't you want me to love her?"

"Of course I do. Every child should be loved and loved abundantly." She pressed her lips together as if trying to find the right words. "But Mack loves her, too. I'd hate to see that boy lose his chance at raising Sarah if it turns out your sister is Sarah's mother."

Thea nodded. She didn't want to see Mack hurt any more than Ms. Aurora did. But regardless of what she wanted, either she or Mack was going to end up with a broken heart. "If I'm given custody, I wouldn't think of cutting Mack out of Sarah's life. She loves him and I want her to be—what was that phrase you used?— loved abundantly."

"And if she isn't your niece?"

The thought stole Thea's breath away. Maybe a week ago, it would have mattered whether or not Miller blood ran through Sarah's veins, but now that Thea had held her, had nursed her through the chicken pox, had heard her baby giggles, she couldn't imagine her life without Sarah. "I'd still love her and only want what is best for her."

"I believe you would." Ms. Aurora smiled before taking another sip. "It must have been hard, coming back here after the war, trying to pick up the pieces of your life."

"Some days, I think the war was easier."

If Thea's pronouncement spooked the older woman, she didn't show it, laughing instead. "Family can be that way sometimes. Mine cared so much for their standing in society that they sent me away rather than keep me at home." She sat the coffee cup back on its saucer. "But every once in a while, I get homesick for Momma, and I think if I could have her back for one more hour, I'd be okay."

"I know exactly how you feel." A tight knot formed at the base of Thea's throat. What she'd give to talk to Eileen, or even Momma in her right frame of mind. To tell them how sorry she was for running out on them, for not being here over the past eight years. She tasted salt and sniffled, willing herself not to cry. What was wrong with her? Grief? Exhaustion? Probably both. Or had returning home turned her into a silly old watering pot? Thankfully, the older woman was too involved in pouring herself another cup of coffee to pay much attention to Thea.

"I thought you were going to let me rock Sarah to sleep."

Thea glanced toward the kitchen door where Mack stood, leaning one muscular shoulder against the door frame, his hair pushed back as if he'd raked it into place with his hands. An uncertain smile hovered on his lips as his gaze turned to the baby resting in her arms.

Ms. Aurora was right, Thea thought. Seeing Mack lose the opportunity to raise Sarah would hurt her, as well. How could this situation be resolved without leaving either one of them with a broken heart?

Thea silently whispered a short prayer as she stood and carried Sarah across the kitchen to where Mack stood. *Dear Lord, I don't have the wisdom of Solomon but You do. Help us find a way so that neither Mack and I come away from this broken. Please, Lord, help us.*

* * *

Mack followed Thea down the hallway, marveling at the way she looked so natural holding Sarah in her arms, dropping a kiss on the baby's brow every now and then, pushing a loose curl out of Sarah's eyes. How would Thea be with Sarah as she grew older? Loving, yes. Strict, after her experience with Eileen, that was a given. And completely devoted to her, as she had always been to her family.

To be loved abundantly. Guilt rippled through Mack. He shouldn't have listened in on their conversation, but when Thea had spoken of her love for Sarah, her desire to include him in the baby's life even if she was the one given custody, so that Sarah would have a life filled with love, he hadn't been able to turn away. It didn't matter that Sarah might not be Eileen's child. Thea would love her abundantly regardless. He'd seen it in the way she cared for her mother and sister, giving of herself without any expectations. And now with Sarah. What would it be like to be the object of such a love? Would his scars, his shortcomings keep him from ever finding that kind of devotion and affection? Or would love, real love, true love, make his physical deficiencies seem insignificant even to himself?

"Mack?"

His thoughts evaporated as he focused on Thea. "Sorry, must have been woolgathering."

She studied him for a long moment, her brows furrowed in concern. "Don't push yourself. If you need to go back to bed for another day or two, there's nothing wrong with that."

Mack smiled at her concern. A man could get use

to that kind of attentiveness coming from a woman like Thea. "I'm fine, really. Just thinking, that's all."

He followed her into the deserted living room. The large faded rug on the floor had frayed edges, and an irregular-shaped hole marred the wool near the coffee table, but the material was thick enough to ease a child's fall. A scarred cedar chest in need of a good sanding and a coat of varnish sat in the corner. Odds and ends of furniture, most likely donated, filled up the room. Nothing was shiny or new, but everything was comfortable and welcoming. A homey place to raise children.

"You want to sit down here?" Thea nodded toward a frilly concoction of eyelet lace that cushioned Ms. Aurora's rocking chair. "Once you get comfortable, I'll hand you the baby."

"It's kind of hard for a man to be at ease with all this girly stuff hanging off the chair."

She gave a throaty chuckle, the sparkle in her eyes rivaling the most beautiful sapphires in Mr. Friedman's jewelry display. "There's nothing wrong with a woman liking to pretty up her house a bit." She motioned again for him to take a seat, and he dropped down into the chair. The cushions proved more comfortable than he'd thought, and soon he was sinking back, his eyes closed in peaceful rest.

"You look better than you have in days." The warmth in her voice soothed him, like warm honey sliding down a parched throat. He opened his eyes, surprised to find Thea barely a breath away, watching him. The memory of their almost-kiss fluttered though his mind. What would she do if he rocked forward, breached the space between them and covered her lips with his own?

Sarah squealed.

Mack pressed his feet against the floor and rocked backward while the squirming baby jumped up and down in Thea's arms. Mack couldn't help but smile. "I always feel good when I get to see my doodlebug here."

"Well, she's happy to see you, too."

Sarah showed her agreement by bouncing with excitement, her bright blue eyes watching Mack like a hawk. She had a few remaining spots but nothing compared to what his imagination had drummed up in the last few days. Her arms and legs fluttered, but Thea kept a firm hold on her until she was safe in his embrace.

Sarah stared up into his face, her gaze darting from one scab to the next as if in concern. Then, as if deciding he was okay, she stuck her tiny sock-covered fingers into his mouth and he nibbled on them lightly. "I missed you, doodlebug."

"She missed you, too," Thea said as she dropped down on the couch and stretched her long legs out in front of her. "I've never seen her this animated. Almost like she got her favorite playmate back," she teased.

Mack gently tugged the baby's fingers out of his mouth. "I hate that I haven't been here for you, baby girl."

"Baby girl?"

He brushed a kiss against Sarah's brow. "My other nickname for her."

"My daddy used to call me that."

Mack glanced over the baby's head to where Thea

sat. In all the years he'd known her, she'd never once mentioned her father. Back then, he'd thought she might have been too young when he died to have many memories of him, but now, knowing Thea's love for her family, he wondered if it simply hurt too much to talk about him. Mack turned the baby around so that she sat up in his lap, his chest against her back giving her the stability she needed. "What was your dad like?"

She shrugged. "I don't remember much. He died when I was four." A sad, sweet smile graced her lips. "But I do know he always carried around lemon drops in his pants pockets and played guitar as well as some of those folks on the radio did."

"And he called you his baby girl," Mack added. "What did he do for a living?"

"He was a farmer. Momma said he loved working outside in the dirt, had a knack for growing things. She said it was like he never grew up from being a little boy playing in the mud."

A thread of sadness laced her voice, and Mack found himself wishing he could find a way to ease her pain, obvious even now, years later. So much loss in Thea's life, and if Mrs. Miller was telling the truth about Eileen's baby, another disappointment hung on the horizon. "Do you have a favorite memory of him?"

She sat quietly for several long moments. Had it been wrong to ask? Did Thea even have a good memory of her father to hang on to?

"When I was a little girl, I loved to follow Daddy out into the fields." She smiled more to herself than for him. Her eyes had a dreamy faraway look to them as she got caught up in the distant memory. "In the spring when he had to plow the fields to get them ready for the planting, he'd hitch our old mule to the plow then let me ride up on Bessie's back. Each row we'd dig, he'd sing a song with these silly lyrics that he'd made up just for me and Eileen. Momma thought it was vulgar for a little girl to straddle a mule but Daddy never paid her any mind. I loved every second of it."

"Sounds like your father was a good man."

She nodded. "He was. I just hate the fact that Eileen never got the chance to know Daddy the way I did. A father is so important to a little girl."

Had Thea realized what she had said? Was she conceding that Sarah needed a daddy? *And what about a momma?* Would he give too much away if he conceded, as well? "A girl needs her mother, too."

Thea fell back into the cushions and crossed her arms around her waist as if to protect herself. "What are we going to do about the baby, Mack?"

Now was the time to tell her about his conversation with Beau, but he wasn't ready quite yet. Instead, he shrugged. "That's the question that's been keeping me up at night."

"Me, too." She drew in a deep breath and sighed. "Either way, one of us misses out on raising Sarah. It just doesn't seem right, does it? Not when we both love her so much."

Mack pressed the baby close to his chest. He hadn't been certain when he'd overheard her talking to Ms. Aurora about allowing him to play an important part in Sarah's upbringing, but now Thea had confirmed it herself. "You almost sound like you're worried about my feelings."

Pain flashed across her features before her mouth flattened into a straight line, her eyes suddenly dull. "Of course I have to consider your feelings. You obviously love Sarah a great deal, just as she loves you."

Mack kissed the top of Sarah's head. It said a lot about the woman Thea had become, her understanding of his feelings for the little girl. Could he be as generous to her? He prayed so. "You know, Sarah loves you, too."

Thea snorted a short humorless chuckle. "She's only known me for a few days."

"That's the beauty of children. A week feels like a lifetime to them."

"She's a baby, not a puppy."

"Yes, but to her, you've been here for as long as she can remember."

Thea didn't look convinced. "Okay, I get that. But what makes you think she loves me?"

Mack smiled. He had her now. "Haven't you noticed how her attention follows you around the room, always watching your every move? I noticed it the first second you gave her to me. And she doesn't usually like to cuddle, but she'll curl into your neck and fall asleep just like she's found a home."

"Really?" A tremulous smile lit up Thea's face. "You think she loves me?"

The woman was so beautiful, especially when she looked at Sarah with eyes full of love and devotion. What would it feel like to have that smile turned on him? Mack cleared his throat. "Yes, I do."

"Thank you." It was almost a prayer, whispered to Sarah or to the Lord, Mack didn't know. Thea leaned forward, extending her hand to the baby, her eyes widening as Sarah grabbed one finger and drew it into her mouth.

"You think she's hungry?"

Thea didn't answer right away, instead remaining quiet, her focus completely on Sarah. "Maybe, but I think she could be teething."

Mack tilted his head to the side and glanced down at Sarah. "I thought so, too, but isn't she a little young to be doing that?"

"No." Thea lowered her face until she was level with the baby. "She's perfectly in line with what's normal."

Mack remained skeptical. All the books he'd read said baby teeth didn't come in until later in infancy. But Thea was a pediatric nurse. Surely she would know. "Are you sure?"

She straightened and held her hand out to him, palm up. "Here, I'll show you."

Her hand felt soft and delicate against his as she guided him to the spot, his finger gliding over the wet, bony section of Sarah's gums once, twice. On the third time, he felt it, the tiny ridges erupting through the skin. "I feel it, a little tooth right up front."

"I know." Thea's smile almost blinded him with its excitement. "Soon our little doodlebug is going to be able to grin at us with her own set of pearly whites."

Our little doodlebug. It shouldn't sound right to Mack's ears, but it did, just the way it felt right for them to be sharing this moment. What about the other milestones in his little girl's life, when she took her first steps, her first day of school, her first homecoming dance? Time was slipping away. Sarah was growing up, and he was missing it every minute the adoption papers remained unsigned.

Mack refused to miss anything else. There was one way to make sure Sarah became his daughter and to give the woman beside him the family she longed for. "Thea?"

"Hmm." Her attention was still focused on the baby. She loved Sarah, more than he'd ever imagined. At least that played in his favor.

"I think I've come up with a way for us both to raise Sarah."

Blond curls bounced lightly against her shoulders as she lifted her head, her clear blue eyes fully focused on him. Boy, a man could die happy staring into those eyes every day. "You have?"

Mack nodded. He might live to regret this, but as he glanced from Thea to the little girl who would be their daughter, he wondered if this could possibly be the best decision he'd ever made in his life.

"We could get married."

Thea blinked, as though the words had stunned her. Well, she wasn't the only one stunned by his proposal. "What did you say?"

He swallowed, suddenly nervous she'd say no. At least she hadn't rejected him outright, and as surprised as she might be, her question had also held a note of interest. Mack clung to that thought as he worked up his nerve to ask the question that would secure their daughter's future.

"Thea Miller, will you marry me?"

Chapter Nine

Thea's thoughts went all fuzzy. Mack couldn't have said what she thought he'd said. "Could you repeat that, please?"

"I asked you to marry me."

This was a joke. It had to be. Though she'd never known Mack to be unkind. But this—offering her a chance to be his wife, to raise Sarah as their child—was just too cruel for him to kid her about. And yet, the determined set of his jaw, the intent expression on his too-handsome face told her he was altogether serious. "Why would you want to do that?"

"Think about it." He leaned closer, and she felt the air go out of her lungs. "If we got married, Judge Wakefield would let us adopt Sarah without a second thought."

Marriage with no mention of love. For some reason she was afraid to ask herself, the thought left her depressed. "I thought you wanted to raise Sarah on your own."

"I did." Mack hesitated for a moment. "Or, at least, I thought I did. But the more I think about it, the more

I know Judge Wakefield was right. Sarah needs both a mother and father who love her very much. Who better than the two of us?"

She couldn't fault his reasoning. Still...

"If you're worried you won't get to see enough of Sarah, I've already told you I'd give you time. I want you to be part of her life."

"And I want you to be a part of her life, too, Thea. What better way to do that than become a family?"

A family of her very own! Her heart fluttered, her fingers and toes numb with joy, the future unfurling before her. She could see them chasing lightning bugs and reading stories together before bedtime, sharing Christmases and Easters and all the other holidays in between, curling up on the couch together in front of the fireplace after the children had gone off to bed and sharing about their days.

Whoa! Where had that thought come from? The man proposed marriage, not love. A means to an end to raise only *one* child. A way to secure Sarah's future while assuring their positions in her life.

To secure a family for herself.

She needed to think. Thea stood up and paced across the room, rolling her bottom lip between her teeth. Marry Mack? There was a rightness to it, but was that because marrying him offered her what could be her only chance to raise her niece? Or had the crush she'd nursed for him so many years ago matured into more than a childish fancy? "What makes you think the court will automatically agree to us adopting Sarah?"

Mack stood, Sarah braced against his chest, and walked across the room to stand by her. "Judge Wakefield has never kept it a secret that he would give my adoption file more consideration if I were married. In fact, he said more than once that he would sign the papers the minute I presented my wife to him in his chambers."

The old coot sounded pushy to her, forcing a man to choose between the baby girl he clearly adored and his possible future happiness with a wife. Mack deserved more; he deserved to find someone who would treasure his kindness and determination, a woman who could make him proud, not bring shame upon him because of who she was, who her family was. Not that she wouldn't cherish being Mack's wife, but he could do better than someone like her. *So much better.*

"There's something else you should know."

A sister gone, a mother ill, a chicken pox epidemic. A marriage proposal from a wonderful man. How much more could she take?

"What is it?"

Sarah wiggled her fingers at Thea and, without much thought, she dropped tiny kisses along the baby's arm. She glanced up from the baby's shoulder and caught Mack watching her, his blue eyes dark with longing. Did he want the same thing she did, a family to call his own? Mack had to, didn't he? Why try to adopt Sarah if he didn't?

"There's been talk…about us."

"Us?" Thea straightened, a familiar knot of dread tightening in her throat. "Why would anyone be talking about us?"

"The town council is considering expanding the police force in Marietta, so of course there's been some discussion about what role I might play. Apparently, there were some who—" he hesitated for a moment as if searching for just the right phrase "—voiced concern over the amount of time you and I have been spending together lately."

"What are they—?" *Oh, no,* Thea thought. *They couldn't mean...*

"Are they talking about our time here? Don't they know there's an outbreak of chicken pox? That there are six—" she glanced over at him "—seven people who are sick. Not to mention, my mother's staying here, too. There's nothing inappropriate about that."

"Well, yes, but we were also seen together at the diner. And in the hospital waiting room. And at the wedding."

When Mack put it like that, no wonder rumors were flying around town about them. Thea dropped down into a wingback chair close to the window. How had this happened? A couple of innocent meetings, an offer of help to a poor woman, and her name and Mack's were being dragged through the mud all over town. Were they calling her the same names they'd used to describe her sister? How would she find a job now? How would she take care of her mother?

She glanced at Sarah. What judge would give her custody with rumors like this floating around?

What about Mack? He was the sheriff in this town—and apparently his position was currently under review. What kind of repercussions would there be for him if they didn't marry? Thea pushed a loose strand of hair behind her ear, her stomach tied in painful knots, her heart beating out a pained rhythm. "Can I ask you something?"

"Anything you like. We need to be honest if we want this to work."

She sucked in a deep breath. "Why aren't you married already? I mean, there's got to be someone you're interested in, maybe a girl you've been dating?"

He shrugged in that self-deprecating sort of way that Thea found endearing. "I hate to tell you this, but I'm not considered much of a catch."

Mack not a catch? Where in the world had the man gotten such an idea? Any woman would be blessed to have someone as kind and considerate, someone who loved the child in his arms so abundantly. Had he been hurt by a woman in the past? Or had she bruised his ego by dismissing the notion of marriage so quickly? "What I'm trying to say is there has to be someone else you want to marry besides me. Isn't there?"

"No." He hesitated. "I'm not even sure I'm the marrying type."

From the way he said it, she was now certain that Mack had been hurt deeply. The thought caused an ache in her chest. Thea swallowed hard. "I don't know that I am, either."

"Marrying kind or not, we have to consider this for Sarah's sake." His expression turned sober.

But what about them? What about their future? Sarah would one day grow up and make her own life. Had he thought what the next forty or fifty years might hold for them? Would a loveless marriage be fair to Sarah? To either of them? "Then I guess the next question I have is, why me?"

"You make it sound like there's some reason I *shouldn't* ask you."

"It's not that." She hesitated. As he had said, they owed it to each other to be truthful with their concerns. "Well, maybe there is. I mean, you know my family's reputation. Not the kind of people that the sheriff would usually want to associate with, at least, not without an arrest warrant."

The corner of his mouth lifted in a wry smile. "Everybody's got an uncle or a cousin who makes them shake their head. That's what makes life interesting."

"And what keeps the local gossips' tongues wagging," Thea muttered.

"Sweetheart."

She lifted her head at the endearment until her gaze met his, and almost sighed. What made this man holding this darling baby girl in his muscular arms so utterly irresistible?

"I know your family," Mack started. "But more important than that is that I know you. You love Sarah as much as I do. I've always admired the way you're so devoted to your family, loving them unconditionally even when they don't deserve it. It's what I want for Sarah. What she needs from her mother."

Thea's heart lifted slightly, but there were so many other questions that needed answers before she'd even consider something so drastic as marriage. "What about you, Mack? Don't you want to fall in love?"

He shrugged, adjusting the napping baby to a more comfortable position. "After four years of being one of the only marriage-aged men in town without any takers, I figure love isn't in God's plan for me."

Love not in God's plan for Mack? If anyone deserved that kind of happiness, it was this man. Irritation threatened to clog her throat. "Who are these silly women not to know a good man when they see one?"

His lips twisted as if he thought her question funny. "There've been a few."

She swallowed the sudden pang of jealousy. "Then they don't have the sense the good Lord gave them."

"I don't know. They may have thought it was a lucky escape."

The uncertainty Thea heard in his voice didn't sound like the confident boy with all the big dreams she'd known in high school. What had changed him? Why was he settling when he could still find love, have children of his own?

"I don't expect for this to be a marriage in the real sense of the word. Sarah needs our full attention for right now, at least until we get her through the surgery."

Thea wasn't sure why, but his statement disappointed her. "So, a marriage in name only." She sank back into the couch. "I didn't know people did that anymore."

"I'm sure they do. You just don't hear folks talking about it much."

Thea certainly never thought she'd be having this conversation. Of course, if they agreed, it would be a marriage of convenience. It wasn't as if they loved each other. Friendship, yes. Attraction, most definitely. But what was a marriage without love?

"What are you thinking?"

Thea felt a slight smile curve her lips. "You've always done that. Even when we were kids, you'd ask me what I was thinking."

"That's because I like to know what's going on in that beautiful head of yours."

Her heart fluttered, though from nerves or at his compliment, she wasn't sure. "I can't pinpoint one thought right now. They seem to be scattered all over the place."

He nodded as if he understood. "Just know this. If you marry me, I'll be there to protect you, to help shoulder whatever the future may hold, to partner with you in raising this child, to be your friend and helpmate for as long as I live."

A vow, but still no mention of love. And yet she knew that marriages have been built on much less. If she turned him down, it was almost a certainty she would lose whatever chance she had at raising Eileen's child. But if she agreed, what did Thea risk losing then? The promise she made to Eileen so long ago roared through her. She'd let her sister down then, had never brought Eileen's first child home. She refused to fail her again. It didn't matter what she lost as long as she played a part in raising Sarah.

"Mack, could you ask me again?"

"Ask you? Sure." He stood, then bent down and placed Sarah in her lap.

Thea shook her head. He really was the most handsome man she'd ever known, spots and all. But when Mack straightened, then knelt down at her feet, Thea almost forgot to breathe.

Mack took her free hand in both of his, his thumb making tiny circles on the inside of her wrist that sent delightful sparks shimmering up her arm. He lifted his head, his blue eyes gentle and with a touch of vulnerability that made Thea's heart ache. "Thea Miller, will you do me the honor of marrying me?"

Someone's heart will be broken, and I fear it will be mine.

Sarah whimpered. For now, Thea would settle for the chance to help raise this child she loved more than life itself. Eileen's child. Her family.

Thea lifted her chin a notch and with a steadiness she didn't feel, gave Mack his answer. "Yes, Mack. I will marry you."

Mack packed his razor and aftershave into his leather bag and dropped it in his suitcase, the tangy lemony-lime scent of his shaving cream refreshing after days of lying around in bed. He scraped his hand against his clean-cut jaw and relaxed. No beard or itchy spots for the first time in a week.

Beau had given him, along with the rest of Thea's patients, the all clear this morning, right before he'd packed Mack's bride-to-be and her mother into his car for a ride back to the Millers' place. Mack hadn't been keen on the idea. He'd wanted to escort Thea home himself, just to make sure she got her mother settled in without any problems. Wasn't that his duty as Thea's future husband, to make sure she was safe and got the rest she so desperately needed?

But Beau didn't see the situation in quite the same way. Tongues were already wagging all over town about his and Thea's quick engagement. No sense giving folks more ammunition than they already had.

Mack shoved his pajamas into the case. Most of them could hang for all he cared. Rumors were easier to believe than the truth. But it was Thea he worried about. She'd gone through years of shrugging off gossip about her sister, buried beneath the weight of Eileen's sins. If Beau driving Thea and her mother home protected them from being at the blunt end of someone's tongue, Mack would step aside.

But it didn't mean it sat well with him. Maybe it would be better for both their sakes to marry sooner rather than later. When he got back into town this afternoon, he'd work out a plan. If Thea agreed, they could be married by the end of the week.

"Almost ready to go?"

Mack glanced up from his packing to find Ms. Aurora hovering in the doorway, a bundle of clean clothes loading down her arms. Her hair had turned a shade grayer and her wrinkles were more pronounced since her heart scare last spring, but there was still a vivid spark in her tired eyes, as if she knew the work she'd started with these children wasn't quite finished. Still, tending a houseful of sick children couldn't have helped her any. *Thank You, Lord, for Thea.*

"Ready to be rid of me?"

A faint smile graced her face. "You know you're welcome here anytime."

It was true. Since his mother's death a few years ago, Mack had found himself at Ms. Aurora's door more and more often, like a stray dog looking for food scraps. She'd befriended him, allowed him to mourn his loss, given him a sounding board when something troubled him and always spoke her mind, even when it was something he didn't want to hear.

Like now.

Mack dropped his robe on the bed and turned to her, crossing his arms over his chest. "You've got something to say, Ms. Aurora?"

She didn't even pretend she didn't know what he was talking about. "You're going to marry Thea?"

Mack drew in a deep breath. This morning before Beau arrived they had told Ms. Aurora their plans to marry and adopt Sarah. She'd appeared to understand the reasons behind the match, had even seemed thrilled as she offered them congratulations on their impending nuptials. But obviously the older woman had reservations. "I thought you were happy for us."

"I am. I think outside of knowing the Lord as your Savior, Thea might just be the best thing that's ever happened to you."

That surprised him. Considering Thea had been spying on Ms. Aurora, Mack would have guessed the old woman wouldn't have thought so highly of his future bride. But then, Ms. Aurora had always had a soft spot for those folks who cared about her children. "Then what's bothering you?"

Her pale gray eyes turned almost sorrowful. "I know the two of you love Sarah, but don't you both deserve something better than a marriage in name only?"

"Maybe." He turned back to his suitcase, picked up his robe and bunched it into a ball. "But neither of us can bear the thought of losing Sarah. If we marry, we stand a very good chance of the adoption going through."

"And what about love?"

Thea had asked him almost the same question. What *about* love? It wasn't as if he'd never opened himself up to the possibility; he had, more times than he cared to admit. But no woman had ever indicated any hint of love toward him. They wanted a soldier, a man ready to die for his country. A whole man, not someone carrying around a physical disability. His lack of military service was considered a flaw in his character, and his refusal to give any kind of explanation simply fueled that belief. "I haven't exactly had women lining up for a chance to marry me, now have I?"

"And whose fault is that?" She took the wrinkled mess that was his spare uniform shirt out of his hand and smoothed it to fold it properly. "There were a couple of lovely ladies who showed an interest in you at church but you were too involved in your work."

"If you're referring to that Mason woman, I caught her selling ration stamps she'd lifted off of some of the girls at the bomber plant. And Susan Bailey told me right from the first she didn't want any kids."

Ms. Aurora pressed her lips together. "I didn't say they were perfect, just that there were ladies in town you've known for a while, someone you might have fallen in love with."

Oddly enough, Thea's face came into focus. Other women had never fascinated him the way she did. Never talked straight to him instead of sugar-coating every word. He respected Thea's opinion, admired that she gave as good as she got. But was that enough to build a marriage on? Could it eventually lead to love, or would she be like all the others when he didn't come up to scratch? Maybe he was asking too much from God to even hope for love in his marriage. He'd have his daughter, a job that he liked, his renewed friendship with Thea. That would have to be enough. "Love just muddies the waters. Better for us to have a straightforward understanding."

"That's not the only thing that muddies the waters in a relationship." Her voice hinted at sarcasm.

"What are you talking about?"

She put the neatly folded uniform on the dresser then joined him in folding his remaining clothes. "When were you planning to tell Thea about the night you got that scar?"

"I already told her about the car accident."

"And the extent of your injuries? Have you told her that?"

Mack's stomach fell into his shoes. "Did she ask you about them?"

"No." Ms. Aurora spared him a glance then went back to folding. "I wouldn't have told her, anyway. It's not my story to tell."

He breathed a sigh of relief. "You're making a mountain out of an anthill."

She took his uniform pants and shook them out. "That night changed the way you looked at yourself."

"No, it didn't." Mack grimaced. "Everyone else changed the way they looked at me."

"Mack, no one can take away what we believe about ourselves unless we give them the power to do so."

Sounded like something his mother might have cross-stitched into a sample. Only there wasn't any truth to it. "They can when they cancel my college scholarship or tell me I'm not good enough to fight for my country overseas."

"I know you were disappointed when the military turned you down, but look what you did. You kept our town safe for the people who stayed behind to build the equipment our boys needed to win the war." She rolled the pants into a neat little bundle. "As far as school goes, you could have gone to college without your scholarship. It might have been a tougher row to hoe to pay your way through, but you would have had your degree."

"And do what? Who would have hired a partially deaf lawyer?"

Ms. Aurora's mouth quirked up into a sweet smile. "Marietta hired a partially deaf sheriff, and I hear he's doing an outstanding job."

When he wasn't fighting the town's rumor mill. Mack stuffed another pair of socks into the suitcase. "They hired me out of pity after the military declared me a 4-F."

"Those old coots? They don't do anything unless they feel it's the right thing for the city." She cupped his face in the palm of her hand the way his mother used to when he was a small boy. "You're the right man to police our town, Mack Worthington."

He wanted to believe her, but how could he? How would he measure up against men who'd experienced battle firsthand? He couldn't. All he'd done during the war was hand out parking citations and mediate neighbor disputes. No, now that war heroes were back in Marietta, his days as sheriff were numbered. Disappointment settled over him. For a job he'd never wanted, Mack was going to miss it. "Maybe I'll look for a job in a smaller town. I hear Hiram is looking for a sheriff. Or Rockmart."

"Then you'll have to talk to Thea. You can't expect her to move that far away without some reason as to why."

Mack hadn't thought about that. Leaving Mrs. Miller behind in her fragile mental state was out of the question, but how could he expect Thea to balance motherhood and being her mother's caregiver in a new town without any friends to support her? "I'll figure out something."

"Hmm." The older woman moved to the bed and started stripping the sheets. "Have you ever asked Thea why she left town that night?"

"At the time, she said it was a family emergency, but she didn't explain beyond that." And for years he hadn't cared, too busy dealing with the consequences of the accident to think too much about Thea and her family's problems. But since her return, the question of what could have sent her running that night had stayed on his mind. And what had kept her away in all the years since.

The more he thought, the more questions he came up with. How would Thea feel when she learned the whole truth behind his scar? Sympathetic for his loss? Angry he'd kept the truth from her? Hurt that, until the past few days, he'd held her at least partially responsible for what happened to him that night?

"Are you going to talk to her, Mack?"

He didn't know that he could, but if he wanted answers he'd have to try. Eventually. "I'll think about it."

"Well, when you do, think about this." Ms. Aurora bundled the soiled sheets up and headed for the door. "It's not your deafness that's holding you back. It's your attitude."

Chapter Ten

"We're here."

Thea could barely keep her eyes open, her body heavy with exhaustion from the past week of caring for a houseful of sick kids. She drew in a deep breath and willed herself awake as she glanced over to the driver's seat and found Beau Daniels pushing the gearshift into Park. She struggled to sit up. "Sorry, I wasn't very talkative. I guess the week's caught up with me."

His mouth curled into a slight smile. "I'm used to it. Edie's at that stage in her pregnancy where if she's not sick to her stomach, she's asleep on the couch."

Thea smoothed her wrinkled skirt down over her knees. "So what you're saying is everything is absolutely normal."

"Yes." His smile widened. "And don't worry. You weren't the only one who fell asleep on me." He nodded toward the backseat.

Thea turned slightly to see that Momma's hat had fallen down over her eyes and her mouth was pursed as she released small, almost ladylike, snorts of air. Her features were relaxed, not tensed into the frantic stiffness Thea had seen in her mother in recent days. Once she got them some lunch, maybe she could convince her mother to take a nap. Thea knew she could use one herself.

Beau got out of the car and walked around to open her mother's door, then Thea's, before stepping to the trunk to retrieve their suitcases. Both she and her mother were waiting by the time Beau joined them, a bag in each hand.

"That was so kind of you to bring us all the way out here." Momma snapped open the clip of her patent-leather purse and dug out her wallet. "How much do I owe you?"

Oh, no! Thea stepped forward, her arm coming around her mother's shoulders. "Momma, I don't think that's—"

Beau interrupted, bowing slightly. "Mrs. Miller, just the pleasure of your company is all the payment I need."

Momma blinked, then broke out into a wide smile. "Well, aren't you a sweet boy! Though your boss might not be too happy with you, passing up a fare and all."

"Momma, why don't you go on up to the house while I settle things with Beau?"

Her mother nodded and shot another smile at Beau before turning toward the house.

"I don't think anyone's used *sweet* or *boy* in the same sentence to describe me since I was in diapers," Beau said, as they watched her mother struggle with the door for a moment before disappearing into the house.

Thea chuckled. "No, but then you've been teasing

little girls almost from the moment you could walk. Remember how you use to pull my ponytail in Mr. Miley's science class?"

"Only because I knew it would get a rise out of Mack." Beau laughed. "He's always been an easy target where you were concerned."

Mack was protective of her even then? "You must have read too much into the situation. Mack and I, we were just friends back then."

"Really?" Beau's smile widened as if he had a multitude of secrets he'd like to share. "You remember Todd Armstrong?"

Thea went completely still. Of course she remembered Todd. Junior year, she'd been almost certain the boy was going to ask her to the Junior/Senior Prom. But just as suddenly as he'd started paying attention to her, he stopped. Next thing she heard, Todd had asked Barbara Emerson. Thea had ended up taking another girl's shift at the movie theater and working that night. "What about him?"

"Word got back to Mack that Todd was bragging about how he was going to take you up to Kennesaw Mountain on prom night. I'd never seen Mack so mad. He took that kid out behind the boy's gym and told him if he even looked at you funny, Mack would knock him into next week." Beau chuckled. "Now that I think about it, he did that to every guy who thought about taking you out."

No wonder she'd never had a date in high school. All this time, she'd thought it was her, or her family's reputation that had scared the boys off. To think it had been Mack! She would wring the man's neck the next she saw him. Protective, huh! More like overbearing, butting into her business. She snorted out a breath. "I should…"

"Come on, Thea. Mack did you a favor. You didn't want to go out with a jerk like Todd."

Maybe, but it didn't take the sting out of missing the prom that night, of watching the other girls walk by in confections of satiny blue or silky white from the ticket counter at the movie theater, the boys she'd grown up with dressed in suits and ties. She'd been in her silly uniform, working that night at the movies. Her heart skipped a beat.

Alongside Mack.

His father had taken ill by then, so Mack had taken the job to earn extra money to help his mom out with the bills. It said a lot about him, about the kind of person he was, working so hard to take care of his parents while he worked on his grades to get into college. But then he hadn't gone to college after all. Did his accident keep him from accepting the scholarship he'd gotten from the University of Georgia?

"You know, you're doing the right thing marrying Mack." Beau's voice drew her out of her thoughts. "He's always been sweet on you, and it'll just be better for all of you in the long run."

When had Mack had the time to confide in his friend about their situation? "At least it will give Sarah the stability she needs."

"And quiet all the talk going on in town."

Thea felt her jaw tighten. "Let's see how that goes."

Beau pushed his hat farther down on his head. "I wasn't sure Mack would tell you."

"Mack's honest with me, Beau, just like I have to be honest with him. It's the only way this marriage is going to work." She crossed her arms over her waist. "But I do believe Mack would try to protect me from the worst of the gossip."

"You're right. It's why he didn't drive you home himself. He didn't want to generate more rumors."

She'd wondered why Beau had brought them home. "So, how bad is it?"

He grimaced. Yes, she'd put him in an awkward position, but she needed to know what they were dealing with. "You know how folks are," he finally answered. "A pretty nurse and the town's sheriff holed up in a house for almost a week. It gets people to talking."

When he said it that way, it sounded so...*scandalous*! Like something her sister would do. The kind of thing Thea had worked hard all her life to avoid. "They did know we had a chicken pox outbreak on our hands, didn't they?"

"Yes, but you know how people are. Take a couple of nice people, throw in a few unfortunate incidents and add some busybodies with nothing better to do with their day than gossip, and they'll cook up a scandal that'll travel faster than a jackrabbit during hunting season."

Her breath hitched. She'd hoped it wasn't as bad as Mack had made it out to be, that with time the rumors would die down and this marriage he'd proposed wouldn't be necessary. But from the way Beau described it, it was even worse than she'd thought.

Mack was right. Even if they could get the judge to allow someone unmarried to have custody of a child, neither of them would be considered a good candidate to adopt Sarah with these rumors hanging over their heads. Marriage seemed their only choice to quiet people's tongues and bring Sarah home. And even with a marriage, there would still be some who would never forget. If Judge Wakefield allowed them to adopt Sarah, she might have to live with the rumors, the kids from school who'd taunt her, tell her how her real mother had abandoned her. How her adoptive parents were forced to marry.

And what about Mack? He'd built a solid reputation in this town. Not only could he lose Sarah, the town council might decide he wasn't fit to be their sheriff. She couldn't live with herself if she caused him trouble. "Mack's not going to get fired, is he?"

Beau shook his head, oblivious to the turmoil going on inside her. "The news of your engagement has stemmed any talk of relieving him of his duties for now."

She nodded, but found no relief in his words. Because of her, because of her family's reputation, Mack had become the focal point of shameful gossip that could even now cost him his job and steal any hopes he had of adopting Sarah.

And now he was stuck marrying her.

Thea swallowed hard against the knot in her throat. She should never have come home, should have built a new life as far away from Marietta as she could, where she couldn't hurt or disappoint the people she cared for. Like Eileen, and now Mack.

If there'd been any other way around this mess,

she'd have taken it, but she'd do whatever it took to save Mack's sterling reputation, to save his job.

Even marry the man.

"Have faith, Thea. This situation hasn't taken God by surprise," Beau said.

Thea gave a humorless chuckle. "No, but it sure has thrown me for a loop."

Beau studied her for a long moment, then sent her a slight smile. "The more I think about it, the more I'm convinced you are the perfect person for Mack. You don't mind saying what you think. Mack needs that in the people closest to him. He admires it."

"Then he'll be admiring me a lot."

Beau laughed. "It wouldn't surprise me at all if the two of you fell head over heels in love."

Thea snorted softly. "Spoken like a man who's hopelessly in love with his wife."

"Guilty as charged." He bent the brim of his hat toward her. "See you later."

Thea waited until the car engine revved up before waving one last time, then turning toward the house. Edie Daniels was a very blessed woman to have someone like Beau to love her as deeply as he obviously did.

A sense of disappointment settled over her like a heavy quilt at the memory of Mack's response to her questions about love. He'd once believed in falling in love. She'd heard him talk countless times about finding that special girl, someone he could settle down with and raise a family. What had changed his mind? Who had hurt him so badly that he'd lost faith in his own happily-ever-after?

Thea picked up the suitcases Beau had left at the

front door and walked inside, her shoulders heavy, the weight of the emotional roller coaster she'd been on this last week or so pushing in at all sides. What she wouldn't give for a long hot bath and a good book to read. She eyed the stairwell that led up to the bathroom where the claw-footed tub beckoned her.

But there were bags that needed to be unpacked, laundry sorted, lunch made. Thea gave one last wistful glance up the stairs before turning toward the kitchen.

"Thea, is that you? I thought I heard the front door."

Her heart sank. Momma had done so well at Ms. Aurora's, had even been a help with the children at times. Had she already forgotten that they'd driven home together? "Yes, Momma. It's me."

"Is that nice Worthington boy with you?" Pots and pans clanged together as she dug through the cabinets, her best hat lopsided on her head. "I saw the way he was smiling at you across the breakfast table this morning, like you were the sweetest thing since sugar was invented."

Momma was more than confused, she was hallucinating. Mack had barely glanced at her over his bowl of oatmeal this morning, too busy answering questions from Ellie and the twin boys to pay her much mind. Meanwhile, Thea had had her hands full, feeding Sarah watered-down oatmeal that ended up on her blouse rather than in the baby's mouth. "Mack was more than likely watching me because Sarah was in my lap. If he was smiling, it must have been at her."

Her mother sat back on the kitchen floor. "No, this was when you were at the sink, getting cleaned up.

Reminded me of how your father used to look at me, as if he couldn't get enough of me."

Had Momma, in her confusion, seen something in Mack's glance, tenderness or affection maybe? Wishful thinking on Thea's part. But perhaps she could use this chance to ease her mother into their marriage plans rather than springing it on her all at once. She'd discussed it with Mack and he'd agreed, even told her to take as much time as she needed to get her mother used to the idea. Who knew how much her mother absorbed these days? But Thea had resolved to try to explain.

She picked up the dish towel that had fallen from the stove and threw it on the countertop. "You remember Mack and I told you we're courting, don't you, Momma?"

"Of course I do, which is why I thought he might come by this afternoon. Gentlemen who are interested usually call around suppertime so they'll be invited to stay." She glanced up, her hands going to her hat and plucking it off her head. "Do you think I should make some chocolate chip cookies, just in case? Your daddy just loves my cookies."

Momma baking cookies? She'd barely known where the kitchen was when Thea was growing up. Thea walked over to where her mother sat and helped her to her feet. "Mack's got a lot to do at his office today. Why don't I make us grilled cheese sandwiches, then maybe we could take a little nap. I know I could use one."

"Well, I am a bit tired." Momma pulled out a chair from under the table and dropped down into it before glancing up at Thea, a confused look crossing her expression. "Where's the baby?"

For the fifth time today. "Sarah's back at Ms. Aurora's, remember? She's going to stay there until Mack and I can bring her home."

"Why?" Momma's salt-and-pepper brows crinkled together. "I don't understand."

Thea walked over to the counter and snatched a stale loaf out of the bread box before carrying it back to the table. "Sarah doesn't have a birth certificate, remember? Without one, I can't prove she's Eileen's little girl, so I can't take custody of her without the court's approval. A judge won't allow a single woman to adopt a baby so Mack and I are going to adopt Sarah together."

"Adopt?" Momma straightened in her chair. "But that's our baby!"

Thea settled a hand on her mother's shoulder. "Momma, Mack and I have it all worked out. Sarah's going to be okay, and we'll be able to bring her home soon. Everything will be fine." Thea wasn't sure if she said that for her mother's benefit or her own. This whole "marriage in name only" had thrown her usual orderly world off-kilter.

Maybe a grilled cheese sandwich and a long nap would put things into perspective. She walked over to the icebox, opened it, pulled out butter and cheese, and set them on the table.

But she couldn't find a frying pan. She crawled further inside the cupboard, picking through the pots and pans until she finally found a small one in the back corner under some cookie sheets.

"Do you always climb around inside the cupboard?"

Thea jerked up and yelped as the crown of her head met a low-hanging plank. Stars exploded behind her closed eyelids as a sharp pain echoed through her head, then dulled into an ache.

The inside of the cupboard went dark as Mack sat in the cabinet doorway. "Are you okay, sweetheart?"

Something—either the endearment or the hint of concern in his voice—made her heart flutter so hard she thought it might stop. Somewhere along the way, her feelings for Mack had changed. Or maybe they had laid dormant all these years, waiting for the right moment to bud and bloom into the love she'd always dreamed of while she was growing up.

"Thea?"

"I'm fine," she whispered. But she wasn't. She was falling in love with a man who didn't think himself worthy of being loved.

"You want me to come in there and get you?"

The thought made her smile. "And have us both get stuck? I don't think so. Just give a minute to brace myself."

"Okay, but if you take too long, I'm coming in there."

And he would, Thea had no doubt of that. Because Mack had a soft spot for her. He worried about her. He would do anything in his power to protect her, even marry her if need be. But was that enough to build a life with this man on?

Maybe.

She backed out of the cupboard slowly. Before she could stand on her own, Mack pulled her free of the cabinet, his hands gently clasping her arms, his gaze locked on her. "Are you sure you're all right?"

Thea nodded, despite the ache knocking around in her head. "I may have a small knot on top of my head, but it will serve me right for scrounging around in the cabinets like that."

"Let me see." Without any warning, Mack cradled her face in his hands and tilted her head down. Sharp needles of awareness lanced through her as he gently massaged his fingers against her scalp, tenderly working his way back until his fingertips closed over the knot. "You didn't cut yourself, so you won't need stitches, but you could use some ice for that bump."

Mack lifted her head up, studying her eyes. "Look at me."

Common procedure to check for concussion, but it felt like much more. Thea couldn't breathe, could barely think as Mack's fingers slid through her hair, catching her behind her neck and holding her still. His eyes studied hers, their vivid blue depths a warm indigo.

"Thea? Are you all right?"

Momma. Thea took a step backward and banged into the cupboard. Mack put out a hand to steady her, then stepped away to put some distance between them. "I'm fine, Momma. Just a little clumsy today, that's all."

"You've always been something of a klutz," her mother answered in that sharp tone Thea recognized from her childhood. "Let's hope the baby doesn't pick up your bad habits."

Thea leaned back against the cabinet as if struck.

This was the woman she remembered from her youth, sharp-tongued, always finding fault in everything she did.

She couldn't look at Mack, couldn't bear to see the pity in his eyes. She'd never wanted him to know this about her mother, never wanted him to look at her any differently because she couldn't live up to her mother's expectations. No one could.

"Thea…"

Before she could finish, Mack interrupted. "Mrs. Miller, why don't you go upstairs and lie down for a little while? You look like you could use a nap."

Momma rested her chin in the palm of her hand as if giving it serious thought. "I am tired."

Thea hurried around the table to where her mother had started to stand up. "Let me help you upstairs, okay?"

"That's very sweet of you, dear," she said as she leaned her full weight against Thea. "Everything will be all right once we get the baby back. Then my daughter will come home and take care of everything for me."

Dread tightened like a steel band around Thea's chest. "Who are you taking about?"

"My daughter, silly girl! Eileen Miller."

Pain exploded through her, as if her mother had reared back and slapped her as hard as she could. Momma didn't know the pain she'd inflicted when, for the briefest of moments, she couldn't remember who Thea was.

Thea straightened on wobbly legs. War had not broken her, the years of endless shifts and dying children might have taken some part of her, but she'd held fast, stayed strong. But the weight of this loss, of losing her mother slowly, of watching her fade away second by agonizing second, fell heavy against her soul. "Let's get you to bed."

Minutes later, the scent of lilacs—her mother's favorite—faintly hung in the cool air of her mother's room as Thea sat Momma in a chair, then pulled back the handmade quilt that had graced her mother's bed since Thea was a little girl. By now it was worn and frayed along the edges, and for the life of her, Thea couldn't understand why her mother hung on to it after all these years. A question never to be answered, perhaps.

Downstairs, Mack had peeled back the wax paper from the bread and was pushing a knife through the stale crust as Thea walked back into the kitchen. She lit the stove, took one slice he'd already cut, slathered it with butter, then placed thinly sliced pieces of cheese on the bread and sat it in the frying pan.

Mack handed her a spatula. "You want to talk about it?"

"Not right now."

"Okay, but you know I'm here when you need me."

She buttered another piece of bread and sat it on top of the other one, then took the spatula and turned it over, the butter sizzling against the hot pan. "You've always been a good listener."

Thea couldn't be sure but she thought she saw him grimace. He ducked his head and went to work on another piece of bread. "Mind if I have a sandwich, too? I've been busy since I left Ms. Aurora's.

"Sure." Thea opened the cabinet and pulled down two plates before flipping the finished sandwich onto one. "Trying to get caught up with work?"

"Nope." He handed her a slice of bread and started sawing off the next piece. "Busy making plans for our wedding."

Their what? "That was quick."

He gave her a lopsided grin that could have melted the butter without the pan. "I figure the sooner, the better."

The sooner, the better. Maybe he thought he was doing her a favor, but shouldn't she have a say in her own wedding? She planted her fist on a hip and glared at him. "And what do I do during all this, just show up?"

She almost smacked him with the spatula when he laughed. "No, that's why I'm here. I wanted to get your opinion and make the decisions together."

"But your plans…"

"Aren't carved into granite. This is your wedding, too, Thea. I wouldn't do anything without asking you first."

Thea smacked the flat end of the spatula nervously against her skirt. Mack's rush to the altar had thrown her for another loop, but she should have heard him out before she barked at him. "I'm sorry. I just wasn't expecting you to want to get married so fast."

"I know, but I think it's best for everyone." He handed her the last slice of bread then rewrapped the leftover loaf in the wax paper. "This way, we put an end to the rumors going around and get our adoption petition into the court before Medcalf sets another sur- gery date."

Mack had been doing a lot of thinking since she'd left this morning. Thea slid the spatula under the sand- wich and moved it on to the other plate. "When were you thinking we could get married?"

"In two days."

Two days! "Have you lost your mind? Two days!"

"Is that too soon for you?"

She'd marry him this moment if she thought there was even the slimmest chance Mack could love her. But never once in all their discussions about getting married and adopting Sarah together had love been mentioned.

Sarah. Mack was right about one thing. Now that Sarah had recovered from the chicken pox, Doctor Medcalf would waste no time rescheduling the sur- gery. If they wanted a say in her care, they would have to act quickly.

If only there was a hope that Mack loved her—or even that he would come to love her in time. It would make everything so perfect. But life never fell neatly into place that way, at least it never had for her. Rais- ing Sarah and her friendship with Mack would have to be enough. Thea handed Mack his plate and picked up her own. "If we're getting married in two days, we'd better get to work."

Chapter Eleven

Thea glanced at the bedside clock and bolted upright in her bed. Nine o'clock! She had an appointment to meet Mack in the hallway outside of Judge Wakefield's chambers at two. There, the judge would marry them and sign the reworked adoption papers, which Red would file with the court this afternoon. In a few short weeks, Sarah would legally be their daughter. She lay back on the mattress, her heart bursting from the joy of it.

A family of her own!

But not if she didn't get moving. Thea pushed back the heavy quilts, her toes curling up against the cold as she sat up on the side of the bed. *Mrs. Thea Worthington.* Mack's wife. A tiny thrill ran through her.

In name only, remember?

The thought tempered the excitement she felt. Okay, so maybe she and Mack wouldn't have a full and complete marriage, but the past couple of days, working on their makeshift wedding, they'd drawn closer, rebuilt the relationship that had cracked under the strain of Thea's desertion all those years ago. And she'd be

Sarah's mother in every way that mattered. That would be enough to make her happy. A heavy knot tightened in Thea's midsection. It would have to be, wouldn't it?

A soft rap drew Thea's attention to the door as Maggie peeked her head around the corner. "Oh, good. You're awake." She nudged the door open with her elbow, a small tray in her hands. The scent of fresh coffee, warm blueberry muffins and shortbread cookies filled the small space as she crossed the room and sat the tray down on the nightstand next to Thea's bed. "I thought you could use a little pampering this morning. It's not every day a girl gets married."

"That's so sweet of you to do this." Thea grabbed her robe off the end of the bad and threw it around her shoulders. "I don't know how I can ever thank you enough."

"You haven't tasted the muffins yet. Mine aren't as moist as Merrilee's and I can't for the life of me figure out why." As if to demonstrate, Maggie picked up one of the small muffins and peeled back the paper, bringing bits of blueberries and crumbs along with it.

"You've still got me beat, though I do make a killer grilled cheese sandwich." Thea pulled a coffee cup toward her, splashed a small amount of milk into it, then reached for the coffeepot.

"If you want more milk, don't mind me. Most everyone around here drinks it black. I only brought some up because Mack said you liked a lot in your coffee."

"Well, thank you." Thea poured in a generous splash then filled her cup. The porcelain cup warmed her fingers as she took a long sip. How sweet of Mack to remember such a small, insignificant thing as how she took her coffee. What other little habits of hers had he remembered? Just the thought that he'd made a note of it made her feel unique and special.

"Thinking about Mack?"

Thea's cheeks grew heated as she glanced over the rim of her cup. "Just wondering how he talked you into letting me stay with you on such short notice."

"Mack thought you wouldn't have to rush trying to get to the courthouse if you were staying in town." Maggie grabbed a shortbread cookie from the plate and broke it in two. "A wise man knows a woman needs a little bit more time to get herself ready on her wedding day."

"That was kind of him."

"He's a sweet man, just as good as they come." Her friend gave her a smile before popping a small portion of cookie into her mouth. She covered her mouth as she spoke. "But a two-day engagement! What's the rush?"

"That's exactly what I said," Thea muttered over the rim of her cup. "But Mack was determined."

A giggle escaped Maggie's covered mouth. "I'll say he was. Planning the whole wedding. Arranging for your mother to stay with Ms. Aurora until after you're able to take Sarah home. I guess when Mack met you again, he didn't want to wait longer than he absolutely had to."

It would have been nice to carry that thought around in her heart, but it was nowhere near the truth. "Is that how it was for you and Wesley?"

Maggie pushed a crumb at the corner of her lips into her mouth and chuckled. "Oh, no. When I first met Wesley, I thought he was this hotshot pilot who couldn't bear the thought of a woman flying one of his precious planes. But as I got to know him—" her voice softened, her hand resting against the soft curve of her swollen belly "—I couldn't help falling in love with him."

Thea smiled against the rim of her cup. It was wonderful that Maggie had found contentment and happiness with her husband. In fact, it appeared most of the Danielses had made marriages based on love and trust. A tiny pang of envy sobered Thea's mood. This marriage she was about to enter into may not be the kind she'd dreamed of when she'd been a little girl. But dreams changed, didn't they? The opportunity to raise Sarah alongside Mack, to grow as a family, to put down roots, was far more than she deserved.

"You'd better get moving if you want any hot water for your bath." Maggie stood, brushed a stray crumb or two off her skirt then arched her back, resting a fist near the base of her spine. "Grandpa mentioned the weather being warm enough to wash the windows today, though why he'd want to do that right before winter sets in is beyond me."

Thea replaced her cup on the tray, then stood, belting her robe at her waist. "From everything I've heard about Wesley's grandfather, he's always been an active man. Maybe he's bored."

"I hadn't thought about that. I wonder if he'd want to help me work on the nursery. The room could use a new coat of paint, and we haven't put up any decorations. Wesley won't let me near a ladder to hang curtains, much less paint."

"Of course the man won't," Thea teased. "He adores you too much to see you get hurt."

"There's adoring, then there's annoying." Maggie flashed Thea a knowing smile as she picked up the service and headed for the door. "But you'll find that out soon enough."

Would she ever know that feeling, of being so loved it was annoying? Both she and Mack had agreed Sarah would be their focus, at least for the foreseeable future, but what about later? Mack had always wanted a large family. If they could find their way to loving each other, there might be a chance at more children. To have his child nestled right under her heart started an ache deep in the pit of her stomach.

"There's bath salts and body cream in the bathroom in case you want to use them. I also put some extra towels out, just in case."

How sweet of Maggie! "That's really very nice of you."

Her friend opened the door before turning and looking back at Thea. "Mack deserves all the happiness the world has to offer this side of heaven. You do, too." She gave Thea a watery smile. "I've always thought the two of you belonged together, even back in high school. You're going to make each other very happy."

How could Maggie be so certain? Thea almost asked but the door had already clicked shut before she could get the question out. The mattress sank beneath her as she sat at the foot of the bed. Marrying Mack might make her happy, but what about him? Didn't someone so good and decent deserve more than a bride thrust on him because of cruel gossip? A woman whose family carried more baggage than the Union Pacific railroad? She vowed never to give him a chance to regret this decision. Because at this moment, Thea knew what choice she'd make.

She chose Mack.

Excitement thrummed through her veins as she rushed over to the dressing table, grabbed her vanity case and headed down the hall to the bathroom. Warm, moist air perfumed with the scent of ginger filled the tiny room, swirls of stream rising from the tub, a trickle of water coming from the faucet. Another gift from Maggie. Setting her case on the vanity, Thea slipped out of her nightclothes and into the fragrant water.

Less than an hour later, Thea emerged from her room, powdered and primped, feeling more like a woman than she had since shipping out to Sheffield four years ago. Looping the strap of her purse up her arm, she tugged on her chocolate-brown gloves, the perfect match for the pale gold dress she'd splurged on for the ceremony. She was still chasing the last button on her glove when she became aware of someone watching her. Thea glanced up to find Maggie and Beau waiting at the bottom of the stairs.

"My word! Mack won't know what hit him when he gets a look at you!" Maggie exclaimed as she took hold of Thea's hands and held them slightly out to her sides to get a better look at her dress. "You're absolutely gorgeous!"

Thea knew her friend was exaggerating a bit but couldn't deny the compliments helped boost her confidence. "Thank you."

Beau nodded. "My friend is a very blessed man."

Thea hoped Mack viewed their marriage that way. "You don't know how much Mack and I appreciate your help with this."

Beau glanced down at his wristwatch. "He won't be so grateful if I don't get you to the courthouse on time. We need to get going."

"Hold on just a second." Maggie gave her cousin a look of mild annoyance. "A bride is supposed to keep her groom waiting for a few extra minutes, at least long enough for us to say a quick blessing for the new couple."

Both Danielses looked at Thea. She nodded. "Mack and I could use all the help we can get."

They each lowered their heads, clasping hands as Maggie began. "Dear Lord, we're coming to You today to ask for Your blessings on Mack and Thea as they begin their lives together. Guide them as they become parents to little Sarah, and take their hearts and shape them into one guided solely by You. In Christ's name, Amen."

As Thea lifted her head, a peace that wouldn't have been possible even five minutes ago flowed through her. Now she felt certain that God would bless this marriage and this new family they were forming today. A bubble of happiness lifted the corners of her mouth as she glanced at Maggie and Beau. "I guess it's time to go and get me married."

"One more thing." Maggie waddled across the foyer to the hall table and came back with a small bouquet of deep burgundy-and-gold mums, sunny daisies and baby's breath. "Mack brought these by this morning.

Said he wanted his bride to have flowers on their wedding day."

"He did?" Thea whispered into the bouquet as she took it from Maggie, a slight dampness seeping through her gloves. Mack had thought of even the smallest detail, almost as though this was a real marriage.

Maybe it would be, Thea thought, following Maggie out the front door. In time.

Mack read over the first page of the case file for what seemed like the fourteenth time, then tossed it to the side, unable to concentrate on the finer details of Officer Sydney's report. His recent bout of chicken pox had left him with a mountain of paperwork and correspondence that needed to be addressed. A good way to pass the time until the nerves he'd been outrunning all morning finally caught up with him.

He was getting married today.

He glanced up at the wall clock that hung over his door and smiled. Maggie would have given Thea the flowers by now. Had she noticed, as he had, how the gold mums matched the color of her hair in the sunlight? Or that the ribbon holding her flowers was the same vivid shade of blue as her eyes? Red had thought it nonsense standing in Wilson's Flower Shop as Mack picked out the blooms. Said his brain must have been attacked by chicken pox for Mack to throw money away on flowers for a marriage in name only. But to Mack's way of thinking, this wedding needed flowers to let Thea know that what they had was special, no matter the circumstances of their marriage.

A rap on the door lifted Mack's head just as his secretary, Nell Jamierson, peeked inside. "Judge Wakefield is expecting you in twenty minutes."

"Thank you, Nell."

"Have you got the ring?"

Leave it to a woman to remember that kind of detail. Mack opened his desk drawer, took out the small box he'd picked up at Mr. Friedman's just this morning and opened it. A slender and delicate band of gold, decorated with a light blue stone, it had instantly reminded him of Thea, as if it had been made especially with her in mind. He held it out to his secretary. "What do you think?"

Nell stepped forward. "I don't know any women who'd turn that rock down. Your Thea is a very lucky girl."

His Thea. Something about the phrase pleased him, maybe because after today they'd be bound to each other, as friends, as parents raising Sarah. *As husband and wife.* Mack gave himself a mental shake. Maybe Red was right, maybe the chicken pox had muddled his brain, though truth be told, he'd been in a tangled mess since he'd spied Thea peeking out from underneath that oak at Merrilee's wedding. At first, it had been only because she'd threatened the hopes he'd built around raising Sarah as his own, but that had all changed. Lately, he'd found himself thinking about her all the time— wondering what she'd done during her day, whether she'd had a good day with her mother. Not to mention the time he spent thinking about kissing her, holding her close. The need to comfort and protect her from the crazy world they lived in just about drove him mad.

"Now, you don't worry about anything. I'll hold down the fort while you're gone. Don't want to keep your bride waiting."

"Right." Mack stood, straightened his tie, then grabbed his suit coat off the back of his chair and put it on. Once he had the coat buttoned, he reached for the ring box and, with one last look, closed and dropped it into the safety of his coat pocket. He came around the desk and headed for the door.

The walk to Judge Wakefield's office usually took five minutes, but the news of his impending marriage had traveled around town as if Betty, the operator at Marietta Telephone Company, had made it her personal job to be the town crier. Folks all along the square stopped him with congratulations and well wishes, so the short trek from his office took three times as long as usual. As Mack rounded the corner on Main Street and hurried up the courthouse stairs, a horn honked behind him, and he turned to see Beau pull up to the curb with his cousin Maggie riding shotgun in the front seat.

Where was Thea?

Mack's heart jumped into his throat. Had she changed her mind? Had she decided marrying him wasn't worth the opportunity to raise Sarah?

Beau waved to him as he rounded the front of the car and opened the door for Maggie. She stood, then, seeing him, hurried across the brick sidewalk toward him, her green eyes flashing with happiness, her wide smile as big as the skies she loved. She playfully pointed her finger at him. "You, Mack Worthington, are a very blessed man."

He was? Being blessed wasn't something he'd felt

much over the years, at least not since the accident. "Why do you say that?"

"Just wait. You'll understand in a minute." She turned back toward the car and Mack followed her gaze.

And felt as if all the oxygen had suddenly been sucked out of the atmosphere.

Thea stood next to the car, her full skirts swirling around her legs, a tiny bow belted at her trim waist and another at the neckline of her bodice. Her blue eyes were hidden by a wisp of a veil, her hair restrained by a band of dark chocolate brown. A cloud of curls gathered about her delicate shoulders, giving him a tempting glimpse of her long, elegant neck.

"Breathe," Maggie whispered to him.

Easy for her to say. Her heart wasn't racing a million beats a minute. Thea had to be the most beautiful woman he'd ever seen, and she was about to become his wife.

In name only.

Disappointment lanced through him, and he sucked in a much-needed breath. Mack couldn't expect their union to be anything but a way to adopt Sarah, to share in raising the little girl, not with the baggage he carried. He still hadn't told Thea about his bad ear, or the part she'd played in the accident that caused it, but he would. Ms. Aurora was right; Thea needed to know the entire story about the night she left town. Just not today.

Mack started toward her, but Thea met him halfway, her skirts brushing against his legs. "Hi."

"Hi."

"You look…so beautiful." The words tumbled out in a husky whisper.

"You think so?" Thea glanced up then, her gaze meeting his, a faint hint of skepticism clouding their blue depths. Did the woman have any doubt as to how lovely she truly was? Had no one ever bothered to tell her?

Mack took her free hand and held it in his. "You're the most beautiful woman I've ever seen."

A ghost of a smile danced in the corners of her full lips. "You clean up right nice yourself, Sheriff."

The simple compliment warmed his heart. "Well, thank you. I try."

"And thank you for my flowers." She lifted the buds to her nose and drew in a deep breath. "It was very sweet of you to think of it."

Heat crawled up the back of his neck as if he were some schoolboy going to his very first dance. "Couldn't have my girl walking down the aisle without her bouquet."

"Still, it was sweet of you." Her cheeks turned a lovely shade of pink that matched the mums in her hand.

He threaded her gloved hand through his, his heart crashing against his breastbone at the touch of her slender fingers against his forearm. "Ready to do this?"

Silky curls fluttered against her shoulders as she nodded. "How about you? Any second thoughts?"

Oh, yes. Second, and third, and fourth and…but looking at Thea now, feeling the warmth of her hand against his arm, all the reasons they shouldn't marry dissipated like the morning mist on Sweetwater Creek. "Not a one."

"I don't mean to interrupt," Beau broke in. "But it's warm out here. Mind if we move this indoors?"

"I didn't even notice," Thea whispered to her flowers, almost as if she hadn't meant to be heard.

So she'd felt the same thing he had, as if the world had faded away, leaving them completely alone. Her eyes widened when she finally looked up and met his gaze. She lifted her hand from his arm as if to retreat, but he gently kept her there, pressing his fingers against hers. Mack leaned closer, the faint scent of ginger and tea imprinting itself on his memory, growing stronger as her hair brushed against his cheek. "I'd forgotten Beau and Maggie were even standing there."

She pursed her lips into an impish grin, and he had to force himself not to focus on the temptation of her mouth, instead holding her close as they started up the stairs. "Let's get inside."

Not more than a minute or two later, the group stood outside the massive doors that led to Judge Wakefield's chambers. Mack knocked on the door, then waited until it opened slightly, a young man Mack recognized as Wakefield's clerk lodging himself in the opening as if guarding the gates of the city of Oz. "Mr. Lemmon, we're here to see the judge on a private matter."

The young man nodded. "I'll let him know you're here. It will be just a few minutes." He gave Thea a long look, then smiled. "I'll come and escort you into his chambers when he's ready."

Mack's stomach twisted. Little runt had a lot of nerve, eyeing Thea like that. He tightened his fingers over hers. Didn't the man know she was about to become Mack's wife? Just proved he had more brains than common sense.

Why am I getting so worked up over this, anyway?

The steady clip-clop of work boots against the marble floor drew Mack's attention to the stairwell where a tall, lanky man stood, the leather bag on his back almost as brown as his weather-worn face. Judson Marsh was the town's mailman. He was tall and lean, and some folks thought he looked the spitting image of Jimmy Stewart, but Mack didn't see the resemblance.

Maybe a string bean, but nothing like the Hollywood actor who had fought in the Army Air Force, and risen to the rank of Colonel.

"Well, howdy folks. Miss Maggie, Dr. Daniels, Sheriff." He gave Thea a speculative glance. "Don't reckon I know you, Miss."

"This is my fiancée, Thea Miller. Thea, Mr. Marsh, our mailman."

Mack felt slightly deprived when Thea let go of his arm and held out her hand to the older man. "Nice to meet you, Mr. Marsh."

The older man took her hand in his and shook it. "Getting married, are ya? I've heard what people are saying around town, about the two of you being out at Ms. Aurora's, and I've got to tell you, I find the whole situation shameful, just shameful."

Thea tensed beside him, but the expression on her face was resigned. It infuriated Mack. Was this what she'd dealt with when people use to talk about Eileen? Or had she heard some of the rumors that swirled about her, guilt by association? Well, government employee or not, he'd deck the postman before he'd let him bad-mouth his future wife. "Mr. Marsh…"

"I know how bad it can be, taking care of a houseful of youngsters who're sick." He leaned close to Thea as if he wanted to share a secret only with her. "Me and my wife had eight girls and a boy, and when they were down with the measles or the chicken pox…" He shuddered. "Besides, anyone with eyes in their head can see why the sheriff decided to marry this little lady." A toothy grin split his weathered face. "Married my Edna just so I've have someone that pretty waiting at home for me." Marsh slapped Mack on the back. "You've done good picking this one, Sheriff."

"I think so," Mack answered. Thea relaxed against his side, and without even thinking, he dropped a kiss against her hair. For Marsh's benefit, and for Thea's, he told himself.

The man swung his bag around, lifted the leather flap and rifled through the contents. "Seeing as how you're here, Sheriff, mind if I give you your mail now? It'll save me a trip to your office this afternoon." Marsh gave them a cockeyed grin. "My daughter-in-law is bringing our grandbaby home from the hospital today, and I sure would like to be there when they get home."

"Of course you would." Thea glanced up at Mack. "We both understand how you feel."

Mack felt for the man. He'd lost his only son in the liberation of Paris and his grandchild was his last link to the lanky boy Mack remembered from church. The stack of letters needing to be stamped and sent from his desk could wait until tomorrow. "Sure, Mr. Marsh. I can take them back to the office."

The door opened. "The judge can see you now."

Mr. Marsh handed a small pack of envelopes tied with string to Mack, then closed the flap on his bag. "Well, good day to you, Miss Thea. Miss Maggie. Doc." The older man gave Mack a sly smile. "And congratulations to you, Sheriff. You've got yourself a mighty sweet lady here."

For once, Mack agreed with the old coot. "Thank you, Mr. Marsh."

"Mr. Marsh," Thea added. "You have a good visit with that grandbaby of yours this afternoon."

"I'm going to try, ma'am. Thank you." He tipped his hat, then turned and headed back toward the stairs, giving them one last look before walking down the hallway.

"Sheriff Worthington." The impatient edge in Mr. Lemmon's voice grated on Mack's nerves. "Judge Wakefield doesn't have all day."

This scrawny kid was just begging for a lesson in manners. But Mack pushed back his temper. "Would you please tell the judge I'd like to have a few minutes alone with my bride before the wedding?"

Lemmon pursed his lips as if he'd been sucking on an unripe persimmon, then nodded. "Please be advised that the judge has another appointment on the hour."

Mack glanced down at the woman beside him, then back at their friends. "Could you give us a moment?"

"Sure." Maggie reached out and hugged him as best as she could, turning to one side to accommodate her growing midsection. "Be happy, my friend," she whispered on a sniff.

She turned then and hugged Thea while Beau

walked over and shook Mack's hand. "You're doing the right thing by Sarah, giving her a mom and a dad. Remember that."

Mack nodded. Yes, he needed to remember that every time he thought of Thea, of the tumble of emotions she caused just being near him, of the attraction that made him wish this was something more than a marriage in name only. He waited until his friends had stepped into the judge's chambers before turning back to his bride.

She looked so lovely, standing there in her dress made of gold, nibbling on her bottom lip in that nervous way he found endearing, the little bouquet he'd brought her this morning clutched between her hands.

She pushed a loose curl behind her ear, another nervous habit that he found equally appealing. "Is everything okay?" she asked.

No, but then he hadn't been okay in almost two weeks, not since he'd seen her at Merrilee's wedding. His mind felt muddled, his feelings tangled up in knots all because of this woman. But that night eight years ago still remained unresolved between them, and until Mack had laid all of that to rest, he had to keep his feelings in check.

Mack reached out and pried one of her hands free of the bouquet. "I thought I'd give you a minute. Figured you might need a breather before all the excitement."

She tilted her head to the side. "Maybe you wanted to take a breather yourself?"

Thea always did know how to read him. Mack chuckled softly. "Things *have* been going at a record speed."

"Mack, if you've changed your mind, I'll understand."

"No," he barked, then cleared his throat. "I mean, no. What about you? I just sprang all this on you a few days ago. Any misgivings?"

Her smile widened, her blue eyes taking on a glow that enveloped him in its warmth, made him feel as if he'd finally come home. She slipped her hand into his and gave it a reassuring squeeze. "None."

His heart collided with his ribcage, his senses punch-drunk. That Thea—wonderfully smart, assertive Thea—had no qualms about marrying him gave him hope. "Beau's going to be crowing about this for years."

"Beau?"

"He's the one who thought it would be a good idea if we got married."

Thea tilted her head slightly to the side, her eyes glittering with mischief beneath the lacy veil. "So we should thank Beau for this mess we're in now?"

"Yeah, let's blame Beau," he answered, pulling her arm through his. Mack glanced down at her once more, his heart quivering like a jar of Merrilee's apple jelly. "Ready to get married, Miss Miller?"

For a brief instant, all her lingering doubts clouded those expressive eyes of hers, but then a smile that seemed to come from the very depths of her heart bloomed across her face as she pressed into his side. "I'm ready."

In fifteen short minutes, he'd have everything he'd dreamed of most of his life: a wife and child, a family to come home to in the evenings. Everything he'd searched for over the last eight years.

Well, almost everything.

Becoming Sarah's father, being Thea's husband in name only would have to do for now. Mack turned the knob and opened the door, standing to one side, waiting, watching as she walked into the judge's chambers.

Chapter Twelve

"If you'll take her left hand in yours, Sheriff."

Thea swallowed, the bravado she'd felt just a few minutes before gone, nerves choking the very air out of her lungs. They were really going to do this, get married and raise Sarah together. Thea would have the family she'd been longing for over the past eight years, people she could pour out all her love on, devote herself to, love and be loved by in return.

Only Mack didn't love her.

She didn't realized she'd lifted her hand until Mack's warm palm closed over her fingers, his hand like its owner—sturdy yet infinitely tender, strong yet unbelievably kind. His thumb swept over the top of her knuckles, grazing the gentle peaks and valleys as if memorizing each one.

"Do you, Marcus Fletcher, take Theodora Grace to be your lawfully wedded wife?"

Thea's breath hitched, the steel band around her chest tightening with each second as she waited for his answer. What if he'd changed his mind? What if he realized she wasn't nearly good enough to be his wife? To raise the child he'd claimed as his own? What if she made the same mistakes with Sarah as she'd made with Eileen? Then she would be all alone. *Not alone, Lord, never alone. But so very lonely without an earthly family to cherish.*

She glanced up and found herself lost in the inky blue depths of his gaze, the sparks in his eyes lighting a way through the darkness. His fingers tightened slightly around hers as if he never intended to let her go, then he gave her the most tender of smiles.

"I do."

Her heart fluttered in a wild rhythm beneath her breast. Was this what love felt like, this indescribable joy at just being near him, of hearing him pledge his life to hers, anxious for the moment when she could do the same?

And then the moment was upon her.

"Do you, Theodora Grace, take this man, Marcus Fletcher, to be your lawfully wedded husband?"

"I do."

His irises darkened, light flaring to a brilliant glow in his eyes. Could it be possible he felt some of the same emotions she was experiencing at the moment? Or was he simply counting on her to hold up her end of their bargain, a marriage in name only for a chance to raise Sarah?

"The ring, please."

A ring? Thea hadn't thought of that. Had Mack? Would they still be married if…? Reaching his right hand into his pocket, Mack fished around until he pulled out a slender golden band and slid it into place on her finger, then, without warning, bent and press his lips against the cool metal.

Her knees wobbled, and she feared there was a very real chance she'd melt into a puddle at his feet. The ceremony needed to end as quickly as possible or Mack would realize what she'd wrestled with these past few days.

That she'd fallen in love with him. Completely, totally in love with a man who only wanted a marriage in name only.

"I now pronounce you husband and wife. You may kiss the bride."

Thea sucked in a breath and butterflies fluttered in her midsection as if freed from their cocoons for the first time. For years she had developed a sterling reputation, holding herself in check, holding fast to the hard lessons she'd learned from her sister's behavior. Only now she found herself completely unprepared.

Mack's warm breath sent a sweet shiver down her spine. When had he moved to stand so close? Or was she the one who'd moved to be near him? His lips brushed softly against the sensitive shell of her ear, his voice barely a whisper. "Is this your first kiss?"

Heat flooded her cheeks. How had he known? Of course Mack would know. Mack, to whom she'd confided her girlish disappointments, who understood how much her sister's behavior had influenced her own. "Yes."

"Then trust me, Thea."

He stepped back slightly, just enough for him to lift the lacy veil and push it back away from her face. Yes, she trusted him as she'd trusted no one else in her life.

All other thoughts splintered as Mack lifted his hands to cradle her face, his thumbs tracing the line of her cheekbones, his eyes dark and unreadable as his gaze floated over her eyes, her cheeks and nose, before settling on her mouth. His handsome face blurred as he moved closer, lowering his head to hers as her eyelids fluttered shut.

Mack brushed his lips against hers, and Thea forgot to breathe. When he finally settled his mouth over hers, she looped her arms around his neck and drew him even closer. This was the man she'd married, the man she'd raise a family with. The man who'd stolen her heart.

Somebody cleared their throat. "I hope you two don't plan on acting like that in front of an impressionable child."

The judge's words sank in. *Sarah.* The only reason Mack had asked her to marry him in the first place. That, and a feeble effort to save her reputation, as if that could ever be repaired. Thea broke off the kiss and pressed her lips together. How long would they tingle like this? When had the room grown so warm? Did kissing always drive every thought from your mind, or was it just kissing Mack?

She stole a glance at him through thick lashes. He looked as shell-shocked as she felt. Did that mean he'd felt something, too, that the vows they'd made, the kiss they'd shared had forged an unbreakable bond between them? Or was she reading more into his feelings because her own were such a tender mess?

A hand at her shoulder turned Thea around to where

Maggie stood, happiness lighting her eyes. "Congratulations."

"Thank you."

The women watched as Beau gave Mack a hearty slap on the back.

"And bravo!" The redhead waved a hand in front of her face as if she was warm. "I'm going to have to go home and kiss my husband after watching that."

Thea had never blushed as much as she had this morning. "I made an idiot out of myself, didn't I?"

"An idiot, for kissing your husband? If so, then there's a lot of us idiots who enjoy kissing our husbands."

Thea didn't have time to respond before Beau swooped over and gave her a kiss on her cheek. She absently accepted his congratulations, her thoughts still in a tangle. After the way she'd returned his kiss, did Mack think she was anything like her sister? Would her behavior ruin their chances of adopting Sarah?

A loud pop echoed in the room as Judge Wakefield slammed a book shut, shaking Thea out of her thoughts. "If you all are finished pawing at each other, we've got other business to attend to before my next appointment."

She risked a glance at Mack. He looked as if he held himself on a tight leash, the muscles across his back and arms stretched with tension like a lion ready to jump its prey. What good would it do to strike out at Wakefield when the man had already made up his mind? She pressed a hand to his arm, steeling herself against the anger she knew would be reflected in his eyes.

Mack turned, his eyes flashing as his hand covered

hers, all the protectiveness he'd shown toward Sarah now focused on her. "I won't let him talk about you like that."

If possible, Thea's heart melted a little bit more. She curled up against his side. "Let's just sign whatever papers he needs and get this over with."

Mack nodded, then turned back to face the judge. "What is there left for us to do?"

The older man glanced past them to where Maggie and Beau stood. "As this is a private matter, you're free to go. Thank you for your participation."

The judge continued to shuffle papers as Mack and Thea said goodbye to their friends. Maggie pulled Thea close for a hug. "If you need someone to talk to, I'm here. Just know there's a whole bunch of us praying for you."

People prayed for them? The thought touched a place in her heart that had been numb for years. "Thank you," she managed.

After their friends had been escorted outside, she and Mack returned to their place in front of Judge Wakefield's desk. "Again, I ask you," Mack started. "What is there left for us to do?"

"Nothing, really." The older man shucked off his robes, hung them on a nearby coatrack then pulled his chair away from his massive cherrywood desk and sat down. He shuffled through some folders before finally pulling one out and opening it. "I've already approved the two of you to act as Sarah's guardians until the final decree comes through. Until then, the state will monitor the child's progress, so they'll be sending out a social worker in the next few weeks."

"No!" The word burst out of Thea without warning. She didn't want anyone from the state near Sarah, not after what she'd witnessed Georgia Tann and her political cronies do to countless children and their families during her time in Memphis. Stealing children away, never to be seen by their parents again for trumped-up legal reasons, signed off on by Miss Tann's pet judge.

Judge Wakefield studied her over his wire-rimmed glasses. "Do you have a problem, Mrs. Worthington?"

"Thea?"

She glanced up at Mack. Questions clouded his expression, questions she'd have to answer sooner rather than later. But not now, not in front of the judge. How could she convince Judge Wakefield to change his mind without going into the sordid details?

"It's just…" The hairs on the back of her neck rose. What could she offer as a perfectly reasonable explanation for her outburst? "Your honor, Sarah has just recovered from the chicken pox and is due to have major surgery in a matter of days. Her immune system has already been compromised, and the more people she's in contact with, the more likely she'll contract something else."

"Which will delay the surgery even longer," Mack interjected.

God bless Mack! He may not understand her reasons, but he was backing up her explanation as any good husband would. "So you see, sir, I'm thinking about Sarah's well-being."

"I see." The man fell back into his chair, his fingers steepled over his waist. "I know it seems as if I've given you a difficult time with this adoption, Sheriff,

but I only want to do what's right by the child." He
shook his head. "So many judges don't take their responsibility as seriously as they should and the child
is always the one who suffers for it." He leaned forward and rested his forearms on his desk, studying
them for a long moment. "While I can waive most of
the social worker's visits, she will need to visit your
home at least once to check out the child's living conditions. Maybe that can be arranged before you bring
the baby home from Ms. Aurora's. That should satisfy
the state requirements."

Thea didn't know what to say. Everything she'd
ever heard about Judge Wakefield had left her with
the impression he was a stickler for the law. An old
coot, she'd once called him. Maybe the man had a
heart after all.

Mack recovered before she did. "That's kind of you,
sir."

"'Thank you' will do just fine."

Mack's face broke into an extraordinary smile.
"Thank you. I can't begin to tell you how much this
means to us."

"You're welcome." The man closed the file in his
hand, pushed it to the side, then grabbed another one.
"Now, get out of here before I change my mind."

"Yes, sir." Mack caught Thea's hand in his and
tugged her toward the door.

Thea felt as if she were floating. Married and with
a new daughter all in one day. A real live family of her
own. Maybe not the way she'd always dreamed, but she
didn't care. She had Mack and Sarah. At the door, she
turned back toward the judge. "Thank you again, sir."

Judge Wakefield glanced up at her, a glimmer of a smile playing along his lips. "Wait until you've been married to that one for a while. Then let's see just how grateful you are."

The evening sky had turned a bruised purple by the time Mack turned the squad car onto Cheatham Hill Road. The chill of the late-fall evening nipped at Thea's fingers through the thin cloth of her gloves. A comfortable silence had fallen over them since they left Maggie and Beau back at the diner, an array of tin cans and old shoes tied to the back of the squad car, announcing their marriage to the folks in Marietta.

Thea stole a quick glance at her husband. In the fading light, she could barely make out the pink edges of the scar that peeked out from under his hair. The ache she felt at the hurt and confusion he had to have suffered was almost overwhelming. But had that accident been enough to make him give up his dreams?

Mack could still go to college and do all the things he'd planned. Be a lawyer, settle down and have the family he'd dreamed of having. An image of him, dressed in a well-cut wool suit, briefcase in hand, coming through the door to her and Sarah popped into her thoughts. Her putting the last touches on dinner while Mack played with their daughter. Him wrapping his arms around her waist, his lips brushing a gentle kiss behind her ear right before he whispered *I*...

A sharp turn onto an unfamiliar dirt road jerked Thea out of her daydream. She whipped around to face Mack. "Where are we going?"

"We need to talk somewhere where no one is likely to bother us."

"What's so important that we can't talk about it at home?"

A smile played along the corner of his lips. "I like how you said that, as if you already consider my house your home."

Anywhere Mack was would be home to her, but he didn't need to hear that right now. "So why can't we talk there?"

"My sources tell me that some of the guys are planning an old-fashioned shivaree at our place this evening."

Thea laughed. "I thought that kind of thing went out with hooped skirts and parasols."

"There are some in our community who still live by the old ways. So while they're trying to figure out where we are, I thought we'd talk about what happened with Judge Wakefield today. I want to know what you have against social workers."

Thea straightened, her hands clasped in a tight knot in her lap. She wanted to let the topic drop, but she knew that wasn't fair. If she had the opportunity to pry the facts out of him about his injury, she wouldn't let him back away from the truth, no matter how painful it was. Why should she expect any less from him now?

They bumped along for several minutes until they reached a small clearing shadowed by a circle of tall trees. Long stems of wild grass swished against the metal doors as Mack maneuvered the car into a patch of fading light.

Recognition dawned as she glanced around, then back at Mack. "This is Lover's Pass."

"You've been here before?" he growled as he shoved the car into Park.

His question felt more like an accusation. "Petey Henderson brought me here after a basketball game my junior year. But we didn't stay long once he found out I was nothing like Eileen."

"And that was the only time you've been here?"

"I figure the answer to that question would be obvious, seeing how I'd never been kissed until…" Her words faded into the waning light. *Until you kissed me.*

She thought she heard him mutter "Good" as he turned off the engine.

The keys jangled in the ignition as Mack turned to face her, propping one knee on the seat beside her. "All right. Now, I want you to explain to me why you have this problem with a social worker coming to evaluate us."

Thea swallowed. How could she ever explain everything that had happened without making her sister sound worse than she was? There wasn't any way, and Mack deserved the truth. All of it.

But that didn't mean it would be easy for her.

"Eileen spent most of her life looking for love, wherever she could find it. When she got into her teens, she started looking for anyone who could make her feel special. Most of the boys were willing to give her lots of attention, but only in exchange for a good time, and after it ended Eileen would be heartsick about what she'd done. But that didn't stop her from searching.

Midway through her sophomore year, Eileen realized she was pregnant."

Mack shifted back slightly in his seat. "She never looked…you know, while we were in school."

It was kind of sweet, his awkwardness with discussing such a delicate matter. If only the topic didn't involve her sister. "Eileen didn't start to show until she was six months along, and by then, school was out. That summer she stayed close to home. She talked about keeping the baby and becoming the kind of mother we never got to have." Thea drew in a steadying breath. "I really believed she was going to turn over a new leaf."

"But in the end, she gave her baby away."

If only it had been that simple. Thea shook her head. "No, Eileen wanted to keep her baby. She told me as much. But Momma…" She swallowed against the thick knot forming in her throat. "The shame of having a pregnant teenage daughter was just too much for her, so the thought of an illegitimate grandchild was unbearable. Weeks before Eileen's delivery, Momma got in touch with someone she'd grown up with in Memphis—a woman named Mrs. Cook who knew how to handle adoptions."

"Your mother thought she could change Eileen's mind?"

Disgust for what her mother had done almost cut off her breath. "Momma didn't plan to give Eileen much of a choice. She had heard about a woman up in Memphis who'd had a lot of success getting children adopted to wealthy people, like movie stars and such. Mrs. Cook promised to deliver the baby to that woman. She arranged to be in town, and met Momma that night at the train station, just hours after Eileen gave birth."

"That was why I drove you to the train station that night."

She nodded, sorry she'd had to involve him in her family's sordid problems. "Eileen called me at work, half out of her mind with grief. She'd overheard Momma on the telephone with Mrs. Cook." Thea hesitated. "I would have told you what was going on that night, but I was so ashamed. What kind of person would give her grandchild away?"

In the fading light, she could make out the sharp angle of his jaw. "Is that why you left that night like you did?"

There was a harshness to his voice she couldn't decipher. "Eileen was so desperate for her baby. She wanted to go after him herself, but she was in no fit state to travel. I couldn't sit back and do nothing. I knew if I didn't follow Mrs. Cook, my chance at recovering the baby would be less than zero. I had my savings for college in my pocket so I bought a ticket and followed her."

"You went after the child," Mack whispered.

She nodded. "I promised Eileen I'd bring him home. But it wasn't as easy as I thought it would be. The first couple of times I went to see Mrs. Cook, she denied knowing what I was talking about. I finally got in touch with the woman who ran the children's home where the baby had been placed, a Miss Georgia Tann. She told me the baby had died."

Mack shifted forward, his particular scent of lemon-lime aftershave and something purely him comforting her frazzled nerves. "There have been rumors floating around about Miss Tann for years."

"You mean the rumors of her stealing babies from their families and then selling them to the highest bidder?"

"I didn't want…"

He'd tried to spare her feelings. "Thank you. But I've faced the truth of the situation many times over the last eight years and it still didn't bring Eileen's child home."

Mack's hand covered hers. When had he moved so close to her, his shoulder brushing up against her own? "It's not your fault, sweetheart."

The endearment wound its way around her heart until she thought it would burst, but the joy quickly faded. He just wanted to comfort her, that was all. "That's not how Momma and Eileen saw it. When I called to tell them what had happened, Eileen refused to speak to me and Momma, she told me not to bother coming back home."

"That's why you're so sure Eileen wouldn't give up her baby girl? Why you thought Ms. Aurora stole Sarah away? Because you thought she was like Georgia Tann?"

Thea gave a shaky shrug. "I only knew what my mother was telling me, and from what I'd seen of Miss Tann and her allies, I thought it was a possibility. But not now. I was so wrong about Ms. Aurora. I told her as much when I apologized to her. She adores those kids and they love her to death." She sighed. "I guess I just wanted my family back, that's all."

"But Thea, you *have* a family, one with you and me

and Sarah." Mack took her hand in his, warmth running up the length of her arm at his touch.

Yes, Thea thought. She did have the family she'd always wanted. Why, with all she had, did she still feel all alone?

Chapter Thirteen

"Got some news from Judge Wakefield's office this morning I thought you'd like to hear." Red burst through Mack's office door a week later without so much as a knock.

"Good afternoon to you, too." Mack finished the thought he'd been writing on an upcoming case, then lifted his head to see his friend had made himself comfortable in the leather wingback chair in front of his desk. "Did it ever occur to you that I might be busy?"

"Still trying to catch up from your bout with the chicken pox?

"Yes." But that wasn't altogether the truth. Since marrying Thea he'd been keeping shorter hours. Work hadn't held the same appeal as going home to find his lovely bride poring over cookbooks or covered in paint from decorating the nursery. Their drives out to Ms. Aurora's to see the baby and Mrs. Miller included interesting discussions of the news around town as well as updates on their friends. It was a vast improvement over what his life had been, yet he craved more. More time with Thea, more laughter. He smiled to himself. And lots more kisses.

"Well, I figured this news would be worth taking you away from reports on parking tickets and petty theft."

Mack filed the report in his desk drawer, then turned and grabbed the next one off the stack. "One of your clients get caught doing something illegal?"

Red leaned back into the chair and stretched his long legs out in front of him. "If you don't want to hear about Sarah's birth certificate, I certainly won't tell you."

That news brought Mack up short. "What do you mean? Mrs. Williams hasn't come back home, has she?"

"No, but she did send Judge Wakefield all the particulars of the baby's birth so the necessary documents could be filed. Wrote in her letter that she'd sent you a copy, too, seeing how there was a dispute over the identity of the baby's mother."

He hadn't received any correspondence from Mrs. Williams. Reaching for a stack of mail Nell had brought in earlier, Mack shuffled through the envelopes, then went through them slowly in case he'd missed something. When he'd completed his search, he turned back to Red. "She must be mistaken. I haven't gotten anything from her."

"It's possible it arrived last week. It didn't get filed with the court until today, according to Mr. Lemmon."

Last week. Could it be in the stack of mail Judson Marsh had given him the day of the wedding? He'd been so occupied with Thea and the baby, he'd plumb forgot. Mack pushed back his chair and hurried over to the small closet where he stored his coat. Shuffling through the hangers, he came across the jacket he'd worn the day of the wedding and reached into the pocket, coming out with a stack of envelopes along with bits of rice and confetti from the wedding lunch he and Thea had shared with their friends.

"Well, did you find it?" Red asked.

Mack untied the string binding the letters and shifted quickly through the stack. Second from the bottom, a small envelope in Mrs. Williams's nondescript handwriting stared up at him. "It's here."

All the answers he'd been looking for in the last month sat at his fingertips. Sarah's parentage. Thea's claim. But now, instead of being evidence he sought, Mack felt a stab of the pain at the possibilities the answers might reveal. If Thea lost her certainty that Sarah was her niece, she lost her last hope of making peace with the memory of her sister. Not that it mattered to him. In his heart, Sarah was as much Thea's child as if she'd given birth to her. Burdening Thea with a new loss would hurt her too much, and her pain had become his own.

I'm in love with Thea.

Mack let the admission settle over him, amazed it had taken him this long to admit what his heart had been trying to tell him from the first. Of course he loved her, had loved her ever since she'd worn her hair up in those adorable pigtails while they were still in high school; admired the generous, loving woman she had become despite the sorrows she'd borne.

"Well, what are you waiting for? Open it."

Mack glanced over at his attorney. Red would never understand his reasoning, but then he wasn't paid to understand Mack's every move, now was he? "I'm not going to open it."

Red sat up. "But you've been waiting for a month to find out the truth, and now that you have it, you're not going to read it?"

What Mack felt for Thea, for Sarah, the relationship he shared with his Savior. Those were the only truths he needed to know. Mrs. Williams's letter could only deliver news that either wouldn't matter, or would cause pain.

What about Thea? Shouldn't she have a voice in this matter? Shouldn't she make her own decision about knowing the contents of the letter? Of course she should. They had promised to base their marriage on trust.

Mack scraped a hand across his jaw, shame rising inside. A hollow vow, considering he hadn't confessed the anger he'd felt toward her since the night she'd left. If he wanted a chance at making this marriage real, he had to bring it out into the open, lance this old wound once and for all.

Mack threw the rest of the mail on his desk, grabbed his coat off the back of his chair and rounded his desk, heading toward the door.

Red jumped to his feet, his expression one of bewilderment. "Mack, what are you doing?"

"I need to talk to Thea."

"Don't you think you need to make a decision before bringing her into this?"

"You can find your own way out." Mack took one last look at his lawyer, then hurried across the room and walked out the door. It didn't matter who had given birth to Sarah, only that Thea was her mother now and always would be.

He'd made his decision.

He was going to follow his heart.

Thea stepped out onto the sidewalk in front of the white marbled bank, the soft fall sunlight doing nothing to ward off the chill that had taken up residence in her bones over the course of the past two days. Tending to her mother's scant finances had led to another dead end. The latest one was a safety deposit box. Momma had kept the key to it in her dresser drawer since before Daddy died. If Thea had hoped to find a life insurance policy or jewelry inside to help fund her mother's care, she'd been disappointed.

Another worry for Mack to deal with, Thea thought as she tugged on her black gloves, their color matching her mood. Her mother was her responsibility, not his. She'd find a way to cover Momma's bills. Maybe the hospital knew of a doctor who needed a nurse. Of course, she'd have to consider Sarah's needs, and she wouldn't do anything until she talked to Mack.

Thea tucked her purse against her side and glanced out over the square. The trees in the park had been shaken bare, a happy occurrence if the children running and jumping into the piles of red-and-gold leaves had anything to say about it. Two women sat together on a bench, each rocking a stroller, deep in conversation as if comparing notes on motherhood. The earthy fragrance of pumpkins from the corner market next door lightly scented the air.

The perfect place to raise a family.

"If only that was all I wanted," Thea muttered as she shoved her purse under her arm.

"You always talk to yourself like that?"

Thea's heart did a funny little flip, her standard response to her husband's voice. She lifted her chin a notch. "Sometimes, when I get lonely and don't have anyone else to talk to."

Her blunt honesty caught him off guard, and even left her feeling a little flustered. What had possessed her to confess that she got lonely at times? Mack, Marietta's golden-haired boy, would have no idea what it was like to feel all alone in a world full of people with no one to talk to or confide in.

But when she lifted her gaze to his, a shock ran through her at the hint of vulnerability in his eyes. Was it possible Mack felt the same loneliness? His parents were gone, and though he had dozens of friends, it wasn't the same as having someone to count on, someone who cared enough about you to tell you when you were making a mistake, someone who loved you despite your flaws.

They'd been friends once, and this past week had seemed to erase all the years they'd been apart. She was his wife, his partner. He'd never be alone again, not if she could help it. Thea slipped her arm through his and gave him what she hoped to be a flirtatious smile. "You're looking mighty good for a man who just got over chicken pox not that long ago."

"Well, I owe that to the good care I received. In fact, the nurse who took care of me was so wonderful, I married her." He leaned down and whispered as if they were sharing a secret. "And I finally got the last of the oatmeal out of my hair this morning."

"I'm glad to hear that, Sheriff." Thea brought her gloved hand up to stifle the giggles. "I wasn't expecting to see you until tonight. Have you heard from Ms. Aurora today?"

"Sarah is fine, as always." Mack pushed the brim of his hat back on his head, revealing more of his handsome face. "John and Merrilee are back from their honeymoon and stopped by Ms. Aurora's to check on everyone. John even dropped your mother back at your house to pick up some things. He'll go and check on her throughout the day, then take her back to Ms. Aurora's this evening."

Worry flashed through her, then slowly dissipated. Ms. Aurora wouldn't have agreed to this unless she felt Momma would be all right. "Has Momma been giving her any trouble?"

He shook his head. "Not any that she mentioned. She seems to think your mother does better when she's kept occupied, so she's been helping with the twins."

"Ms. Aurora's a wonderful woman to take Momma in for a few days but it's got to be exhausting. Maybe I should go stay with her? Let Ms. Aurora get some rest."

Mack gave her an approving smile that warmed Thea to the tips of her toes. "That's sweet of you, but John and Merrilee are staying with Ms. Aurora until their house is ready. They'll help her."

"That's good to know."

"Besides, we have other things we need to take care of."

"What exactly is it we need to do?"

"I figure with Sarah recovered, Judge Wakefield will be pushing for the surgery again very soon."

There was a tone in his voice she hadn't heard often. Irritation? Annoyance? "You're not a big fan of the judge."

Mack glanced over her head, his eyes trained on a building behind her. Thea glanced over her shoulder to where the county's courthouse stood. "He made this whole adoption situation more difficult that it had to be."

An interesting admission from this man. The Mack she'd grown up with never had a bad word to say about anyone. What had changed him? Something about Judge Wakefield bothered Mack more than a little bit. He needed to talk this problem out. Maybe she could be his sounding board. "There's something more to it, isn't there?"

"More to what?"

Now the man was just being evasive. "Why you don't like the judge."

The muscles in Mac's jaw tightened, and she could feel the sudden tension in the air. "I guess it just bothers me the way Judge Wakefield stonewalled me about adopting Sarah almost since the moment I filed the paperwork. As if he thought I wasn't good enough."

"Why would you think that?"

His humorless chuckle caused a pang of pain near her heart. "Because he gave me one reason after another why I wasn't capable of raising a child, the biggest reason being that I'm a single man." Mack's lips flattened into a grimace. "He felt that a little girl needed a mother in order to be brought up properly.

The judge thought I'd be cheating Sarah out of the family she deserves."

"But having a mother doesn't guarantee you're going to raise the perfect child. I mean, look at my sister." Thea felt Mack watching her and glanced up at him. He'd stopped glaring at the courthouse and was watching her with that same stubborn protectiveness he always showed toward her when her sister was mentioned. Her heart overflowed with affection and tenderness. If only he could find a way to love her. "Still, the judge did apologize."

"When?"

She playfully swatted Mack's arm. "At our wedding, silly man."

"He did?" His blue eyes turned almost black, a pale light rimming the irises drew her deeper into his gaze. "I was kind of preoccupied at that moment."

Her heart fluttered to a wild beat in her chest. It almost sounded as if he didn't regret this marriage to her, as if he was open to the possibilities a life with her could bring. Could Mack ever care more for her than the friendship they'd rekindled between them after all these years? Was it possible Mack might love her someday?

No, her mother's voice whispered through her. Why would a man like Mack, so good and decent, someone who could have anyone he wanted, pledge his life to someone like her?

Thea walked slowly toward the crosswalk, not sure if Mack would follow, only knowing she needed to move. She had to make this marriage work for his sake as well as Sarah's. Mack deserved so much more than being forced into a marriage with her.

"Did I say something wrong?" Mack asked as he caught up with her.

She should have expected he would follow her. Mack had never liked seeing her upset, even back in school. He'd always managed to tease a smile out of her or make her laugh after a rough night at her house. He was the only reason she'd made it through some pretty bad days back then. Thea shook her head. "No, it was kind of sweet, really. Like something Cary Grant might say."

One blond eyebrow quirked high on his forehead. "I'm betting that if Mr. Grant had said that, you wouldn't have taken off as if your life depended on it."

"Probably not," she teased, pressing a gloved finger to her cheek. "But then, he is quite handsome."

His face collapsed into a sorrowful expression but his eyes twinkled with playfulness. "You wound me, dear lady."

The laughter she'd worked so hard to suppress bubbled up in her throat. "I'm so sorry. That was rude of me to walk away from you like that." She struggled to find the right words. "You don't have to sweet-talk me."

"I didn't know I was." The laughter slowly drained from his eyes. "There was a lot going on that day. It was more an honest observation than anything."

"Oh." Disappointment flooded through her. She was just being a romantic idiot, twisting Mack's words to mean something they obviously didn't.

Thea had to contain the light shiver that ran the

length of her spine when Mack gently touched the small of her back and guided her across the street. "We've already stood through two lights. Folks are beginning to notice."

They'd been standing there that long? Thea glanced around and noticed a couple of older ladies on the other side of the street stealing looks at them. The same kind of looks she'd gotten whenever she'd come to town with Eileen. Had they heard the false rumors going around town about her and Mack? Had they already tried her and found her guilty before she'd even been given a chance to clear his name?

"Good afternoon." Mack tipped his hat toward the ladies. "Nice day to get your errands done."

The darker-haired woman looked as though she'd swallowed her gum, but the silvery blonde gave them a friendly smile. "Yes, it is, Sheriff, and not too cold just yet. I can't handle the cold. My arthritis, you know."

"Yes, ma'am. I remember."

The woman took a cautious step forward as though she thought Thea might bite. "It's good to see you back on your feet. Zelda was just telling me you were under the weather a couple of weeks."

I bet that wasn't all Miss Zelda was saying. Thea shouldn't feel like this, but she'd had enough experience with people to know better. Thea shifted away from Mack but his hand remained firmly at her waist, almost possessive, as if he was staking his claim.

"That's true, Miss Helen. I was in bed with the chicken pox, as were all of Ms. Aurora's children. Fortunately, we had a wonderful nurse to care for us while we recovered." Mack gave her a grateful grin that made her stomach do little flips. "Ladies, I'd like you to meet my wife, Thea. Thea, this is Helen and Zelda Shirley. They moved down from Chattanooga to work over at the bomber plant."

"We *did* work at the bomber plant until the war department cut our shift," Miss Zelda muttered.

"Now, sister," Miss Helen cajoled, then she turned back to Thea and Mack, an apologetic smile on her face. "We should be counting our blessings that this horrible war is finally over and that our boys are coming home."

"And our girls," Mack added. "Thea here was an army nurse. Followed the troops onshore at Normandy."

That bit of information sent Miss Helen to twittering. "How exciting, and oh, how brave you must be! I guess a chicken pox epidemic is boring compared to what you must have seen."

"Both can be challenging." Thea slid Mack a teasing glance. "It all depends on who your patient is."

Miss Helen glanced from one to the other so fast, Thea was sure her eyes must hurt from the exertion. "Well, it must have been exciting, seeing how the two of you are married now."

So, word of their nuptials had gotten around. How fast would word get around town if anyone ever learned the truth, that Mack had married Thea to adopt baby Sarah? What would folks say then? *One more thing I have to leave up to You, Lord.*

"All I have to say," Miss Zelda started, glaring at Thea, "is marry in haste, repent at leisure."

"Sister!"

"Well, it's true."

Miss Helen's cheeks flushed a deep red. "You'll have to ignore Zelda. She's got the manners of a billy goat."

Thea could think of another barnyard animal the older woman emulated more. "That's all right, Miss Helen. I believe in complete honesty." Thea gave Miss Zelda her sweetest smile. "That way, I know exactly where I stand."

Mack choked on a chuckle beside her. Miss Helen gasped while Miss Zelda studied Thea for a long moment, then nodded, something close to respect glimmering in her eyes.

"Ladies," Mack said. "I hate to break this up but Thea and I still have an errand to run before we need to get home, so if you'll excuse us."

Miss Helen nodded. "Of course, Sheriff. It was nice to meet you, Thea."

Thea smiled. "Nice to meet you, too."

As her younger sister walked away, Miss Zelda lingered, finally holding out her hand to Thea. "Pleasure to meet you, young lady. And thank you for serving your country the way you did. We appreciate it."

Thea took her hand and gave it a firm shake. "Thank you."

She and Mack watched as Miss Zelda limped over toward her sister, then turned and headed down the sidewalk. Mack gave a low whistle and shook his head. "Thought I was going to have to break up a tussle there for a moment."

Oh, dear. Thea hadn't thought how this episode might embarrass him. "I'm so sorry, Mack. I wasn't thinking how this might look for you."

"Are you kidding? That woman's been a burr in everyone's side since the second she and her sister got off the train." Her skin tingled when he pushed a dislodged curl behind her ear. "But you, you had her tamed in a matter of seconds."

"I'm not so sure she's tamed. All I did was be honest with her."

"Well, that was enough to earn her respect." Mack took her elbow and leaned closer, his breath a soft rustle against her ear. "I was mighty proud of the way you handled yourself."

Mack was proud of her? How was that even possible? Her presence at Ms. Aurora's house, as innocent as it was, had caused a scandal that could have robbed him of his livelihood and his one chance to adopt Sarah. Of course, this marriage gave him what he wanted most, the opportunity to raise Sarah. But children grew up. One day in the not so distant future, Sarah would leave home and build a life of her own. What would become of their marriage then?

"I can hear that brain of yours working all the way over here."

She shook her head slightly. "Just thinking."

"Want to talk about it?"

"It's nothing." Thea pushed the thoughts away and focused on the present. "What exactly is this errand we're supposed to be on?"

"We kind of got sidetracked, didn't we?" He maneuvered her around a parked car and across a deserted side street. "Anyway, Sarah's not going back to Ms. Aurora's after the surgery, not if we want to keep her from catching something else. I know you've been painting the nursery but if we want to get the social worker's approval we really do need to look at buying a baby bed and stuff."

"You're right." And here she'd been thinking of something of a more romantic nature, like another trip out to Lover's Pass. She should have known better. Thea unclenched her hands. "You know, we've already got that dresser in the guest bedroom that's not being used. I thought I'd sew some padding together and make the top of it into a changing table so we wouldn't have to go out and spend money on one."

"I hadn't thought of that. I'd picked out a crib for her before we got married, but it's up to you. I know you'll want to make it perfect for Sarah." He hesitated, and for a moment Thea thought she caught a glimpse of color in his cheeks. "I'm not real good at this decorating stuff. I only bought the house right off the town square because I wanted Sarah close by to where I work so I can drop in on her during the day, maybe take her to the park in the evenings."

Thea tried to drum up some degree of annoyance, but how could she? Mack not only wanted to be a part of Sarah's life, he'd planned his life around her. What a blessed little girl she was, to have that certainty of Mack's love. What must that feel like, to be loved so completely, so unconditionally by this man? Maybe, one day, she might have that kind of love, the kind of family she'd always wanted with this man who was so good and kind, better than she deserved. If he offered her a chance at love, she'd embrace it with her whole being.

And if he couldn't love her? She'd take whatever

he was willing to offer as long as she could stay with him and Sarah.

Thea cleared her throat. "Well, if you want me to, I could stop by Mr. Hice's department store and make a list of the items I think we'll need. Then we could talk it over at dinner tonight."

"I was kind of wanting to do the shopping together. Maybe pick out something that we both liked."

It was such a sweet gesture, the kind of thing a real married couple would do together as a way of welcoming their new baby into their home. Thea could almost envision Mack sitting cross-legged on the floor, wrestling with the directions for the crib while she folded each diaper and nightgown, all the tiny bibs and playsuits, and arranged them lovingly in the dresser, anticipating the arrival of their little one.

Oh, dear! She really needed to stop daydreaming like that before Mack figured it out.

"I took the afternoon off so that we could do this together."

An entire afternoon with Mack! Thea intended to savor every moment. "I was in Hice's Department Store the other day and noticed they had a nice selection of baby things. Why don't we go there and have a look first, then decide where else we might like to go?"

Mack gave her an easy smile. "Sounds like a plan to me."

"Good." Thea took a step in the direction of the store but Mack's hand at her elbow stayed her. She tilted her head back to look at him. "What is it?"

"I just wanted you to know."

Her pulse quickened. "Yes?"

"When I decide to sweet-talk you," he whispered, his blue eyes pinning her, robbing her of what little breath she had, "you'll definitely know it."

"What would you like to look at first?"

Mack glanced around the baby department of the store and suddenly felt overwhelmed. Along one high wall was every conceivable item a baby would ever need—diapers, washcloths, soaps and blankets in a rainbow of pastel shades, decorated with tiny stitched emblems of ducks, frogs and rabbits. Racks of tiny clothes filled out the area, making him feel like a giant out of one of those fairy tales he read in the evenings to Sarah. Along the other wall, a row of cribs stood at attention, ready for their inspection.

He glanced down at Thea, her expression bright with anticipation and excitement. "It's a lot to take in."

Thea leaned into his arm and gave him a playful shove that sent his senses reeling. "We're not buying out the entire store, silly man. Just the necessities."

That was a relief. He wasn't sure his bank account could take another hit so soon after buying a house. "Do babies really need all this stuff?"

Thea shook her head. "Babies just need to eat, sleep and be kept warm and clean. And, of course, be loved."

"And this?" Mack swept his arm out to take in the entire section.

"For the parents. Makes them feel like they know what they're doing."

Mack gave a bark of laughter. It was nice to hear a woman say exactly what she thought. "Then what would you suggest we look at first?"

"The crib you picked out would be a good start."

"This way." He held out his elbow to her, the air crackling between them as she looped her arm through his, her hand a warm weight. It felt so natural to be with her like this. But he couldn't help worrying that the fragile relationship they were building might crumble at any moment.

The letter from Mrs. Williams burned a hole in his pocket. What would Thea do with the letter? Would it change how she looked at Sarah, at their marriage? Mack knew how he felt. Thea was the only mother Sarah needed, and the only woman he wanted as his wife.

"What do you think of this one?"

Mack jerked himself out of his thoughts and glanced at the cherrywood baby bed Thea was examining. "Looks like one of the jail cells down at the county lockup."

She shot him a quelling look. "This is important."

Goodness gracious, but she was taking this much too seriously. "It's a crib, Thea."

"Where Sarah will sleep for a third of her day, every day for the next two years or so."

A third of her day? How had she come up with that number? Eight hours in a twenty-four hour day is… Mack studied her with new appreciation. "I'd never thought of it that way."

Thea pushed up on the railing then gently slid it down to the floor. "It's something my nursing professor told me right before she began scheduling our class for thirty-six hour shifts." Her lips turned up in an impish grin. "Guess she didn't figure nursing students fit into that category."

"Understaffed sheriffs don't, either." Mack walked over to the other side of the crib and stretched his arms across the top of the railing. "Did you like nursing school?"

"It was all right. A means to an end." She pressed her hand into the mattress as if to test it, then nodded. "My clinicals were particularly tough because the staff at the hospital where I studied relied on nursing students to pick up the slack. I don't think I slept for the entire two years I was in school."

"Then you joined the army and didn't sleep for four more."

"That's about the gist of it." Her eyes sparkled with humor as she turned and walked over to the crib behind him.

Mack twisted around, the fragrance of ginger and sweet tea floating around him as she moved closer, the urge to take her hand, tug her into his arms and kiss her almost unbearable. But common sense stopped him. Their marriage was an arrangement, a "means to an end" as she put it. The thought of the years ahead, married yet not truly in a marriage with Thea, left him feeling more alone than he thought possible. At least he'd be Sarah's father, but even that wasn't enough, not when he loved Thea more than he ever could have believed.

"What about you? Do you like being the sheriff?

He shrugged. "I guess. It pays the bills."

Thea glanced back at him. "That doesn't sound like you."

Of all the things she could have said, he wasn't expecting that one. "How would you know that? You haven't been around for the last eight years."

"Maybe, but I know you used to pore over law books when you didn't think anyone was watching. And you interned during the summer with Judge Huffman your junior and senior year so he'd write you a recommendation for college." Thea turned and leaned back against the crib's railing. "You were always so passionate about going to college and then to law school. What happened?"

Mack's gut tightened. Wasn't this the opening he'd wanted, to come clean and be honest about that night? If he wanted a future with Thea, he needed to tell her what had happened to put his life on a different course. Discussing it in the baby section of the town's department store just hadn't been his plan.

"I shouldn't have asked you that. It's none of my business."

Mack reached out and took her hand, her cool tapered fingers a balm to emotions roiling around inside him.

Mack cleared his throat. "I didn't go to college because I couldn't afford it."

A tiny line of confusion formed between her perfectly arched brows. "But you had a full scholarship to play football."

He'd hoped she wouldn't remember that part. "After my car accident, the doctors wouldn't sign a medical release. So the university rescinded their offer."

Her face paled. "You were that badly injured? A doctor would only do that if you had a long-term medical issue or if there was a risk of doing further injury to yourself."

Mack gave a humorless snort. "Yeah, that's what the doctors told me, too."

Thea's gaze shifted to the area where the scar lay hidden under his hair. "From the placement of the injury, they must have thought you'd lose your eyesight or your hearing."

Mack couldn't help the slight smile. Thea always had been sharp as a knife. "Cochlear concussion, they called it. I'm partially deaf."

Thea's eyes widened, her creamy skin a ghostly white, concern etched in her expression. She nibbled at her lip as if to keep it from trembling. "That must have been a horrible accident."

"It didn't look too bad at the time. The doctors were more concerned with my broken jaw than anything." He hesitated. "Then I noticed I couldn't hear what was going on right beside me. That's when the doctors sent me for a hearing test and discovered the problem. They felt that there was a chance another blow to my head would make me completely deaf in that ear."

And there it was. That look on her face was the reason he hated telling anyone what had happened to him. Who wanted to be pitied? To have their lives defined by one random moment? Pity colored how people viewed him, how he saw himself.

As if he were less of a person. Sometimes it felt as if he'd never been that boy Thea had known back in high school. The accident had taken more than his hearing and his dreams of being a lawyer. It had taken a part of his very soul.

Consider it all joy, My brethren, when you encounter various trials.

Okay, God, I get it. You never promised life would be a rose garden. But when does this trial end so that I can experience the joy?

"You could still go to college."

Mack grimaced. *He* was the one with the bad ear, not her. Had she not listened to a word he'd said? "That's not possible."

"Why not?"

"You're not serious." Mack jerked his head around toward her. Everything from her earnest gaze to the determined set of her jaw spoke of her sincerity. "I'm almost completely deaf in my right ear."

"Someone once told me that nothing worth having ever comes easily." Her blue-gray eyes challenged him.

Leave it to Thea to remember some motto he'd tossed out at her when things were tough back in high school. But, as much as he hated to admit it, there was a grain of truth to what she said. "I thought nurses were supposed to have the gift of mercy."

"Sometimes it's more merciful to be honest than to allow someone to drown in self-pity."

Ouch! Mack stepped back as her words sank in. Was that what he'd been doing, wallowing in self-pity? He thought for a moment. Why hadn't he found another way to go to school when the scholarship fell through? Had it been easier to not try rather than face his limitations every day in the classroom?

But it was too late for him. He'd missed his chance. He had a house payment, a job, and a wife and daughter. Or was he just using them as more excuses not to try?

Pinpricks of awareness raced up his arm as she joined him, her warm hand closing over his. "I'm sorry, Mack. Sorry that you had to go through all of that. But I believe in you, and if you want to go to school, we'll find a way."

Thea wanted to give him his dream. Before he knew what he was doing, Mack grasped her hand and tugged her into his arms, all the hurt and anger over the past few years that had borne down on him finally, blessedly, lifting. She fit neatly under his chin, her feminine curves a perfect match for the hard plains of his body, the scent of ginger and tea invading his senses as she nestled closer. "Aw, Thea. I can always count on you to tell me what you think about things, even when it's hard for me to hear."

The brim of her hat softly bumped his chin as she tilted her head back. "Then, can I tell you something?"

Mack braced himself. No telling what the woman might say this time. "What's that?"

Thea tilted her head back, that impish grin he was coming to adore flashing at him. She nodded toward the crib behind her. "I love this baby bed."

A bark of laughter erupted from Mack's throat. The next hour flew by as they looked through bedding and blankets, diapers and safety pins, bottles and bibs. A seemingly endless pile of baby items awaited them as they followed the sales clerk to the register. As the order was being rung up, Mack turned to ask Thea a question but she wasn't there. He scoured the clothing racks before finally finding her in a small selection of rocking chairs at the corner of the department.

Mark turned back to the clerk. "Can you wait just a moment? I may need to add something to the bill."

The young woman's smile brightened. "Of course. Take all the time you need."

Mack skirted around the racks until he stood just a few feet from Thea, sitting in one of the rocking chairs lining the wall. Sooty lashes rested gently against the curve of her cheek, several strands of silky blond hair fell free from their place behind her ear, giving her a mussed look that was in perfect contrast to the orderly woman Mack knew her to be. Life and experiences had changed her, molded her into the strong, capable woman she'd become. Yet Mack sensed a vulnerability beneath her strength, and a heart for others that risked being hurt. A surge of protectiveness welled up inside him. He would do whatever it took to keep her heart from being broken.

Even at the risk of my own.

Her eyelids fluttered open, the soft dreamy look in her eyes tugging at his heart. "Did I fall asleep again?"

"Looks like it." Mack slipped down into a chair next to her. "Maybe you need to have Beau check you out."

She drew in a deep breath through her nose and stretched her back into a slight arch before resting back against the chair. "Got to grab some shuteye whenever you can."

Mack glanced around. "Even in a department store?"

She gave him a gentle smile. "Even in a hedgerow outside of Caen during a forty-seven hour bombing raid and nonstop surgery."

His respect for her grew even more, if that was

possible. "Sarah's a lucky little girl to have you for a mother."

Thea tilted her head toward him, the soft glow in her eyes snatching what breath he had. What would it be like to make Thea light up like that for him? "That's a sweet thing to say."

"It's true. You're going to be a wonderful mother."

"I just hope I'm better at it than I was at being a sister."

She'd always done that, beaten herself up over how Eileen had turned out. Maybe Thea was ready to hear a few truths of her own. "You were a great sister, Thea. It was Eileen who had a problem."

"I know. She was hurting so much." Thea drew in a defeated breath. "Maybe if I'd been here when Sarah was born, things would have turned out differently."

"You don't know that." He couldn't stand to see her blame herself for Eileen's decisions. Mack reached out and covered her hand, surprised when her fingers threaded through his as if by habit. "Your sister probably would have given up her baby, anyway."

"Maybe, but I'd like to think that eventually she would have learned from her mistakes. That she'd grow up and find love, real love, with somebody who wouldn't ever think to let her go."

"She did."

Thea glanced over at him. "What?"

Mack couldn't believe no one had told her. Not even him. Customarily, he wouldn't give out information on other victims in a car accident. But it was important Thea knew the truth of the night her sister died. "Eileen didn't die by herself in the accident. Gene Allgood was with her that night. His parents said they were on their way to the justice of the peace."

Thea's eyes glittered. "Eileen was getting married?"

Her fingers felt cool against his as he squeezed her hand. "I never found a marriage license at the scene of the accident, but Mr. Allgood said his son had been seeing Eileen since he'd come back from the war. They'd been dating about a year when they died." They rocked in silence for long moments before Mack spoke again. "I really thought someone had already let you know. I'm so sorry I didn't tell you."

"You have nothing to be sorry about."

It didn't seem like that to him, not when he could feel the pain she bore. "But…"

She interrupted. "You just told me my sister had found love, was on her way to get married to the man she loved. I remember Gene from Sunday school. He was a good guy who loved the Lord. Maybe he took Eileen to church. Maybe she had a chance to meet the One who loved her most of all."

Thea would look at the situation that way, with a hope and optimism no one else who'd gone through what she had would lay claim to. It was one of the many reasons he loved her. Mack reached into his pocket. Maybe now was the time to give her Mrs. Williams's letter and resolve Eileen's memory once and for all— so they could move on from it together.

"Mack, would you mind if we checked on Momma? I don't like the idea of her being out there in that house all alone."

"We can run her back over to Ms. Aurora's." Leaving the envelope in his pocket, Mack pushed to his feet. Then they would go home, and he'd lay his heart out to her. Tell her he wanted their marriage to be real. Mack could only pray she wanted that, too.

Chapter Fourteen

Thea straightened in the passenger seat and stared out over the inky blackness yawning before her. "I sure did have a good time with you today."

Mack glanced over at her as he turned the squad car out of the square. "Are you saying you usually have a bad time with me?"

She laughed. "You're fishing for a compliment."

"No, I'm not." But there was a teasing quality to his voice, a playfulness that almost made her think she was back in high school. "I just like to know I can still show a lady a good time."

"Taking her shopping for a crib. That's always a good first date."

"Hey, don't forget the rocker."

"Sarah is going to love that rocking chair, especially when she doesn't feel so well and she wants to cuddle."

They fell into spurts of conversation followed by moments of companionable silence that felt so easy. Within minutes, they were working their way through the shadows until they reached the smooth surface of the paved road.

Mack broke the awkward silence. "Do you smell that?"

Thea sniffed, the taste of salt and something acrid coating her throat. "Is that smoke?"

In the dim light of the dashboard, Mack reached down and unhooked the receiver from its place next to the radio and brought it to his mouth. "Myrtle, this is Mack. I'm out on Cheathem Hill, and there's a distinct smell of smoke in the air. Has anyone called in to report a fire out here?"

The radio cracked and hissed for what seemed like an eternity before Myrtle replied. "Just got a call in. Sent the fire crew to number twelve Cheathem Hill Road."

Number twelve! The air shot out of Thea's lungs as if she'd been struck by a baseball bat. Frantic, she pushed herself up to the edge of the seat and dug her nails into the leather dashboard as she searched the darkening sky for signs of smoke. "Momma."

The radio receiver dropped to the floor at her feet, then Mack's strong arm pushed her back into the seat as he gunned the engine. "Hang on, sweetheart. We're almost there."

Time slowed to a crawl as the world narrowed, her heart pounding out a frantic beat in her ears, her palms moist beneath her gloves. A glimmer of light sparked through the trees up ahead, growing as they drew nearer. When Mack pulled into the front yard, Thea opened the door and jumped out even before the car slowed to a stop. Reddish-gold flames shot high above the treetops in the rear of the house, casting an eerie silhouette against the night sky. Embers floated

in the air like the lightning bugs she and Eileen used
to chase across the front yard as children. A loud crack
to her right caught her attention and she watched as the
awning crashed into the front porch railings, sending
sparks high into the air.

"Momma!" Thea dashed from one end of the house
to the other, then surged forward.

A familiar pair of arms caught her around the waist
and pulled her back against his chest. "You can't go
in there."

"But Momma's in there, Mack."

"I know, sweetheart," he whispered against her ear.
"But let's look at this a moment and see if there's a
way we can get your mother out without getting either of us killed."

Mack was thinking of going into that inferno? No!
What if something happened to him? How could she
live if he walked into the flames and never returned?
Thea looped her arms around his waist and hung on
for dear life. "You can't go in there."

"Listen to me." Mack gave her a gentle shake that
caught her attention. "I have to do this, you know that.
But you're going to have to let me go if we want any
chance at saving your mom."

Thea knew what he said was true. No matter how
hard she fought him, eventually he'd go in after her
mother. It was his nature, to protect those under his
care even unto death. It didn't make it any easier for
her to let him go.

Mack studied the house for a long moment. "It looks
like the fire started in the back right-hand corner, near
the kitchen."

Thea nodded, her eyes burning from the smoke. "But Momma doesn't stay in there much. At night, she usually sits in the front parlor and listens to the radio while she knits. Maybe that's what she was doing instead of packing." Thea didn't know the woman her mother had become in her absence.

Mack eased his hold just a bit as if he didn't trust her not to bolt. "Do you have a rain barrel?"

"Over there, under the downspout, but…" She grasped the arms that held her. "Let's check around first. Maybe she got out on her own."

"I don't have time to argue with you about this." He circled her wrists in one hand and gently pulled her toward the back of the car and opened the trunk. In the distance, the sound of sirens filled the night air. After a brief search, Mack pulled two snowy-white cloth diapers from their recent purchases and wadded them up in his hand. "Rain barrel?"

She pointed to the far corner of the house. "Mack, please."

"Stay here, Thea or I'll handcuff you to the car."

Of all the… "Fine, go get yourself burnt to a crisp."

Mack cut her next words short as he trapped her chin between his thumb and forefinger and stepped closer, the lines of his handsome face blurring into a pleasant haze. Her breath caught as he lowered his head, his lips a gentle brush against his own before settling over her mouth in a too-brief kiss.

She felt disoriented by the time he lifted his head and pressed something into her hand. "This is for you, sweetheart, with all my love."

Before she could react, he ran across the yard to the

rain barrel then, with wet cloths in hand, Mack disappeared into the fiery inferno.

Mack pressed the wet cloth against his nose and mouth, and sucked in a heavy breath, the heat pressing at him from all sides, as if he'd stepped inside a raging furnace. A watery film formed over his stinging eyes. The smoky fog that settled in the front hallway grew thick and dark toward the back of the house, tiny flames licking the doorway to the kitchen.

He didn't have much time. When lit, these old houses went up like seasoned kindling. He only had a few minutes, maybe less, to find Mrs. Miller and get them to safety.

Father God, help me find her.

He turned left, took a quick look around the dining room then headed to the room across the hall. Dust motes stirred in the murky air, a cloud of whitish gray smoke billowing from the lit fireplace, piles of folded paper crinkled like an accordion into black ash. With one corner of the wet cloth, he wiped soot out of his eyes and glanced around. In a wingback chair near the hearth sat Mrs. Miller, her head slumped to one side, her mouth gaping open, the irregular rise and fall of her chest a sign she was breathing, but just barely.

Mack hurried across the room, knelt down in front of the woman and folded the other wet cloth he'd been holding against her face as he tied it into place. "Hang on, Mrs. Miller. I'm going to get you out of here."

A loud crack beside him split the opposite wall into two sections, fiery fingers burning a path along the seam up to the ceiling. Time was running out. Grabbing her hands, Mack dragged the woman to the edge of the chair, planted his shoulder against her midsection and lifted her onto his shoulder. He shifted her weight to get a firmer grip on her then turned.

The smoke had thickened, leaving the room obscured in shades of black and gray. He moved forward until his knee connected with the blunt end of a table, and then he retreated. Without a clear path, there was no way he could get them to the hall and out the front door. Mack's lungs tightened, his nose and throat on fire despite the makeshift mask plastered to his face. Watery tears blurred his vision, and his legs wobbled underneath him.

The imagine of Thea, the devastation he'd seen in her expression as they'd pulled up to the house, pushed to the front of his thoughts. She'd lost so much already—her father, her sister. Mack would do everything in his power to help save the only person in this world she had left.

Please, God, for Thea's sake.

A glimmer of light from a nearby window caught his eye. Heat closed in around them, the struggle to put one foot in front of the other becoming more difficult as he pushed toward the exit. Mack punched the elbow of his free arm through the glass, felt a sharp sting against his back as he stepped across the window sill. Drops of water sizzled against his skin, his lungs bursting for air. Just a few more steps…

"Mack!"

Thea! He opened his mouth to speak but the words caught in his parched throat. His legs buckled and he collapsed to his knees. A weight lifted from his shoulders as the darkness he'd tried so hard to evade overwhelmed him.

Thea pushed back a matted lock of hair from Mack's face, her fingers lingering a moment longer than was necessary. Reassured by the steady rise and fall of his chest, she felt his skull, telling herself she was checking for any lumps or cuts the medics might have missed. Though she couldn't deny the comfort she found in touching him, in knowing he'd survived.

Crazy man! What had he been thinking, running into the growing flames like that? Didn't he know how close he'd come to being killed? How close she'd come to losing him without ever telling him how much she loved him? How much she wanted him in her life? The thought sent a cold shiver down her spine.

"Here's some water for when he comes to." The fireman who had introduced himself as Bobby handed her a glass jug. "The medic just finished checking out your mother. She's fine, though little confused. I do have to ask. Was there a child in the house we didn't know about?"

Thea shook her head. "Why would you ask that?"

"It's just that…" Bobby stopped, as if searching for the right words. "Your mother keeps talking about someone called Eileen and how it's her fault the baby died."

Thea shook her head, the sudden pain that tore through her being almost physical. She remembered what Ms. Aurora had said about the three days Eileen had been in labor. Had Eileen's baby not survived her traumatic delivery? Had her mother buried the loss so deep that she'd latched on to the idea of Sarah as Eileen's baby, even though it wasn't true?

"The medic is giving her some water. Sometimes dehydration can cause confusion, too."

"Thank you, Bobby." Thea swallowed. "I appreciate all you guys have done."

A set of white teeth smiled sympathetically from a soot-stained face. "I just wished we could have saved the house, but these old places go up so fast. It was a wonder Mack was able to get your mother out like he did."

Mack! How would he respond when she told him that Sarah might not be her niece? She drew some measure of comfort watching his chest continue to rise and fall. "Why hasn't he come to yet?"

"Probably got a little smoke inhalation. What he did, going in after your mother, takes a lot out of a person. Give it some time," Bobby said before heading back toward what was left of the house.

All things she knew as a nurse, but knowing it didn't calm the unsettling fear she had. If only Mack would wake up. Thea unbuttoned her coat, tugged it off then folded it and gently lifted Mack's shoulders slightly to angle it under his head as a pillow. She grabbed one of the clean cotton diapers she'd brought from the car and soaked it with water, wringing out the extra fluid before gently wiping away the patches of soot on Mack's face.

Even wearing grit and cinders, he was still the most handsome man she'd ever known. Smoky lines of soot marred the intelligent slash of his brow as well as the high cheekbones that were a throwback to some Cherokee ancestor. She skimmed the cloth down the ridge of his nose and detected a small knot unnoticeable to the eye. When had Mack broken his nose? As a boy in a playground scuffle? Or maybe later in his duties as sheriff? Thea shivered at the other dangers Mack might have faced.

She stilled as she came to his mouth, the memory of that brief kiss before he ran into the flames making her lips tingle even now. Well, maybe it was more of a brush of his lips against hers but she'd felt it down to the deepest depths of her soul. Her pulse picked up speed. What would it be like if she never had the chance to kiss him again? Never had the opportunity to bask in the warmth of his smile again? Her heart would never recover.

"Like what you see?"

Thea lifted her gaze and met Mack's dark blue eyes. There was a playful gleam in them, as if the past two hours had never happened, but she also found something that hinted her answer mattered to him. The thought sent a tiny thrill up her spine. She sniffled and leaned close, pushing her hands through his hair. "Are you fishing for a compliment?"

"Would that be so bad?"

Thea shook her head. "After what you've done, I don't think there would be enough words to tell you…" The thought of what could have happened, of all that had changed in the course of the last hour, clogged her throat.

"Come on, you can do better than that."

"I know what you're doing, trying to get my mind

off of…" She waved her hand toward the burning structure. "That."

"Thea, you can do this."

His way was probably better than her making a fool over herself. Thea sat back on her heels as if she needed to get a better look. If the man was fishing for a compliment, she'd certainly give him one. "You're… passable."

"That's it? Just passable?" He leaned up on his elbows, his face within a whisper of hers.

Maybe she should lean forward just a hair and kiss him. Her heart stepped up a beat at the thought. "You know you're terribly handsome."

Her breath caught as he came even closer, his handsome features blurred. "I'm glad you think so."

Her eyelids fluttered shut, his warm breath a soft caress against her cheek. The fear she'd felt as he'd run into the burning house seized her again. She could have just as easily lost him. *Thank You, Lord, for this man.*

"How's he doing?"

Thea pulled away, heat rushing up her neck and into her cheeks as she glanced up at the fireman. She sat back, her hands pressed into the folds of her skirt. "The patient is doing fine."

"Patient, huh?" Mack whispered with a hint of laughter in his voice.

"Good," Bobby answered, then addressed Mack. "You gave the little lady here quite a scare. She was worried sick."

"Nice quality for a man's *wife* to have, don't you think, Bobby?"

The man glanced at Thea, then looked at Mack and

gave him a crooked grin. "I thought I heard something about you getting married. Congratulations." He turned and headed back toward the men near the house.

"You were a little worried about me?"

"Maybe," she conceded. She'd been more than a little worried. She'd been frantic. Why wouldn't she be? She loved him, more than she'd ever believed it was possible to love another person. The man had been willing to risk his life to save her mother, knowing the kind of person the woman was. Knowing what she had done with Eileen's first child.

If Mack did ever come to love her, he wouldn't care what other people thought about her family, only how he felt about her. That was why she loved him so completely. Is that why she'd gone through with this marriage? Because she knew at her very core that there would never be another man she could make her wedding vows to?

"How's your mother?"

Thea cleared her throat. "Fine. The medics checked her out but want to take her to the hospital as a precautionary measure."

"Good." Mack took a deep breath to Thea's relief. "She was breathing kind of shallow when I found her. I wondered if she had some smoke inflation."

"No, just mad she's got to go to the hospital." She glanced toward the ambulance. "I'm surprised they haven't been over here to get you ready for the ride back into town."

Mack tried to chuckle but it came out as a cough. "I'm not bottling up the ER on the count of my sorry hide when there are others in the community who need to be seen."

That's what he thought. Didn't he realize he'd been unconscious for a spell? Smoke inhalation, concussion, each possibility worse than the last, shuffled through Thea's mind. Whether Mack liked it or not, he needed to be checked out by a doctor. "You're going, and that's it."

A stubborn glint flared in Mack's eyes. "It'll just be a waste of time."

Well, bullying only made him dig in his heels even deeper. Maybe there was a more persuasive way to convince him. Thea leaned forward and pressed her cheek against his, the stark smell of smoke a reminder of what she could have lost. She whispered softly into his good ear. "Please, Mack. I couldn't live with myself if something happened to you. Do it for me. And for Sarah. She's lost so much already. Don't take a chance of her losing you, too."

His jaw loosened slightly against hers. "All right, Thea. I'll do it. For you both."

Chapter Fifteen

In the end, Mack got Thea to compromise. No hospital but Beau agreed to meet them at their place after Thea got her mother settled in at the hospital for the night.

"The Lord was watching out for you this evening, Mack," Beau said a couple of hours later as he tossed his stethoscope around his neck and made notes on a piece of paper resting on the coffee table. "What possessed you to run into that house in the first place? From what I hear, it was almost fully engulfed by the time the fire department got there."

"Mrs. Miller was in there."

He'd like to think he would have done the same for any of the folks in his county, hoped he'd respond in the same way as he had tonight. But he wouldn't be honest with himself if he didn't admit the prospect of Thea losing her mother had played a very definite role in his response tonight. The look of absolute devastation that marred her expression in those first few moments after their arrival, the look of complete and total loss haunted him even now. She had borne so much in her life—losing her father, then her sister. Her nephew and niece. If she'd lost her mother, too…

Mack grimaced. But wasn't that what was happening already? Mrs. Miller hadn't been herself in months, even before Eileen had died. The confusion only seemed to grow worse with each passing day. What if Thea had been at home in bed asleep when the fire broke out? Would Mrs. Miller even have remembered her daughter? The thought sent a shudder through him. No wonder Thea clung to the hope Sarah was her niece. The child would be the only family she had left.

I will never leave you or forsake you.

Mack had held fast to that verse in the days after his father and his mother had died. Still, he remembered the deafening silence of his parents' house in the months after Mom's death, the feeling of being totally alone. No one who shared your history. No one to call your own.

Well, he was Thea's family now, and he'd be there for her. All the days of their lives, if she'd let him. She wouldn't have to bear her mother's illness alone.

"How's our patient doing?"

The men glanced up to see Edie Daniels walking quietly toward them, a tray of sandwiches and sugar cookies along with a pot of coffee in her hands. Mack had once fancied himself in love with the beautiful engineer, but what he felt for Thea filled up parts of his heart he hadn't known existed until she'd come back into his life. If tonight had taught him anything, it was that whatever time he had left on this Earth he wanted to spend it loving Thea.

Beau moved the papers to a side table, then stood and hurried to take the tray from his wife. "You shouldn't be carrying something that heavy."

"Really, Beau." Edie flashed her husband a teasing smile. "I'm not going to break."

"Maybe," he answered as he dropped a kiss on her brow. "But you're the only wife I want so I'm not going to take any chances."

The tender look they exchanged made Mack duck his head. Beau's life had not been an easy one. An abusive father and time in a Germany POW camp had seen to that. But the love he'd found with Edie Michaels and his newfound faith in Christ had changed him, set him on a solid path.

How would Thea's love transform Mack? She'd already brought him through the pain of his disappointment, showed him how to serve others with a glad heart. What other lessons would they learn together as the years passed? Could she ever learn to love him?

Mack glanced toward the doorway that led to the hall. "How's Thea doing?"

"Better than I would have been." Edie filled one cup with coffee and handed it to him. "She wanted to get out of those smoky clothes and freshen up a bit before she joined us."

It felt as if she'd been gone forever. Probably a reaction to this evening, but he wanted to be close in case she needed him. "Could you go and check on her? She's had a rough night and I'd feel better if I knew she was okay."

Edie studied him as if he were one of those building plans she used to draw for the War Department, then nodded to her husband before standing and heading down the hall.

Mack glanced over at Beau. "I might have breathed in my share of smoke tonight, but what was that look all about?"

His friend chuckled as he reached for the coffeepot. "We had a friendly argument going, and my darling wife thinks she's won."

Mack wasn't sure he wanted to know, but curiosity got the better of him. "What was the argument?"

Beau glanced down the hall, then settled back, taking his cup with him. "Edie said you would fall in love with Thea."

Mack raked a hand through his hair and chuckled. And he thought he'd played it so smooth. That made him laugh even harder. "How did she figure that out?"

"She recognizes that dog-eared look a man gets when he's pining after a woman." A cloud of steam rose as Beau blew across the hot liquid before taking it to his lips. "Met, matched and married, all within a month. That's pretty quick."

"Eight years and a month, but then who was counting?"

"I told Thea you had a thing for her back in high school, but she said it was my imagination." He took another sip. "I have to say, since she's been back, I've seen more of that guy who didn't have a huge chip on his shoulder."

Mack rubbed his eye. Had he really been that awful? Probably, yeah. "I didn't know how to handle what had happened to me. The accident, losing my chance to go to school. It was a lot for me to lose."

"You blamed Thea."

He was ashamed to admit he had. It had been easier than facing the truth, that he'd caused the wreck that cost him any hopes he'd had for the future. "I realized I was wrong. The accident was all my fault."

"I'm glad you figured that out. Maybe now, you'll consider going to school and becoming a lawyer just like you always talked about doing." Beau nodded slowly as if mulling over that particular piece of information. "Though, after tonight, you may have a hard time convincing the town council to let you out of your contract."

"So now they want to keep me on as sheriff?"

"Are you kidding? You're a hero." Beau laughed. "What do you want to do?"

Mack knew what he wanted. He wanted everyone gone so he could finally tell his wife how much he loved her. Kiss her the way he'd been dreaming of since the day they got married. Try to convince her to make their marriage a real one with children and laughter and love. Years and years of love.

Mack glanced over at his friend. "Thea thinks I should go back to school, too."

"So you told her about the accident?"

"Ms. Aurora convinced me I should." Mack set his cup back on the tray. "But the more I talked to Thea about it, the more I realized I'd blamed her because life hadn't turned out exactly as I'd planned."

"It never does. But I've learned the hard way that God takes whatever mess we make out of things and works it to our good and His glory."

Boy, wasn't that the truth, Mack thought, though

even a few weeks ago, he couldn't possibly have seen the good in the past eight years. Looking back, he would only wonder at God's faithfulness in the face of his anger. Maybe it was past time he talked to the Lord about it.

"So, what are you going to do?"

Mack's shoulder ached when he shrugged. "It depends on what Thea wants."

"And if Thea wants you?"

"Then I'll spend the rest of my life making sure she never regrets it."

Beau reached for a sandwich. "Yep, I'd say you're in love."

"And if Thea doesn't want that?"

Beau chuckled. "Do you know what my part of the argument with Edie was?"

Hadn't his friend heard him? "Well, if you disagreed with her then that must mean you thought that I wouldn't fall in love with Thea."

"No." He leaned back into the sofa. "I thought that Thea would fall in love with you first."

"You thought that Thea would…" The memory of those first seconds after he'd woken up, the tiny worry lines that were etched in her forehead, the shimmer of tears laced within the dark fullness of her lashes played out in his mind. She'd been more than a little concerned.

Thea cared about him?

Even now, the thought that she might somehow have feelings for him radiated warmth though his veins. It didn't matter how deep her feelings went. They'd have something to build on, caring and trust, a base to work from as partners, friends, someone who was committed to him and to their family.

Thea.

Beau and Edie couldn't leave soon enough for Mack.

Thea glanced around the living room thirty minutes later, her robe pulled tightly around her, the letter Mack had given her in the moments before he'd run into the flames in her pocket. Only after they had returned home and she had escaped to the quiet solitude of her bedroom had she looked at the envelope, the return address reaching out and grabbing her attention.

Mrs. Williams. The woman who'd delivered Sarah. Why had Mack given it to her? What did the letter mean?

As if sensing her presence, Mack opened his eyes, exhaustion and worry lining the area around his forehead. "You okay?"

A slight smile lifted the corners of her mouth as she studied him for any signs of distress that warranted medical attention. "You're the one who ran into a burning building tonight."

"All in a day's work," he quipped.

She glanced down at the two cups stacked neatly on the coffee tray then at Mack. "Did Beau and Edie leave already? I wanted to thank them."

Mack nodded. "They needed to get home, but they wanted me to tell you good-night and that they'll see you in the morning."

"Of course. Edie must have been tired." Instead of coming farther into the room, she stepped behind the rocking chair. It was the only thing keeping her from making a complete fool out of herself by throwing herself into his arms.

Telling him she'd fallen in love with him, that she wanted a real marriage might be more difficult than she'd thought. "How are you feeling? Headache, nausea?"

"I'm okay, sweetheart, really I am." Thea's heart skipped a beat at the endearment. "If Beau had had any reason to worry, he wouldn't have thought twice about admitting me to the hospital."

Thea relaxed for the first time in hours. "Good, but I'm still going to keep my eye on you."

Mack gave her a lopsided grin. "I certainly hope so."

Thea's fingers dug into the rocker's headrest. How could Mack be flirtatious after what he'd gone through tonight? Hadn't he lost enough—his dreams, then tonight, almost losing his life—all because of her family?

"How's your mom?"

Thea drew in a deep breath to steady herself. The reality of her mother's illness had finally sunk in. "The nurse said she's sound asleep from that sedative the doctor gave her. He's going to arrange an appointment with a doctor who specializes in diseases in the elderly. She can't stay by herself anymore."

Mack stood and crossed the short distance to her, wrapping his arm around her waist and drawing her close. "I'd like to go with you to talk to the doctor, if you don't mind."

Thea glanced up at him, startled by the sincerity in his expression. How would Mack feel about her mother when he learned she might have lied about Eileen's child? "Why would you want to do that?"

Mack dropped a gentle kiss on her brow. "We're in this together, aren't we? Come on." He guided her over to the couch, then—still holding her close—sat down beside her.

Mack smoothed her hair away from her face. "Let's think about that tomorrow. There's something else we need to talk about right now."

He wanted to talk about the letter now? Thea pushed a few inches away, anything to put some distance between them. Might as well get this over with.

"Is this about the letter from Mrs. Williams?"

"Yes."

Her heart galloped in her chest. "All right, but first there's something I need to tell you." She wet her lips. "Sarah can't be Eileen's baby. Momma told the paramedic that Eileen's baby died."

"We don't know that that's the truth." Mack pushed a stray curl behind her ear. "All we have is your mother's word, and that's not very reliable."

"You knew?" The question came out strangled and high-pitched. Thea cleared her throat. "When?"

"The day the kids came down with the chicken pox and I went by your house so your mother could pack you a bag. Her thoughts were scattered all over the place so I didn't take her talk about Eileen's child too seriously."

Mack had suspected Sarah wasn't Eileen's since before the wedding, before his proposal? "Why didn't you tell me?"

His thumb feathered lightly over her chin before he

cupped her cheek in his hand. "Because we didn't have any real proof and until we had some kind of confirmation, I didn't want to risk hurting you."

That must mean something, but what?

"Do you know why I gave you that letter?"

A sheen of tears sprang to her eyes as she bit her lower lip. "To let me know you knew who Sarah's mother was?"

He shook his head. "I already know who Sarah's mother is." Mack tapped the tip of her nose. "You."

Thea hadn't expected that answer. "Me?"

"Sweetheart, you may not have given birth to her, but Sarah doesn't have any other mother than you."

She was confused. "Then why did you give me the letter?"

"Did you look at it?"

Thea refused to tell him she'd stared at it for the last half hour. "Yes."

"Did you notice anything about it?"

What was there to notice? It was a plain, unopened...

She lifted her eyes to meet his, a spark of hope flaring up inside her. "You didn't open it."

"And I don't plan to. I don't care what it says." Mack reached over and pulled her onto his lap, rocking her back and forth, brushing comforting kisses against her brow. "You poor sweetheart. I really mucked this up, didn't I?"

She sniffed. "I don't know. I think you're doing okay so far."

Mack's laughter rumbled beneath her ear. "When I sent that letter off, I wanted answers about Sarah's mother. And if Sarah was your niece, you needed to know that, too. By the time Mrs. Williams replied, I knew it didn't matter who had given birth to Sarah, only that you were Sarah's mother and that I had fallen very much in love with you."

"Oh, Mack!"

She threw her arms around his neck, her body pressed against his, her tears wet against her cheeks. Mack cradled her head in his hands as he tilted her head back and lowered his mouth to hers.

Several minutes went by before they broke apart, breathless and gasping for air. Thea was still trying to regain her voice when Mack spoke. "I love you, Thea. I love your sweet spirit, and the way you boss me around when I'm sick. I love the way you love our little girl, the way you've always loved your family, so unconditionally."

She buried her face in his shoulder. "I could have lost you tonight."

"But you didn't." He dropped another kiss on her hair.

She lifted her head and met his gaze, his blue eyes dark with longing and just a touch of uncertainty. "I can't stand the thought that you could have died without my telling you how very much I love you."

Mack cradled her cheek, his thumb tracing the path of her tears. "You do?"

Thea leaned into his hand. "I think I've been in love with you since we were in high school. I just didn't know it until now."

All in God's timing. Just like Ms. Aurora said. He kissed her cheeks and the tip of her nose before brushing a soft kiss against her lips. "I sure hope you do, sweetheart, because I love you so much. I want this to be a real marriage."

A brilliant smile graced her lips. "I want that, too, Mack. I want to be your wife."

"Sweetheart, you're more than just my wife. You're the mother of my child. You're my family. And I'll love you forever."

Epilogue

Thea straightened the flat sheet on the baby crib stationed in the hospital room, every corner pulled into a crisp wrinkle-free line, then grabbed the cloth doll from the bedside table and sat it against the railing.

Two muscular arms circled her waist and pulled her back into the familiar warmth of her husband's chest. "You really think she needs the doll?"

"It's her favorite, Mack. She's already going to be in a strange place. I thought it might help."

He dropped a soft kiss on her cheek. "If you think that it will make her feel better, then I'm all for it. I just can't stand to see you so worried."

Thea turned toward him, relaxing against him, her hand pressed to his chest, the sure, steady beat of his heart a comfort to her rattled nerves. "I just need to keep busy. Anything to get my mind off of all the things that could go wrong."

"I've got an idea to help with that." Mack cupped her cheek in his hand, tilted her head back until his lips caught hers.

In the three months since they'd made their marriage into a real one, Thea had found she never grew tired of Mack's kisses. Or the shoulder he gave her to lean on, or the talks they shared after they'd returned from visiting Sarah every night. If possible, she'd fallen even more in love with him as she watched him tenderly care for their daughter and her mother.

Thea broke off the kiss, slightly thrilled by the disappointment registered on her husband's face, and laid her head back on his chest. "Do you know how much I love you?"

She felt his soft kiss against the top of her head. "Almost as much as I love you?"

Thea started to respond, but a knock on the door interrupted them. A young nurse—Corrine—poked her head around the door. "Mr. and Mrs. Worthington, there's someone here to see you."

Thea lifted her head to look up at Mack. They'd both agreed that until Sarah was further along in her recovery, they would limit her visitors. Besides, the Danielses, Hickses and Davenports were camped outside the delivery room, waiting for Maggie to give birth while Ms. Aurora kept busy with Mrs. Miller and the kids.

"Did they give a name?" Mack asked.

"A Judge Wakefield."

Mack threw Thea a quick look before turning back to the door. "Send him in, please."

"Yes, sir," the young nurse answered.

Thea glanced up at Mack, her knees wobbly beneath her, her hands suddenly cold. "What do you think he's doing here? The last time we talked with him, a couple of weeks ago, he said it might take a few months before we heard anything about finalizing the adoption."

Mack gently backed her into a nearby chair, his hands on her shoulders as he stood behind her. Almost immediately, she leaned her head back against his midsection, drawing strength from him for whatever news Judge Wakefield brought.

Another knock on the door, and the judge walked in, his overcoat thrown over one arm while in his hand he held his gray felt hat. He bowed his head slightly. "Sheriff, Mrs. Worthington. How's the baby doing?"

"She's in recovery right now," Mack answered. "Dr. Medcalf says the surgery went very well. We should be able to take her home in a few days."

"Good, good." The judge smiled. "I'm glad to hear that."

The knots in Thea's stomach pulled tighter. Why couldn't the man simply tell them whatever news it was he had and be done with it? Why was he drawing this out? Unless he had bad news and didn't know how to tell them.

Mack squeezed her shoulder. The man had to be on pins and needles, yet his first thought was always of her. She reached up, took his hand in hers and gave it a reassuring squeeze. No matter what happened, no matter what life threw at them, Mack was her family, the man of her dreams, her love. They would get through this together.

"I was down this way on another case and thought I'd drop by to give you the news myself."

Thea's chest tightened and she could barely breathe. "What news would that be, Your Honor?"

The judge reached into his coat pocket, pulled out a thick envelope and handed it to Mack. "This came in the mail this morning. I thought you might like to have it."

Thea felt Mack tremble and stood, linking her arm through his, wanting to give him a small portion of the strength he always gave to her. He pulled out a set of thick papers and unfolded them, skimming over the first page.

"What does it say?" Thea managed to squeak out.

Before she knew what was happening, she was in Mack's arms, rocking side to side as if in a slow dance. "She's ours, sweetheart," Mack whispered in her ear. "She's really ours."

Tears sprang to her eyes, but she refused to cry. She'd wept enough over the past few years to fill the seven seas, now was a time of unbelievable joy!

"We'll still have a more formal signing of the papers once the baby has recovered," the judge said with a smile in his voice. "But as far as the State of Georgia is concerned, you are legally the parents of Sarah Eileen Worthington."

Sarah Eileen Worthington. Thea smiled. Mack had been the one to suggest the baby's middle name, a tribute to the sister she had loved, a way to start healing from the loss. She might never learn the truth about what had happened to Eileen's baby, but Thea had forgiven herself for the mistakes she'd made with her sister.

Still holding Thea close to his side, Mack held out his hand to the judge. "Thank you, sir. We can't begin to tell you how much we appreciate you coming all this way to give us the news."

"No problem at all." The man glanced down at his watch. "I'd better get going if I hope to make my next appointment." He slipped his hat on, then touched the brim. "Sheriff. Mrs. Worthington."

Before the door had even closed, Mack swung her up in his arms again, his blue eyes bright with untethered happiness, his smile the most beautiful she'd ever seen. "You're a momma, sweetheart."

"And you're a daddy." Thea's heart soared as she dropped a quick kiss to his lips.

They stood wrapped in each other's embrace, an unimaginable joy passing between them, drawing them ever closer, twining around them, forging them together.

"If someone would have told me this time last year I'd be a happily married man, completely in love with my wife and father to a beautiful little girl, I would have thought they were nuts," Mack whispered. "But God had another plan."

"I wondered at times. But then He gave me you and Sarah." She chuckled. "What have I ever done to deserve this much joy?"

"You haven't done anything. None of us have." Mack dropped a kiss on her head. "It's only through God's goodness to us that He gives us our heart's desires."

"I'm glad he gave you to me."

A knock on the door was followed by the door being held opened wide by Nurse Corinne. "Mr. and Mrs.

Worthington, we're bringing your baby back from recovery."

   Our baby. Thea and Mack glanced at each other, the
smile they shared full of love and hope for the future.
Fingers entwined, they walked to the door to greet
their sleeping daughter.

* * * * *

Dear Reader,

I hoped you enjoyed *The Baby Barter*. Thea and Mack's journey to their happily-ever-after was quite a bumpy one, but no one ever said the path to true love was easy—in fact, some of the most enduring love stories have been filled with those hard times that my husband says "forges two hearts into one." As you can see, I married a very wise man!

My prayer for you is that even in those rough seas life throws us at times, you'll look for God's goodness, for He's there, ready to hold your hand, to give you that "peace that passes all understanding" if only you look toward Him.

Blessings!
Patty

REQUEST YOUR FREE BOOKS!

2 FREE INSPIRATIONAL NOVELS
PLUS 2 *FREE* MYSTERY GIFTS

Love Inspired® HISTORICAL

YES! Please send me 2 FREE Love Inspired® Historical novels and my 2 FREE mystery gifts (gifts are worth about $10). After receiving them, if I don't wish to receive any more books, I can return the shipping statement marked "cancel." If I don't cancel, I will receive 4 brand-new novels every month and be billed just $4.99 per book in the U.S. or $5.49 per book in Canada. That's a saving of at least 17% off the cover price. It's quite a bargain! Shipping and handling is just 50¢ per book in the U.S. and 75¢ per book in Canada.* I understand that accepting the 2 free books and gifts places me under no obligation to buy anything. I can always return a shipment and cancel at any time. Even if I never buy another book, the two free books and gifts are mine to keep forever.

102/302 IDN GH6Z

Name	(PLEASE PRINT)
Address	Apt. #
City	State/Prov.	Zip/Postal Code

Signature (if under 18, a parent or guardian must sign)

Mail to the **Reader Service:**
IN U.S.A.: P.O. Box 1867, Buffalo, NY 14240-1867
IN CANADA: P.O. Box 609, Fort Erie, Ontario L2A 5X3

Want to try two free books from another series?
Call 1-800-873-8635 or visit www.ReaderService.com.

* Terms and prices subject to change without notice. Prices do not include applicable taxes. Sales tax applicable in N.Y. Canadian residents will be charged applicable taxes. Offer not valid in Quebec. This offer is limited to one order per household. Not valid for current subscribers to Love Inspired Historical books. All orders subject to credit approval. Credit or debit balances in a customer's account(s) may be offset by any other outstanding balance owed by or to the customer. Please allow 4 to 6 weeks for delivery. Offer available while quantities last.

Your Privacy—The Reader Service is committed to protecting your privacy. Our Privacy Policy is available online at www.ReaderService.com or upon request from the Reader Service.

We make a portion of our mailing list available to reputable third parties that offer products we believe may interest you. If you prefer that we not exchange your name with third parties, or if you wish to clarify or modify your communication preferences, please visit us at www.ReaderService.com/consumerschoice or write to us at Reader Service Preference Service, P.O. Box 9062, Buffalo, NY 14240-9062. Include your complete name and address.

LIH15

SPECIAL EXCERPT FROM

Love Inspired HISTORICAL

*Can a grieving woman find happiness with a man who
can't remember his own name?*

Read on for a sneak preview of
RECLAIMING HIS PAST,
an exciting new entry in the series,
SMOKEY MOUNTAIN MATCHES.

October 1885
Gatlinburg, Tennessee

It wasn't easy staying angry at a dead man.

Jessica O'Malley hesitated in the barn's entrance, the
tang of fresh hay ripening the air. The horses whickered
greetings from their stalls, beckoning her inside, probably
hoping for a treat. She used to bring them carrots and
apples. She used to enjoy spending time out here.

This place had become the source of her nightmares.
Her gaze homed in on the spot where the man she'd loved
had died defending her. The bloodstain was long gone,
but the image of Lee as she'd held him during those final,
soul-wrenching moments would be with her for as long
as she lived.

If he'd been honest with her, if he'd made different
choices, she wouldn't be living this lonely, going-
through-the-motions half-life. She wouldn't be a shadow
of her former self, clueless how to reclaim the fun-loving
girl she once was.

LIHEXP0116R

Lost in troubling memories, a weak cry for help wrenched her back to the present with a thud. Her empty milk pail slipping from her fingers, Jessica hurried to investigate. She surged around the barn's exterior corner and had to grope the weathered wall for support at the unexpected sight of a bruised and battered man near the smokehouse.

Hatless and looking as if he'd romped in a leaf pile, his golden-blond hair was messy. "Can you help me?"

"Who are you? What do you want?"

He dropped to his knees, one hand outstretched and the other clutching his side. Jessica belatedly noticed the blood soaking through his tattered shirt. Bile rose into her throat. Lee's gunshot wound had done the same to his clothing. There'd been so much. It had covered her hands. Her dress. Even the straw covering the barn floor had been drenched with it.

"Please…ma'am…"

The distress in his scraped-raw voice galvanized her into action. Searching the autumn-draped woods fanning out behind her farm's outbuildings, she hurried to his side and ducked beneath his arm. She barely had time to absorb the impact of his celestial blue eyes on hers. "What happened to you?"

"I…don't remember."

Don't miss
RECLAIMING HIS PAST
by Karen Kirst,
available February 2016 wherever
Love Inspired® Historical books and ebooks are sold.